the force of the p

Sandro Veronesi was born in Prato, Italy, in 1959. *The Force of the Past*, his seventh book, won Italy's Viareggio-Repaci Prize and the Premio Campiello, and was a finalist for the Zerilli-Marimò prize. It is his first book to be published in the UK. Sandro Veronesi lives in Rome, Italy.

For more information on Sandro Veronesi visit www.4thestate.com/sandroveronesi

the force of the past

Sandro Veronesi

FOURTH ESTATE • *London* and *New York*

This paperback edition first published in 2004
First published in Great Britain in 2003 by
Fourth Estate
A Division of HarperCollins*Publishers*
77–85 Fulham Palace Road
London W6 8JB
www.4thestate.com

1 3 5 7 9 10 8 6 4 2

First published in 2000 by Bompiani,
Via Mecenate 91, Milan, Italy

A catalogue record for this book is available from
the British Library

ISBN 1-84115-653-1

Printed in Great Britain by
Clays Ltd, St Ives plc

To my mother

I can't go on. I'll go on.

—Samuel Beckett

the force of the past

one

Are you," pause, "an unhappy man?"

That's what that journalist said to me. It was her last question, after which a councilman who had just lost the election was going to shake my hand and hand over the envelope with the fifteen million lire that came with the Giamburrasca Children's Fiction Prize. Fifteen million. Well worth the burden of that evening, consisting of a long dinner at the restaurant in the company of the local worthies, the subsequent prize-giving ceremony in the newly inaugurated conference hall (which still smelled of paint), the speech by the outgoing mayor, the speech by the mayor designate, another by the chairwoman of the panel of judges, and in closing, the interview with the winner conducted by a journalist with eyes like those of a boiled fish. And that fifteen million was worth it, worth all the mindless questions that the aforementioned lady had put to me ("How old were you when you stopped believing in Santa Claus?" "What's your favorite

season of the year?" "I noticed you didn't eat any dessert: why?"),
to which I replied with heroic diligence—but suddenly everything
took a chilling turn when a woman burst in and seized the micro-
phone to launch an appeal for help needed to keep her nine-year-
old son Matteo (a faithful reader of mine, she declared) on a
life-support machine. The boy had been pronounced clinically dead
following a car accident and had become the subject of a heated
dispute in the town as to whether it was right for him to take up
for an indefinite period one of the two life-support machines in the
hospital's intensive care unit. "Help me," she said in a firm voice.
"My son is living the life of the tulips, of the laurel hedgerows,
and he has a right to carry on living it until his heart ceases to
beat. But they want to take him off the machine, they want to take
his organs. Do something, I beg you all: they want to kill him!"
The mayor designate reassured the woman that no one was going
to take away the machine that kept her son alive, while the outgoing mayor told her that the decision to purchase another two life-
support machines would be approved the following week, before
the new town council took office; then, to my utter disbelief, she
went back to her seat to watch the rest of the ceremony, and the
journalist resumed the interview as if nothing had happened, asking me this last question: "Are you," pause, "an unhappy man,"
question mark.

I drew a breath but kept silent for three, four, five, six seconds,
enough to make it extremely difficult, later, to give the answer. For
if one immediately says "no," let's say, or "yes," everything is okay,
no one enquires further, and on you go. But if after a question of
this kind one stops to think it over for a long time, then everything
gets more difficult, and the answer must perforce be sincere. *Am I
an unhappy man?* Sitting bolt upright in front of a hundred expec-
tant strangers, stunned by the question and by my own silence
and, while I'm at it, stunned by everything else (by the fact, for
example, that a town with only two life-support machines should
waste fifteen million on a children's fiction prize), I came to a dead
stop, run aground on my own uncertainty. The journalist carried

on staring at me without changing expression, petrified in a smile that was an infinite repetition of the question; and I said nothing and thought. An unhappy man? I was married to the woman I had loved most in all my life, and we had a healthy, intelligent son, whose survival did not depend on any machine; my father had gone into a rapid decline and died two weeks previously, and I had never gotten along with him, which is why his death made me feel guilty; I was doing the job I had always wanted to do and I was receiving a prize for having done it well; I had signed a contract with the publisher for a third book and I had already been paid half the advance, but, after *The Adventures of Pizzano Pizza* and the prize-winning *The New Adventures of Pizzano Pizza*, the vein was mined out and I no longer knew what to write. Was I an unhappy man?

I thought, and I remembered. I remembered that Dominique Sanda, when she must have been more or less my age, in an interview in which she was asked what kind of woman she felt she was, had replied, "I'm not a woman, I'm a girl." I remembered that when I was nine they had had an artist paint my portrait, and the picture came out very gloomy indeed because of all the sadness the artist declared he had perceived in me—but I'd like to know how many kids would be happy to pose motionless propped up against a chair for whole afternoons. I remembered old Marti, the invisible friend I had invented when I was little so that I didn't always have to play on my own, my incomplete collection of picture cards, the interminable years in military college, the thrashings I took at chess when I was on the verge of becoming a master; I remembered a girlfriend of mine, when I was eighteen, who accused me of having made her sad because I had taken her to see *Stroszek,* and then my father's death once more, the funeral in the rain, my mother and my sister leaning on me, but also my wife's extraordinary beauty and, that very morning, my son's silvery laughter as we played the remote-controlled newspaper game—his formidable right to be made happy by me. I thought about and remembered all these things, while I exchanged a murderously long glance with the mother of the little boy who was in a coma, who was staring at me exactly like everyone else, smiling at my embarrassment but confident that I would get over it, and even curious, it really seemed to me that she too was curious to hear my answer, as if she were genuinely interested in it. As if it had something to do with her laurel hedgerows.

I don't know how long that pause went on for. It seemed like a very long time to me, and I really can't say how long it went on for. All I know is that at a certain point the answer slipped out of my mouth on its own account, as tiny and darting as a little mouse.

"Not anymore," I heard myself saying.

two

hen I got off the train it was after midnight. No subway, at that hour; and naturally no cabs, in expectation of which a long line of well-heeled travelers freshly unloaded by a gloomy evening commuter train had already formed. But I was thinking about something else. I was thinking: No more Giamburrasca prize money.

In a moment of madness, I had actually handed over the check to the mother of the little boy who was in a coma. A handsome gesture—everyone was touched—even though an utterly pointless one, since the woman did not seem at all poor and the money could not have helped solve her problem in the slightest. Or could it? The fact was that for the entire journey back to Rome I thought about that money, about its ephemeral appearance in my hands, and I missed it as if it really had been mine. But whose money was it, in reality? To whom did the fifteen million of the Giamburrasca Children's Fiction Prize belong? And—the step is only a short one—to whom, in general, does money belong? Does it make sense to talk of ownership, of money, if it can change master so easily? What kind of stuff is it? There are times when you don't give a thousand lire to a beggar merely because you can't be bothered to stop for five seconds to take a banknote out of your wallet—and then you up and give fifteen million to a stranger. What if it had been a put-up job? What if the town council had been *in league with* that woman, sure, and it had all been no more than playacting calculated to ensure that the loot only just handed over to the winner returned instantly to the council coffers, which led to the conclusion—a devastating one it has to be admitted—that that money did not even exist? Of course not, as far as playacting went it seemed to have been orchestrated really badly: had the woman been homeless, jobless, or an HIV-positive unemployed unmarried mother, then okay; but a middle-class lady with a son in a coma provides no guarantee that the winner might be persuaded to donate the prize money to her. There's no connection. No, come off it: that woman's tragedy was authentic. If anything what had been strange was the reaction to my fit of solidarity, hers as well as that of the public as a whole: no surprise, no embarrassment, no resistance, only an emotional thank you and a lengthy round of approving applause. A madman throws away fifteen million and not one damned person in that town is surprised by the fact.

As I was thinking along these lines, but also, simultaneously, fantasizing about what I could have done with the cash (a holiday in Disneyland with my wife and son; a catamaran, preferably an old Hobie Cat 17, secondhand, with no Genoa jib, to putter about in in August; and especially the famous loft in my son's bedroom, required in order to liberate the room from the space taken up by the bed and me from my guilt over having installed my study in the room that ought to have been his), the hour-long journey flew by without my noticing it; and I got off, and joined the line for the taxis, without having made head or tail of anything at all. The only thing I was certain of was that I didn't have that fifteen million anymore, and that I had never really had it if not for about thirty seconds, between the moment in which the outgoing mayor presented me with the envelope containing the check and the one in which I gave it to the woman, still seated in the front row. Was that half minute enough to make the money mine? Can I at least say that I *donated* it?

Suddenly a shady-looking character all curly hair and gold pendants materialized before me, obliging me to break off my thoughts. "Taxi?" he hissed, with a cigarette butt stuck in his mouth and a furtive air that was really ridiculous if you thought about the transactions of quite another nature that were going on all around. I know these cowboys well: they try to make you think they are risking a jail sentence, and they use this pretext to hit you up for absurd prices. Unlicensed cabbies are the only category of working people I manage to haggle with.

"The Pyramid," I murmured, playing along with his furtive style.

"Thirty thousand," he said, without thinking about it for a second, as if he already had the price in mind even before he knew where I was going.

"The one in Rome," still whispering, "not the one in Egypt."

The man was dumbfounded—he didn't get it right away—then he understood and it seemed to me that he was contemplating flattening my nasal septum with a head butt: but professionalism won the day.

"Twenty-five."

He said it in a whisper, cocking his head to one side, with the air of one making an enormous concession.

"The ride costs fifteen thousand lire," I said, "I do it every day."

The man smiled, then he raised his head using his chin to indicate the long line in front of me, waiting for legitimate taxis that weren't coming.

"Let's see how much change you'll get out of them."

"I'm in no hurry."

It was the truth, after all. I was in no hurry and I wasn't tired. I liked the idea of standing there in the fresh air for half an hour, and I also liked, were I to tire of that, the idea of taking a good stroll while mulling over how I could explain my foolish donation to Anna.

"Twenty thousand."

It was the final offer, I knew. The cowboys have a strict rule about never lowering the fare to that applied by their legitimate colleagues. I looked at the people ahead of me in the line: fifteen, maybe twenty, all still waiting, stranded, enveloped in a murmur of discontent, while other cowboys, stationed at various points, tested their resistance by whispering their inflated prices. For good measure a couple of gypsy women had begun to work their way up the line on the other side: *Please meester Bosnia no home the war much sufferings for to eat meester Bosnia war and sufferings.*

"Sorry, pal," I said, shaking my head. "No kidding: I'm fine right here."

I pulled my wallet out of my pocket and gave two thousand lire to the gypsies, who were passing close by. *Thank you meester good night much happiness.* The cowboy glared at me, a long stare brimming with indignation, during which he transferred his scorn for the two gypsy women onto me. As for the women, he knew what he would have given *them*. He went off without a word.

So, where was I?: the money. Was it technically correct to say that I had . . .

"Fifteen thousand's okay by me."

A second shady-looking character had taken the place of the first: older, this one, shorter, beefier, with a nose that looked as if it had been through the wars, a swollen belly exploding beneath his shirt, and a shabby gray jacket upon whose collar lay a fluffy layer of fresh dandruff. And he smiled.

"The Pyramid, fifteen thousand," he repeated, on seeing my hesitation. And I was hesitating all right, as I continued to garner details of his rather seedy person. One in particular: his naked hairy arms protruded directly from the sleeves of his jacket, half pulled up. Now I am aware that that may seem a trifle, but it was an important detail for me, because there is a whole story behind it, which I am now going to tell.

As I said before, I never got along with my father, and as I also said, my father had died only a short time before, which was why I was feeling bad as well as guilty. No matter what the pretext that led me to think about him, my recollections always held a hint of bitterness that tainted even my grief over his death—despite the fact that the detail of the naked arms beneath the sleeves of the jacket came straight from one of the few flickers of our relationship that I still remember without embarrassment. It was in the seventies and we were watching a party political broadcast on television, shortly before I don't recall which election. Naturally, politics was not the cause of our conflicts, but it certainly provided some excellent opportunities for them to break out, and that evening promised a memorable clash: the neo-Fascist leader Giorgio Almirante was holding a press conference, and that year I was sure my father would have ended up by voting for him, thus revealing himself as the Fascist that he was once and for all. Mom, in the kitchen, was baking a cake; my sister was already in Canada; he and I were alone, without mediators, an ideal situation for degeneration. Almirante was speaking, and I kept quiet in order to let my father make the first move, the better to decide on which attack to unleash; but strangely, rather than his usual opening provocation (something like "he's certainly not wrong there"), this time he kept quiet too. By then Almirante had gotten to the fourth answer and neither of us had yet said a word, when, finally, my father spoke. "Never trust men who wear shortsleeved shirts under a jacket," he said. Starched and sun-tanned, Almirante looked like the president of the Red Cross; but his naked arms peeped out from beneath the sleeves of his impeccable blue jacket, and, once you noticed it, that detail made him look vaguely obscene. It really did. It betrayed a complete slovenliness that not even I would have attributed to him, convinced as I was that it was precisely with elegance that Almirante conned people. But that observation (not mine, damn it, *his*) completely defused him, and at that point it was as if he were talking in his underpants as he was cutting his toenails; he had been unmasked: a wretch, a slimy wretch. Amazed, I waited in silence for my father to say something else, for him to start in on the unions or the communist Pajetta, his favorite targets, in short for him to get back on the usual track; but he didn't say another word, and for the first time a party political broadcast ended without having triggered the slightest squabble between us. What's more, after that devastating remark I had to acknowledge that my father was not a fascist, that *in reality* he was a Christian Democrat—even though the fact that one could really be a Christian Democrat still struck me as incredible; anyway, this much is certain, you cannot make such a scathing remark about the man for whom your heart beats in secret.

I recall that I did not go out that evening, I stayed at home with him and Mom to watch *The Shadow Man*; I remember that during the film we ate the *torta di pinoli* piping hot, and that while we were eating it the telephone rang, but there was no one on the line; I remember that my father fell asleep on the couch, and that my mother covered him with a blanket. I remember it all with great clarity. And I remember that when I went to bed I still couldn't believe what had happened. Things were really bad between my father and me at the time; it was the worst time, even though it wasn't that things got much better afterward. That's why that evening made such a lasting impression on me: it was a demonstration of how things could have gone between us and never did, a kind of fleeting interference from a life different than ours. Apart from the memory itself, all that remained to me of that prodigy was that precept of his, perhaps the only one I ever managed to bear in mind: never trust men who wear short-sleeved shirts under a jacket. This is why that detail was important.

"Well, then?" urged the man wearing the short-sleeved shirt under his jacket, given that I was still staring at him without speaking. He was standing there waiting for my reply, with arms outstretched, on the wrong side of sixty, at a rough guess, and no trace of the moderation, or even of the tiredness that all that time ought to produce in a man: his face did not bear so much as a hint of the smoothness caused by the gaze of a wife or a child, of a superior, of a colleague; what endured, rather, was the untamed bravado of a street urchin, marked by the years but still pure and incandescent as it had been in the days of the orphanage, when from inside a light-blue smock with an embroidered tomato on the front he must have observed classmates and staff with the very same expression he was now favoring me with: the expression of one who has absolutely nothing to lose.

"Fifteen thousand, all right?"

And he wasn't even a cowboy. Cowboys never lower the tariff to that of bona fide taxis, as I have already said. If one did, he would be letting himself in for a good hammering, and rightly, because he would ruin the market. And were he in such straits as to be obliged to do such a thing, then he certainly would have whispered the price, he would never have let the others hear. But this man was talking in a loud voice, careless of the fact that they could all hear him, including the real cowboy who a short time ago had not gone below twenty thousand lire for the same run. He wasn't afraid of reprisals. He didn't give a damn.

No, he wasn't to be trusted.

three

Okay," I replied; and as for the reason, let's put it like this: because I'm full of shit.

The man took my bag and walked off with an electric stride à la Bob Hoskins, all friction and chafing. I brought up the rear, very puzzled about what I was doing: true, I had just lost fifteen million, but was it worth putting myself in the hands of a probable criminal in order to save five thousand lire? And, on the other hand, could it be that my steadily growing certainty regarding his intentions was merely paranoia on my part?

Before stepping off the pavement I looked around for the other cowboy, the real one, in the hope that he might confirm with a grimace these bad feelings of mine, or, better still, that he might step in to complain about unfair competition; but he was already working an elderly couple, and he didn't even see me.

The man's car was double-parked outside the side entrance to the station, where it was obstructing the passage of a streetcar whose bell was clanging hysterically. It was a Jeep, another fact in marked contrast with the man's attempt to pass himself off as a cabby: a Daihatsu Feroza, it was called. Never heard of it. The headlights were on and the hazard lights were blinking, *and the engine was already running.* The man made a hasty nod of apology to the streetcar driver, slipped inside, stowed away my bag, and opened the door. Then, given that this Daihatsu Feroza had only two doors, he started groping around in search of the lever that lowers the seat back, as if he weren't familiar with the car at all; in the meanwhile I had plenty of time to notice the wires dangling loose from beneath the steering wheel, which can mean only one thing.

The streetcar driver was still clanging his bell, the man told him to go to hell with a vulgar gesture, and I hoped that the driver would get out of his streetcar for a brawl, so that he would get the knife wound that was in all probability waiting for me, while in the confusion I would be able to grab my bag and run for it. But, rather than do that, I even went so far as to break the deadlock, by deciding to sit in the front and be done with it. At least I would have an escape route, I thought, a chance to throw myself out at the first opportunity: trapped in the backseat I would have had no way out. I know very well that this is not easy to explain, but by then I was acting and, above all, thinking, as if what was threatening to happen was actually happening; despite the fact that there was still nothing to prevent me from going off freely about my own business, for some insane reason I was thinking as if I were already up to my neck in the trouble that I still hadn't finished getting myself into, and all that I could do was to look for a way out of it. It was either that or I had been seized by panic without even having realized it, and this giving in to my worst presentiments had something to do with those lethal absurdities that we commit in the face of looming danger, when terror takes over our brain and solves the problem by making us feel *protected* by that danger, invulnerable, safe, with an incredibly intense and naturally wholly delusory feeling that drives us to do the exact opposite of what should be done (pheasants terrified by a blaze in the woods plunge into the fire rather than flee from it; Stan Laurel, pursued by the murderer, slips a bucket over his head because he doesn't know where to hide) or even to do absolutely nothing, waiting motionless for the arrival of the irreparable armed with the absurd hope that when it comes *it will not be* irreparable.

So I got into the front seat, and the man drove off with a jerk, as happens—it's a mathematical certainty—when you drive a car for the first time and you are not yet accustomed to the clutch. He must have stolen it a really short time before. And as he entered the feeder lane for Via Cavour, I marshaled all my remaining lucidity and started to put together a plan. First, I groped around looking for the door handle: another thing you can never find in cars you are not familiar with (like the lever for tilting the seat back), and when I found it I kept my hand over it. Second, I mentally ran through the route to my house, in order to pinpoint the limit beyond which for no reason in the world could I afford to remain aboard that car. The Coliseum, I decided: I had to jump out before the Coliseum. Third, I decided on the system. At the first red light I would say, "Here'll do fine, thanks," I would leave fifteen thousand lire on the dashboard (this in the event—which despite everything I was still contemplating—that this was all really just paranoia on my part, a kind of delayed shock caused by the loss of the fifteen million, or heaven knows what, and the man was only a family man betrayed by appearances and forced by grave financial circumstances to defy the unlicensed taxi racket in order to scrape together a little cash), and I would get out, simply. Fourth, I prepared the fifteen thousand, pulling the notes out of my wallet with my free hand, the left, leaving my right over the door handle. Fifth, remember the bag, damnit, because I was already forgetting about that. And that was bad, because my laptop computer was inside it.

In the meantime we had come to the lights in piazza S. Maria Maggiore; red. I was no longer looking in the man's direction: but when the car came to a stop, while I noted with a certain relief that there was a police car parked broadside, to our right, with the cops leaning against the hood and all, I sensed that he was looking at me, staring at me in fact: and so instinctively I turned toward him. And the man really was looking at me, and smiling, again, as he had done shortly before when he had told the streetcar driver and his bell to go to blazes, or as he had done when he had materialized before me in the line for the taxis—as he had always done, you could say, since in reality all I had seen him do was smile. And even though the monstrous youthfulness that had already made such an impression on me was still undiminished on that old man's face of his, it would have been incorrect to say that his was a menacing smile: he was smiling, that's all. The fact was that now, as he sat there at the wheel, the butt of a pistol peeped out from the belt of his trousers. Yes, it was a pistol butt, there was no doubt. And he said the last thing I would have expected from him.

"So," he said, "Franceschino has finally learned to ride his bicycle . . ."

Green.

I didn't see myself leap out of the car, and so I cannot describe myself; but I can say how I felt: shocked. A scooter missed running me over by a whisker. The jeep, which had just moved off, braked violently in the middle of the intersection causing an instant braying of horns, and I found myself praying, really, praying that the man wouldn't shoot me in the back before I had time to talk to the policemen. Afterward, maybe, but not before. And in fact he didn't shoot me, but roared off at top speed with a furious squealing of tires.

Just as I didn't see myself leap out of the car, so I didn't hear myself talk to the policemen. I must have been rather agitated, at times perhaps incomprehensible, also because what I had to say was not simple, and there was no time to stand there and explain matters calmly. The police, however, two young men and a girl, were very understanding, and as soon as they got something of the picture they believed me, which surprised me, given the circumstances. Translated into their language, they believed that a stranger armed with a pistol, after having passed himself off as an unlicensed cab driver and after having forced me to board a jeep that was presumably stolen, had threatened my family and in particular my son, revealing that he was in the possession of some highly personal information, only to vanish with my bag—containing a laptop computer and other personal effects—as soon as I had gotten out of the car to report the matter. The girl even allowed me to call home using her private cell phone, and, when she heard me bombarding my wife with warnings not to open the door to anyone, for any reason, for heaven's sake, until I got back, she took the phone and made an effort to calm her down, saying she was a police officer and telling her not to worry because they were going to accompany me home right away.

I shall always imagine her, Anna, woken up in the middle of the night by that phone call, in the ten minutes it took for us to arrive at the house. What could she have thought? What could she have *done*? How afraid, exactly, must she have been? And of what, since neither I nor the policewoman had so much as mentioned the nature of the danger. The fact was that just as the police officers had taken me seriously, so did she, that's for sure, and in a certain sense it was also consoling, because inside me, in some mountainous region of my brain, a tenacious pack of doubts lingered on. And as soon as I dashed into the house, even before I explained the reason to her, while I was telling Anna that we had to leave, immediately, that very night, to get to a place of safety, I was nagged by the doubt that this entire maelstrom had been generated by the lightly beating wings of mythomania. After all, the scene was practically identical to the one with Kevin Costner and his wife in *The Untouchables*, when they threaten the little girl. I packed the suitcase and I thought: What if I'm going mad? This might be exactly the way that people suddenly blow a fuse and go crazy, it might have been happening to me. When would the others notice it? To what lengths would I have to go? While on the one hand it is nice to realize that you have not toiled in vain to make yourself a courageous and reliable person, on the other hand it is also worrying, because it makes you feel tremendously responsible. Probably this was because I had been brought up by a father who, as a matter of principle, always cast doubt on everything I said, and therefore I must have become inured to such lack of confidence where I was concerned: but the discovery that there was nobody to protect me from myself, supposing I had gone mad, because everyone believed me even though my behavior was so incongruous, increased, if possible, my anxiety. But there was no time to think about this: we had to run for it, run away, fast . . .

It was only on talking things over calmly, later, as we were speeding along the highway toward my in-laws' house in Viareggio, that it all began to seem clearer to me: I had found myself faced with the unknown, simply, and this had caused me to get into a flap. I told Anna about everything that had happened, from the beginning, calmly, and I resisted the temptation to lie to her about the exact expression the man had used. I'm not sure, but given that I had talked of threats against our son I was afraid for a moment that the exact words he had said to me did not entirely justify my reaction, and I was tempted to transform them into something more explicit, like "Of course now that Franceschino has learned to ride his bike it would be a pity if he were to hurt himself." I knew there was no difference but I was afraid that there might have been for Anna. Fortunately, however, I told her the truth, and I realized that there was no reason to lie, because, when she heard the phrase the way it had been spoken, she too was very frightened. And so, from the fear of being taken for an incorrigible liar, I was suddenly gripped by the fear that she might distress herself too much, and I immediately began to play down the importance of my adventure.

Of course, I said to her, maybe I was exaggerating, perhaps the danger was not so serious as to make us flee like refugees under bombardment, and it could even have been a terrible misunderstanding contrived to perfection: but how the devil was I to know? How could I take chances? I am a normal person, as I said, a peaceable writer of children's books who hasn't had a fistfight in twenty years, trained to tackle immense problems, certainly, but ones that have nothing to do with pistols stuck in trouser belts and allusions uttered Mafia-style concerning my son. We *must* run away, mustn't we, Anna?

Anna, I have to say, showed herself to be even better that I could have hoped. I don't know how or what, exactly, she understood, but she understood, and from all the reactions she could have had she chose to go along with mine, thus making everything much easier. Worried yes, but not terrified, she helped me to recover the rational side of the whole business, the only one that was really practicable for both of us, and as we drove up the Tyrrhenian coast, under the moonlight of that mid-June night, she followed me in a serene conversation in search of the dark side of our life. Where is it? we wondered. Even though there was no apparent reason for anyone to threaten us in this way, someone had done so: therefore a dark side has to be around somewhere. It was a question of understanding where.

We started with me. Was I really sure I didn't know that man, that I had never seen him before? Yes, I was absolutely sure. Was I absolutely certain that I had seen him carrying a pistol? Yes, Anna: it was a pistol. Had I perhaps written something that could have been the cause of a reprisal? No. Politics? No; over the years my political commitment had gradually diminished until it was concerned solely with the activities of an association that safeguards children's rights, which Anna knows well because we sometimes hold the meetings in our house. A small affair, very specific: we keep an eye on the television, comics, and advertising, write the odd letter of protest to the newspapers, and we organize one conference a year. Of course, we sometimes tread on the toes of some business interest, but frankly it doesn't seem possible that this activity could have unleashed a campaign of criminal persecution. Moreover, two months had gone by since we last did anything.

We moved on to her—but her life is so transparent that it's hard to find a single question mark. She is a translator, she looks after Francesco, and the house: that's it. She may have had a few secrets, I don't want to deny that, but it is really inconceivable that any one of her personal affairs could have degenerated to the point of taking the form of the maniac that had picked me up in that jeep. "The other day I was rude to the Goblin salesman," she joked. "He kept on pestering me to buy that vacuum cleaner." Yet I found myself asking her a very silly question, one that she had not asked me. Anna, do you have a lover? I don't, I hastened to add, I don't have one now and I never have, and you? Answer me sincerely, I told her, it's important: we all make lots of mistakes in life, you can go to bed with a son of a bitch who then, when the first hassles come along and he is faced with the prospect of counting for nothing anymore, loses his head and sets a cutthroat on your tail. Are you having, or have you had a relationship, Anna?—and as I asked her this I said to myself: What now if old Anna were to answer "yes": perhaps it has nothing to do with this affair, perhaps he might turn out to be an extremely civil man and a better one than me in every respect, but what if it were to come out, here, now, that she has another. Never ask these questions. Never.

She replied without hesitating and without protesting about the fact that I had considered the eventuality. No, she said—luckily. And so what can it be? Who could want to hurt us, why? And it was strange, but the more we failed to make sense of what had happened, the more we calmed down, because while it was true that a threat was looming over us it was also true that our life was clear, clean, and honest. We had known each other since we were kids, and we still loved each other; our son was snoring on the backseat, lost in the simple dreams of his eight years, and there was no jeep following us. Who would want to hurt us, why? And we repeated this question so many times, during the journey, that it was as if we had attributed it with the properties of a Tibetan mantra, reassuring, benign, capable of driving out evil at least from our heads if not from our lives. Who? Why? Who? Why?

Dawn was breaking by the time we reached Viareggio. We couldn't show up at my in-laws' house at that hour, and so we went to a hotel. To the Excelsior, damn it; and to hell with our enemies. A big room with a sea view, with an immense double bed and a single bed behind a partition, entirely useless because that night we wanted to sleep with Franceschino in our arms. But Franceschino, after having slept the whole way and after awakening among unknown marbles and stuccoes, rightly got excited and demanded a whole series of explanations that dragged us down into a mad round of colorful lies, a marvelous world of absolutely clear and reasonable causes and effects, in which no one threatened anyone else and there was no need to flee in the night like rats: exactly the same world, I realized, in which we had lived until five hours ago but one that had now become a fairy tale to be told to children.

Then, right in the middle of our explanations, Francesco fell asleep again. In an instant, as usual: a second before he was still there asking why, then he was sleeping like a log. After all that talk a mild and comfortable silence fell, while the light filtering through the curtains revealed the details of the kind of hotel room I never thought I would ever find myself in: a dressing table, a framed print, a massive wardrobe with upholstered doors. Anna fell asleep too, and I was dead tired myself, because it really had been a long, fatiguing, incredible day, but I stayed awake for a good bit longer. I looked at my boy, peace painted on his terribly delicate and transient features, and I wondered if I would be up to the situation, if I would be able to protect him. Whatever it was that was happening, it was going to be tough to face up to, because it certainly wasn't happening on my favorite terrain; but I had to do it. After all, Francesco had done it, he had won his great battle: after years of repeated failures that were inexplicable for a smart kid who had always succeeded in everything right away— with the consequent identity crisis, loss of faith in himself, psychological block and so on—he had finally managed, on his own account (and *finally,* as the man with the short-sleeved shirt under his jacket had also said), to ride his bicycle without the training wheels. He had told us on the day my father was admitted to the hospital, three weeks before, and he had given us a demonstration in the little square beneath our apartment block. He pedaled away marvelously. And we had not told my father until he was dying, he who had so stubbornly tried to force that block, to make the boy try and try again, with method, he said, and willpower—in my view complicating matters a good deal, but let that pass. After his death, the only ones who knew that Francesco had kicked the habit were Anna and me, apart from that little pal of his from the ground floor, whatshisname, Luca, with whom he would hold races in the courtyard every afternoon. We still hadn't talked of the matter to anyone else, damn it, because Francesco had wanted to surprise everyone, that summer.

four

We spent some lovely, strange days in Viareggio. Just like Francesco, Anna's parents had accepted without objections our version, according to which we had simply wanted to stay with them for a bit, and they took pleasure in the consequences—company, lunches, grandson at their disposal. They did not consider the absurdity of the circumstances: a little boy who still had not finished the school year and two parents who were usually incredibly busy that, out of the blue, one Wednesday, drop everything and go off to the seaside. Or perhaps—more probably—they had considered the absurdity but had not asked for explanations, because they were discreet and because it was not in their interest. The fact is that we spent some serene days there, despite the situation: on the beach, on the paddleboat, in the pinewoods, on the promenade, on the docks, and in the amusement arcades. Yes, probably we were all pretending, my in-laws were pretending that our visit was normal, Francesco was pretending that he still hadn't learned to ride his bicycle (he wanted to wait for my father, convinced as he was that you come back from death), and Anna and I were pretending that no one was threatening us; and perhaps this was the very reason why we weren't worried.

Of course, I was markedly more vigilant, ready to notice the slightest thing that was out of place (like the *Spot the Mistake* section in tests), but I never actually saw anything disturbing, with the exception of a Daihatsu Feroza speeding along the promenade just as we were about to cross the road—but it was a different color and it had Lucca rather than Rome plates, but it gave me a start in any case.

Anna and I kept on putting off facing the problem; and at bottom, while we were playacting, it wasn't hard to let ourselves be borne along by appearances for a few days, imagining we were one of those happy, absolutely ghastly little families of self-sufficiency freaks, who rebel against massification by rejecting details rather than fundamental principles, and so they don't have television, don't give one another Christmas presents, and hold football, sliced pizza, and sweatshirts in contempt. Actually there is something heroic about these families that has always fascinated me: their attachment to supremely irrelevant values (alternative medicine, holidays in June, Nordic skiing, organic fruit) in whose name they stagger departures, plan, save, spend, and travel around Europe with discernment, in a strenuous waste of intelligence that ferries them from a form of consumerism that is barbarous and chaotic to one that is far more Christian and logical, albeit no less voracious. We are not like that—too much effort—but we could be; and above all, as we strolled along the promenade at Viareggio at eight o'clock on the eleventh of June, I with Francesco on my shoulders, Anna with her light, ex–ballet dancer's step, in the fragrant evening air, among swallows high on space, surrounded by a jungle of agaves exceptionally in bloom (they flower every fifteen years, and then they die) and by many other beauties as yet spared the assault that would disfigure them a few weeks later, we might have *seemed* like that. A different family, one of those that the pollsters discard because they spoil the sample group. Besides, Viareggio in June *is* different: it is aristocratic and languid, even exotic, as it must have been in its prewar heyday, when Edda Ciano used to spend her restless holidays there, and porcine Fascist leaders with hair plastered in brilliantine wheeled and dealed between the bedrooms and swimming pools, as anarchist heroes dreamed of blowing them sky-high with the famous bomb-to-liberate-everyone that has never exploded in Italy. Of course, what do I know about the way Viareggio was then. Nothing. But I sometimes imagine it: the air, the colors, and the smells of those days, I don't know how but it strikes me that I *remember* them; and when I found myself, in June, amid the paradox of those empty and rarefied days, but especially in the early morning, along the beach still only sparsely dotted with beach umbrellas, I always got the feeling that such things had reemerged from the rubble of the present. Like when you meet an old lady you have never seen before, and in the way she smiles or withdraws her hand after a greeting you feel as if you can see the beauty of a half century before, a beauty you have obviously never known.

In short, fine days; only four of them, to tell the truth, but it seemed like many more than that. It was only on the second to last day, after having put Francesco to bed, and taking advantage of the absence of my in-laws (they go dancing, every Saturday, in places frequented by older people), that Anna and I got back to the fundamental business, and it was hard to persuade her to accept what I had decided in the meantime, in other words that I was going to return to Rome, but she and Francesco weren't. It was a classic case of the untenable argument, whose first premise contradicts the second, because in saying that I intended to go back to Rome, I had perforce to maintain that it wasn't dangerous, but in asking her to stay at the seaside with the little boy I was implicitly stating that it was. A rational woman, Anna pressed me hard on this point, and dialectically she won all down the line, no doubt about that, except for the fact that in the end she was persuaded to let me go, since she had understood that mine was neither the most brilliant nor the most logical but simply the only solution. And she was splendidly expeditious in resigning herself to this: a brief and lightning-fast sequence that went to join the list of her exemplary gestures—perfectly executed gestures, that is—in which she manages to make form and content correspond like no other person I have ever known.

The argument was in full swing, she had just drawn breath to rebut one of my statements: she suddenly stopped, and instead of speaking she turned her face to one side, lowering her gaze to the ground as if looking for something. Her feet were in the fourth ballet position. She stayed like that for a few seconds, two, three, something like that—all I know is that it was the *right* time: less and it would have been comical, more and she would have seemed hesitant. Then she looked at me once more and said: "All right." End of argument.

So, there I was on my way back to Rome, alone, in the car, on a sparkling Sunday morning traveling along in the opposite direction from almost everyone in Italy, that is, from the seaside toward the city. I had thought that if I had to go back I might as well do so right away, and take advantage of the empty Sunday afternoon to think things over alone, trying to get my thoughts in order. For my misadventure—let's call it that—with the man at the station, four days before, had come right in the middle of what was a rather delicate moment for me, for several reasons. My father had died, as I have said, and this was one reason. By December 31st I had to deliver a new book of the adventures of Pizzano Pizza, and not only had I yet to begin, I had no idea of *where* to begin: I've said this too, and this too was a reason. But there was another reason, although compared to the first two it might seem less objective and therefore less serious: it was a matter of my self-image, which had recently become vague and shaky. I was no longer sure if I was who I thought I was; and this threw me off balance quite a bit, especially in situations that required a certain promptness in decision making. Take the ugly encounter at the station, for example:

I'm not sure if I *recognize myself*—if you see what I mean—in the reactions I had, either in the heat of the moment or later. My getting into that jeep even though I had sensed that I shouldn't have done so, then my diving out at the light and risking getting run over; putting myself so blindly into the hands of the police—with whom I had not exactly had good relations in the past; and then, at home, my absolute certainty that we had to run for it, and at the same time the profound, genuine suspicion that I was blowing things out of proportion; my capacity to remove the problem for the four days that followed, living the tranquil days of the holiday-maker, and even the decision to go back to Rome alone, to face heaven knows what, with heaven knows what resources. Come to think of it, I don't know where all that sprang from; but if I had to imagine myself wrestling with a problem of this kind, then that was certainly not the way I would imagine myself. And this wasn't the last of my doubts. For some time, as a matter of fact, you could say that I had been doing nothing else but doubt myself.

At the root of this insecurity of mine there was also a kind of trauma. I do not deny that this must have been a process with profound and complex causes, which must certainly have begun lord knows how long before, without my realizing it: the fact is, however, that I had become brutally aware of it a couple of months previously, following a curious incident that had occurred with the intercom in my house. Some people had come to dinner, more specifically my agent with his fiancée and a couple of mutual friends, he was an art critic, she was a speech therapist, whom Anna and I see often because they have a son of Francesco's age. We had eaten well, and drunk a good wine brought by my agent, who is a connoisseur, and chatted pleasantly until eleven. At that hour, owing to baby-sitter problems, our friends had to leave, while my agent and his fiancée stayed on. I saw the departing guests to the door and, immediately after closing it, my eyes met those of my agent, who had followed me to the vestibule. He was wearing a very mischievous look.

"I always listen to what people say as they are leaving my

house," he whispered, with a meaningful glance at the intercom hanging on the wall. I thought it was a horrible idea, manic stuff; but, God knows why, I did it: while he continued to stare at me that way I raised the handset and began to listen—which is why I can now give you a great piece of advice: don't ever do it. Never eavesdrop on the things people say when they leave your house.

To get out of my house you have to go down four flights of stairs, then there is a door and a little courtyard to cross before you come to the gate that gives onto the street, where the doorbells are: for a bit, therefore, all I could hear were indistinct little noises, mopeds going past, rustling; then there was the click of the front door catch, and from then on my friends' voices became more and more distinct. Well, it wasn't true that they had baby-sitter problems: they had simply been unable to stand our company any longer. He was congratulating her for having come up with a good excuse, and when he must have come to the point right in front of the doorbells, because his voice was very strong, I heard him saying I was ridiculous because for the umpteenth time I had related a certain anecdote about when I was in military college. Nor did they spare my agent, defined by her as a "parasite," or his fiancée ("neither fish nor fowl"), and the voices faded away as both, absolutely in agreement, said that Anna and I were stingy because despite the tons of money I must have made thanks to Pizzano Pizza we were still living in that shabby little house, with linoleum on the floors, unmatched chairs, and no elevator. Only Franceschino was spared, but perhaps they liquidated him when they were too far away and I couldn't hear them anymore.

It costs me a lot to talk of this—it is distressing, but I think it is important: those two were my friends, and the fact that they could talk that way about me, about my wife, about my house, and about my guests really upset me. On the other hand, apart from the business of the money (I haven't made tons of it at all), it's not that they said things that were false: I often relate anecdotes I have already related, my agent lives on percentages of other people's earnings, his fiancée is a lovely girl but in actual fact is not a sparkling conversationalist, and our house could really use a good face-lift. It's just that I would never have imagined that those two could have minded about such things, after all the years we had been frequenting one another, and especially that they could have spoken about them in such a cutting tone after having used a pretext to flee from an after-dinner party they could no longer bear.

These things disorient one.

When I hung up, my agent was sniggering, and for a moment I hoped that he had set things up with them in order to play a trick on me. But it wasn't like that, those two had been talking in earnest, and he had no idea of the trouble he had caused.

"Nothing," I said to him. "They didn't say a word."

I didn't say anything to Anna either—I was too ashamed, but it was from that moment that I began to doubt myself openly. Although I was strongly tempted, it would have been silly to dismiss the matter by concluding that certain presumed friends were in reality gigantic shits—a conclusion that I had come to regarding those two in any event, but without considering the problem solved. No, they had been talking about me, about my life, and they were in complete agreement, blast them; shits they may well have been, but that's how they saw me: an unbearable, ridiculous skinflint. There was a problem all right, but it was mine, not theirs.

And so I inevitably found myself wondering: What if the correct line of reasoning were the exact opposite of the line I had been following so far? What if growing older did not mean knowing oneself at all, and the gift of experience consisted only in having to insert a big fat "don't" into the phrase "I know who I am"? Everything struck me as frighteningly more plausible. At twenty you still know almost nothing about yourself, because you have never found yourself faced with anything really important, and you think that your confusion is due to that. Then you begin to accumulate experiences, every one of which provides you with information about yourself that you didn't possess before: the resulting portrait is fuzzy at first, but it gradually becomes more and more detailed and credible, until one day you think you have sufficient information to enable you to consider it definitive, and you come to terms with it. You accept it, first of all, and then you laboriously resign yourself to all the limitations and defects that it nails you to, and, by resigning yourself, you feel at peace with yourself a little for the first time—and, precisely because you think that that peace springs from a long process of self-awareness, you begin to rely on it; but since you continue to accumulate experiences, sooner or later one comes along to upset your applecart (you weren't *obliged* to pick up that intercom: anyway, shortly afterward your father was going to die suddenly, and then a mysterious encounter was going to terrify you, and then goodness knows what else), after which the various pieces of information on yourself can no long coexist and begin to war furiously among themselves, thus tearing to shreds in a short time what had been assembled with all that ingenuous patience. In a twinkling, the reassuring, hard-won illusion that you know what to expect from life is swept away to be replaced by the suspicion that from then on, you, a stranger to yourself, in whatever circumstances, would have to content yourself with discovering *in the field* whether friends can bear you or not, whether you are miserly or not, ridiculous or not, knowing that the others, around you, may judge you very harshly even though they have no right to do so, and above all knowing that things will never again be any different; the suspicion that the time that remains to you, in reality, will be none other than this daily damnation—a lengthy and tentative return toward the confusion you began with.

This is why I had been wondering for some time what the devil kind of a person I really was; and this is why I felt that I didn't have the slightest idea. And I was reminded of the journalist's question, there at the prize-giving ceremony: "Are you," pause, "an unhappy man?" The right answer was "I don't know."

In the meantime I had almost arrived. Rome was hot and empty, everyone was away. I drove slowly along the Ostia road; seen like that, with no traffic, shaded by the central rows of sycamores trembling in the breeze, and even silent, it looked like some Cuban *avenida*. It was odd, but after having skirted the sea for three hours, down from Viareggio along the coast of Tuscany and Lazio, it was there that I felt I could perceive the sea, as if before me there stood, not the Cimitero degli Inglesi (*harsh climate, balmy history*, as Pasolini put it), but a harbor breakwater. It was the same thing on the terrace of my house, up there, where the eye roams out over the broad southwestern horizon of the city, open and clear but with so little of Rome about it, centered as it is on the white triangle of the Cestia Pyramid: I felt as if I were in some splendid city on the sea that I had never visited—Salonika, Alexandria, Izmir—and I had the impression that those expanses of rooftops pierced by antennas barely concealed a view of a port in the Levant, sensual and swarming with illicit activities.

I stopped at a red light, but the intersection was deserted. I wound down the window, and a wave of hot, improbably scented air swept over me. My house was up there, on the top of its nameless hill. It could have been a beautiful moment, everything seemed suspended, and when the lights changed to green I could even linger without anyone behind me starting to blare on his horn. I could have even been at peace. But no, peace was far off, and beset by the storm of first times that was raging over me anew, as if I were an adolescent; I was about to park outside the house, where I would go up to the gate with my keys already in hand, warily, for the first time in my life ready to throw myself to the ground in case someone came up to shoot me.

five

L et every man do his duty. May life carry on as normal." These are the shining words that the Emperor of Japan addressed to his people on the outbreak of war with Russia, in 1904. I had written them down, some time before, in my notebook, in expectation of the time when they might have come in handy, and it looked as if that time had come: the only thing was that when I copied them down I had thought to make literary use of them, that is by putting them in the mouth of some character in the next Pizzano Pizza book, or maybe even by having him say them in person, but I found myself having to make *literal* use of them instead. But since on coming back home that hot Roman afternoon everything appeared peaceful as usual, since no one had attacked or followed me, nor had the house been visited by strangers during our absence, for the time being my duty was reduced to dealing with the chores that had accumulated over those days of flight. Correspondence to be answered, undelivered postal packages to be picked up, bills to be paid, seventeen messages on the answering machine—as well as the list I had brought with me from Viareggio, in which Anna had set down all the things I had to do on my own, if I wanted to keep her and Francesco far from Rome; and, considering that I was still behind with other obligations as a result of the upset caused by my father's death, I had four or five days of work in front of me.

Of course, it's frightening to think of how much continuity of action is required by the practical aspects of everyday life. You don't notice until you find them lined up in front of you all together after having neglected them for a while, and it seems indecent, as your father lies dying, or as you are escaping because someone has threatened your family, that they continue to accumulate as if nothing had happened. It seems indecent, but it isn't: it's normal, even right. People like me must acknowledge that their existence, no matter how spiritually intense it may be at times or no matter how it may be troubled by menacing events, is nonetheless founded on this daily metabolism of practical things. And if, as I believe, this existence contains a strength, that strength is *also* due to the acquired capacity to control that metabolism without coming apart at the seams. I played chess for many years, taking some severe drubbings from down-at-the-heels Russian masters who during the tournaments would peddle icons in imitation gold—and *Berkut* binoculars and contraband cameras—and I learned at least two things: the first is that if you are under attack—but also when you are the attacker—you have to pay the maximum attention to the unimportant pieces, defending them and looking after them as if they were not extraneous to the action in the slightest, while maintaining a constant understanding of the overall picture; the second is that in the world, from a certain level upward, there will always be several dozen people who are better than I am at doing this—which is why I gave up chess.

And so, even though it may seem absurd, the first real move I made in defense of my family was to draw up a list of things to do over the days that followed, in order of importance, in order to untangle the knot that they had formed as soon as possible. I was meticulous, continually struggling against the temptation to stretch out on the sun lounger on the terrace and to abandon myself to my worries in the afternoon sun. I did everything on impulse, without ever stopping to think, but even had I wanted to, despite the orgy of inanities I had devoted myself to, I could not have lost sight of the principal problem, since two of the messages on the answering machine were from a certain Inspector Olivieri of the Esquilino police station, asking me to stop by her office as soon as possible to sign my statement; but I restricted myself merely to transcribing these two messages onto a sheet of paper together with the other fifteen, without setting them aside for any special treatment—so that their importance might emerge objectively, and so that they might conquer the top ranking in my list only as a result of fair competition with all other matters pending. "May life carry on as normal," damn it: Japan wiped the floor with Russia in that war.

I also called Anna, naturally, to tell her that all was quiet: and it was only at that point, finally stretching myself on the lounger on the terrace, with a stiff gin and tonic to be downed on an empty stomach, did I allow myself the luxury of thinking.

The afternoon was drawing to a close with exquisite slowness, as can happen only in June, in that part of the world. Before me, in the distance, just above the flat green crest of the Janiculum, pierced by the skyscraper—that's what they call it—in piazza Rosolino Pilo, an airplane was flying at what seemed a frighteningly low altitude. But I knew it was an optical illusion, I've learned that much. The sky was full of swallows soaring and wheeling, and by the time the noise of the traffic below—the blowing of horns, the revving of motorcycle engines, ambulances—came to me, it was muffled and seemed normal, reassuring. I finished the gin and tonic and made an effort to bring to mind all the things that I had tried to keep at bay over the previous four days: an armed stranger had identified me in the line outside the Stazione Termini, he persuaded me, let's say, to get into his car, and then, smiling, had showed that he knew something about my son that no one knew. This had happened, four days before. It was undoubtedly serious, but the time I had allowed to flow over events had already washed away the details, so that, at that point, it was no longer a matter of a recollection but of a sort of *news item*. What had that man been like? Height . . . ? Eyes . . . ? Hair . . . ? If I was going to drop in on that Inspector Olivieri the following day to sign my complaint (for this was how the police had obviously taken my request for protection), I was going to have to provide a minimum of information. Yet, although I was the first to find it strange, I couldn't remember that man anymore. I remembered that he smiled, but I couldn't remember his smile. I remembered that under his jacket he had been wearing a short-sleeved shirt, but I couldn't remember the color, either of the jacket or the shirt. What the hell kind of inquiries could ever be made, if I myself was unable to provide one useful piece of information?

I decided to have another gin and tonic. On going back into the living room to prepare it and on returning to the terrace to drink it, I felt my legs were already pleasantly wobbly, and I liked that. I stretched out again, drank, took a breath: my head was spinning—very nice. I almost never drink, but when I do I want to see results as soon as possible, which is why I prefer to drink on an empty stomach—and by results I mean precisely the light-headed feeling I had then: not real drunkenness, merely a slight fogginess in the brain, just enough to scrape away the coating of rationality and finally let the irrational stuff run free. Yes, I felt fine: the dusk's slow advancing, the rooftops of Rome, the heat, the swallows, my slightly befuddled senses, and my brain prepared to content itself with the most improbable solutions to my problem. For example, the eventuality of a derisively illogical universe—why not?—in which events take place without a cause, without any logical nexus, as in cartoons. Then, at that moment, I would have been prepared to believe it. No natural order of things, only an insensate jumble of events, great and small, individual and collective, which the shamans of reason manage to put in relation with one another only occasionally, locally, and at random: a universe in the image and likeness of the "shuffle" button on compact disc players. No God, no Big Bang, at best a big book like the one imagined by Melville at the beginning of *Moby-Dick*, in which the things that must come to pass are written, but without the mark of the Fates, and without any other artifice, any explanation. People read these things and carry them out as and when they can. That was why the character at the railway station suddenly wasn't a problem anymore, because he had simply been doing his duty: on passing by there, he had read in the big book, *"Let someone steal a car, stick a pistol in his belt and tell a certain Gianni Orzan that his son has finally learned to ride his bicycle,"* and he had done this: but he didn't have it in for me, he didn't even know who I was, and I wouldn't be seeing any more of him. A senseless world, all right: it would have been fantastic, then, to discover that that was how it worked, and that I had gotten it all wrong in life.

Suddenly, almost in corroboration of this hypothesis, a voice began to curse right under my terrace: it was a youthful, broken voice, like that of someone who was yelling at the top of his voice and weeping at the same time. And he was cursing, only cursing. For a while, I lay there on the lounger listening; the cursing continued, so I got up and went over to the parapet—around whose perimeter, about seven years before, when Franceschino had learned to walk, I had erected a barrier of green garden mesh fencing a good meter high to avoid any risk of his ending up like Conor Clapton: it spoiled the view a bit, but without it, peace of mind would have been literally out of the question for Anna and me.

The voice continued cursing: three different expressions, I noted, always repeated in the same order—first the Madonna, then God, then the Madonna again. There was absolute desperation in those shouts, a blend of fury, suffering, frenzy, hatred, anguish, and frustration, which nonetheless seemed to have found a strange equilibrium in this monotonous solo, without a crescendo and without variations. First curse. Second curse. Third curse. Pause.

First curse. Second curse. Third curse. Pause. And again. As regular as a burglar alarm.

Naturally I couldn't see who was swearing. I thought I had spotted the house in which he was at work, on the first floor of the building behind mine: an apparently modest flat, with windows thrown open, peeling gray paintwork, and a little terrace where a flowering jasmine clinging to the wall struggled heroically with brooms and clothes rack in a battle to decide the effective use of the area: open air closet or cool and scented nook in which to smoke a cigarette on evenings like this, leaning against the iron parapet to contemplate the doormat of sky between the surrounding buildings, reflecting on how life might have gone and didn't? But I wasn't even sure if that was indeed the right house. The strange thing was that no other voice came to superimpose itself over that of the swearer, as one might have expected, perhaps the voice of a woman begging him to stop or that of a man threatening blows; nothing: our hero must have been at home alone. And the other strange thing was the absence of any accompanying sound, which produces the improbable image of a young man possessed only vocally, howling curses without storming through the house, without breaking anything, and without—the doubt arose—even being able to move.

A kid tied to the bed and left alone in the throes of a withdrawal crisis: it was the only thing I could think of.

In the meantime the swearing had drawn several people to the windows of the houses all around, and comments were already being exchanged in loud voices, so I beat a retreat. It may be that they knew exactly who was swearing and why; but, although I too would have liked to know this, I didn't want to satisfy my curiosity with windowsill chit-chat.

Then, as suddenly as it had begun, the cursing ceased, and this, at bottom, seemed far more mysterious: why? What the devil had happened? I continued to listen for a little longer, just in case it was merely a longer pause; but it really seemed as if the show was over, and all I could hear was my doorbell ringing. I went back inside the house, and the telephone began to ring too: by then my head wasn't spinning anymore, the cursing had had the effect of a bucketful of cold water, but this sudden concomitance, with all the new questions it brought with it (Who can it be? Which bell should I answer first? What time is it), dazed me a bit. For a second I just stood there midway, then, without having really decided, I awarded precedence to the doorbell and went to the door. If I had heard aright, it was the bell right there on the landing, which sounds a bit different from when they ring from the gate down in the street: and so as I was opening I was expecting some neighbor, who for God knows what mindless domestic reason, perhaps to exchange a few comments on the cursing, but perhaps only because he or she was oppressed by solitude on that first real summer Sunday afternoon, had had the brilliant idea of . . .

But—a fine coup de théatre, this—it was the man with the short-sleeved shirt under his jacket.

I instantly recognized the old-adolescent mug that a few minutes before I thought I had forgotten (obviously he was smiling), and my heart shot straight into my throat, paralyzing me. In the meantime the telephone had rung until the answering machine had cut in to diffuse through the house the voice of a woman (not Anna's): " . . . still out . . . ," it said, ". . . or out to dinner . . ."

"Your bag," said the man, "I've brought back your bag."

I was still paralyzed. It's a strange sensation: I could see everything, perceive everything (in fact, my impression is that in this state one can perceive far more things), but I couldn't move an inch or emit a sound, every single impulse I sent out misfired, and I felt really awful. I can't say that it was a new feeling, because it was more or less what you go through in nightmares, but when you're awake it's another matter altogether. I barely managed to direct my gaze onto the man's hands, which were in fact clutching the handles of my brown leather traveling bag: it was really my bag, the one I had left in the jeep, with the computer inside and all the rest.

"Here you are," he said, and he held it out to me.

The answering machine had finished recording, and it was emitting its end-of-message *boop boop boop*. The man smiled, the bag in midair, proffered in a quasi-votive gesture.

"I saw the car parked outside and . . ."

Then I was suddenly paralyzed no longer. I realized this because I suddenly did what I hadn't managed to do when it should have been done (it should have been done immediately upon recognizing the man), when it would have made much more sense, while at that moment more than anything else it seemed like the firing of an impulse hitherto on hold and its effect was, well, pretty comic, since comedy is a question of timing, as we all know, and in this case the interval between what I should have done and when I actually did it was time enough to contain all the hypothetical unexpected events that gestures of that kind are calculated to protect one from—like a pistol shot, for example, or a blackjack over the head, or a punch in the face, or even only a shove from a big pistol-packing belly that hurls you aside to burst into your apartment, after which God only knows what might happen. Admittedly, none of these events occurred, and indeed nothing at all had happened thus far, since we were both standing motionless in the doorway, me paralyzed, and he smiling with my bag in his hand, so in the end, comical though it may have been, what I did was nonetheless the only intelligent move available to me, in other words: to slam the door in his face (*blam!*) and to slide home the bolt.

six

The door of my house. I on this side, he on the other. Outside, beyond the crumbling cinder-block and mortar walls with which this building was built in feverish haste immediately after the war, in my nameless little quarter and then gradually all over Rome, all over Italy, and all over Europe, at that moment people were preparing dinner, watering the garden, playing with the children, coming home from days out, watching the news, or, as Franceschino was certainly doing in Viareggio, old Japanese cartoons on obscure local TV channels with indecipherable logos. But lord knows what was about to happen to me . . .

"Gianni!" His warm, sweet voice barely managed to carry through the wood of the door: it was in such sharp contrast with his appearance that it seemed as if it had been made afterward, to make up for it.

"Sorry, I didn't mean to scare you!"

I wasn't paralyzed anymore, but I wasn't *moving*. What to do? I could have made a 113 call. Unfortunately, however, the police emergency number was no longer 113 but another number that I couldn't remember, 118, 119—damn it, why did they have to change it? What was wrong with 113?

"Gianni!"

I harpooned the phone book, stretching an arm out toward the shelf by the door where the phone stood—I didn't go there, he could have fired through the door and shot me. I looked up the introductory pages and found that they hadn't changed the police emergency number at all, it was still there, the first of the emergency numbers, to be dialed "only in case of real and imminent danger to persons," as the caption said. So why had I been convinced they had changed it?

"Gianni," the bell sounded again, two rings, "I'm a friend of your father's! Open up, come on . . ."

That was a good one. I knew I shouldn't answer, not before having called the police, because in that case I might as well have opened the door and have done with it. But that was really too much.

"A friend of *whose*?" Perhaps I was shouting too loud, but god knows what the right volume is for speaking through a door.

"Of your father's."

Such a good one it was almost encouraging, I should have said. Or at any rate it wasn't threatening, that's it; which was already something, at that moment.

"That's absurd," I said, still loudly.

"It's the truth, Gianni."

That made four: he was really determined to be on first name terms.

"And what was the name again?"

"Whose name?"

"Yours."

"I'm Gianni too," he replied, "Gianni Bogliasco. My name won't mean anything to you, but . . ."

"That's right, it means nothing to me. Therefore you are not a friend of my father's."

"But I am! You must believe me!"

"Leave me in peace or I'll call the police!"

"I can prove to you that I'm telling the truth!"

"I'm going to call the police!"

"Hey, all I did was bring back your bag . . ."

"Thanks. Leave it on the landing."

"Listen, I realize that I may have given you the wrong impression the other night, but I really am a friend of your father's. Your father's *best* friend, for Christ's sake! We were prisoners together in Russia, we spent half a lifetime together, and his death was a terrible blow for me! How can I prove this to you? Ask me anything!"

Silence.

"What was my father's great passion?"

What was I doing? A moment before, the mere sight of that man had paralyzed me with fear (and, while I'm on the subject, what an *enormous* disappointment to find myself so devoid of resources in his presence, so incapable of reacting, despite the fact that over those last few days it could be said that I had been thinking of nothing else save the moment in which we would meet again, and of how to deal with that moment, and of how to deal with him) and there I was playing quiz games with him through the door. This was a character who went around armed. And in all his life my father had never pronounced that name, Bogliasco . . .

"Translating from Russian," he replied.

Correct. That was something few people knew: my father used to translate from Russian, but he never talked about it and, especially, he hadn't the slightest ambition to publish. He did it for himself, he used to say, for love: love of the Russian language, which he had learned during his imprisonment.

"He translated all of Sholokov," the man continued, "and, seeing that I know Russian too, let me tell you that he did so wonderfully well, not like that garbage they published here. But you never read his translation of *And Quiet Flows the Don*, did you?"

"No," I replied, in a much lower voice, so much so that he probably didn't hear me, there on the other side of the door.

"Oh, I know . . . And your father was hurt by that. He set great store by your opinion, you know. You ought to read it, really, and then compare it with the version published by Bompiani in 1941. You're a writer, you'd appreciate the difference . . ."

It was absurd. There I was talking about translations from Russian with the man who had thrown the last few days of my life into complete confusion, through the door. My fears, naturally, had been dispelled; in an American film this last chunk of dialogue would have intensified them even more, because in films intellectual killers are the worst kind: but this was reality speaking in Italian, and the wild men that go around shooting people have never even heard of Sholokov. At that point I was suddenly overwhelmed by powerful feelings of shame, for having been scared, and so badly scared, until a moment before, and for all the things I had done, thought, and said over the previous four days. Not that the mystery of that man had been resolved, nor was his presence on the other side of my front door any the less incongruous than before.

I slid back the bolt and opened the door, in an attempt to recover a scrap of dignity: taken by surprise, the man started, and for a split second I managed to see him when he was not smiling. On looking at him, I remembered him: his image, then, there on the landing, with my bag between his legs, immediately called up the image of a few evenings before, when he had presented himself before me to offer me his cut rates, and the one superimposed itself perfectly upon the other, like spoons. Gray hair, dandruff on the shoulders, broken nose, distended belly, smile, wrestler's forearms protruding out from the sleeves of his jacket, naked and hairy: more than anything else he looked like some former rugby player of the fifties, a hooker, punchy from scrums and beer—one of those who played with a scrum cap, for teams that were legends in Italian rugby: Petrarca, Fracasso, or Amatori, and were considered irreplaceable even though they had never scored so much as one try, nor were they likely to, in all their careers.

"Weren't you supposed to be an unauthorized taxi driver?" I asked, point-blank.

"No, no," he laughed. "It was, let's say, inappropriate to approach you that way the other evening. I wanted it to be a fun thing, but instead . . ."

He spoke with a slight Tuscan accent—Livorno, or Pisa.

"Are you armed?," I asked.

"Well, actually: that's another thing I have to explain to you, I realize. But I assure you that the other evening I . . ."

"Now, I mean."

"Yes, I am armed."

"Pistol?"

"Yes."

"And do you intend to use it? Are you thinking of having a gunfight with me?"

"Obviously not."

"So why did you bring it with you?"

"Listen, I'll explain everything you want me to, but it would be better if you let me in, don't you think?"

His voice was still completely incompatible with his appearance: it was fine, elegant. I repeat, almost sweet.

"How come you knew my son had learned to ride his bike without the training wheels?"

"Your father told me."

"Like hell he told you!" I blurted out. "He was dying when I told him!"

He didn't bat an eyelid.

"As a matter of fact he told me in the hospital, the last time I saw him," his expression became serious, "two days before he died," then it brightened again. "But do we really have to stand here in the doorway?"

"I'm going out," I said.

"Oh yes? And where are you off to?"

"What d'you mean where am I off to?"

"Are you going to your mother's, by any chance?"

"No."

"Well, when you do see your mother, ask her if I am a friend of your father's or not. Anyway, you'll be going there sooner or later, won't you?"

"I'll ask her."

"Do that, tell her you've met me."

"I shall."

"Do you remember my name?"

"Gianni Bogliasco."

"Perfect."

He rubbed his nose with the back of his hand and sniffed.

"Naturally," he continued, "she will deny she knows me."

"I beg your pardon?"

"I said that your mother will deny knowing me. One hundred percent. But you look her in the eye, while she does so, and with your expert son's eye you'll realize that she is lying."

And he smiled. The taller the story, the more he smiled.

"I see," I said. "Can I go now?"

"The bag."

Right. He held it out to me, and I put it on the floor, in the doorway. I didn't even bother to take out the computer, but grabbed the keys off the shelf and went out. I didn't have the faintest idea where I was going: Mom's place would have been an ideal solution, if she hadn't been in Sabaudia with my sister—who has three children, and a really wealthy husband, and a villa by the sea, and Filipino servants, and a French nanny, a whole series of luxuries that instantly suggested that destination to a seventy-year-old widow whose house had suddenly become carnivorous. I slammed the door and set off down the stairs, heedless of my man.

"Aren't you going to lock up?" he said.

"What?"

"The door. Aren't you going to lock it?"

"No."

"That's bad . . ."

He caught up with me on the landing of the floor below, and from there we went down together, without talking, to the courtyard. I noticed that he had a whistle in his chest, like emphysema: you could hear it distinctly every time he breathed.

"Bye, then," he said, when we got to the gate, "and sorry again for the other evening. I messed up my entry."

He held out his hand and I shook it without looking at him, my glance falling on the wall in front of my house, which had borne the words ELVIS IS A BIG FAGGOT for years and years. God knows how old the graffiti artist was by that time.

"Good-bye," I said.

His hand was as hard and callused as a chimpanzee's.

"Who was doing all that swearing, before?" he suddenly asked me, all cheerful. He might even have been the same age as my father, were it not for the diabolically youthful expression on his face.

"I have no idea."

"You don't trust me, do you?" he asked me. (And, incidentally, how my answer could have triggered that question was another mystery.)

"Not blindly," I said.

He became pensive. He didn't seem to be aware of the fact that such a thing as sarcasm exists in the world.

"You're not all wrong there," he said, "but I'm very fond of you, and I'll give you proof of that," he was caressing my shoulder, no less, "because we need to talk, you and I."

"It's not a particularly pressing need, as far as I'm concerned."

Again, he took my answer literally, very seriously, and nodded with a thoughtful air.

"But it is for me," he said. "There are things I absolutely must tell you."

The caress became a grip: a very light one, of course, but enough to make me look up at him. Naturally, he was smiling. And the challenge was on, the kind that kids hold with their friends, and that some people—not me, but evidently he was one of them—still hold as adults, with strangers on the train, at the traffic lights, or in the elevator, in an attempt to see who can oblige the other to lower his gaze—to establish what, god only knows.

I realized that I was holding up well, I hadn't expected that: without embarrassment I held his gaze, fixing on his beady, close-set eyes, cunning and deceitful as those of a fox terrier, which were shifting imperceptibly from left to right to stare into mine (the usual old story that, in reality, you only look at one eye at a time), and so much did I enter into the spirit of this challenge that I even came to think that by winning it I would have wiped out the sense of shame that was still oppressing me, because of the fear I had felt and had made others feel over the previous days. And while I was staring at him I had the odd dual feeling that while, in reality, on the one hand my fear had been unjustified, since you could see perfectly well that this man had no evil intentions toward me (at most he was a bit cracked, as well as obsessed with my father for some reason that would soon—I felt there was no way out—be revealed to me), on the other hand it *was* justified, because on observing him carefully I realized that in some mysterious way his face reflected the fear that over the years a number of people must have felt in his presence—because there's no help for it, people's expressions, the way they smile or clench their jaw or raise their eyebrows, and I'd even go as far as to say that, with the passage of time, even their features, in other words the permanent physical traits, wind up by retaining a trace of what others have felt in their presence: I have always believed this, and so I could easily believe, even though in the particular circumstance that had led him to me there had been no reason to be afraid, that this man must have aroused a good deal of fear, in his lifetime, and the marks of that were written upon him.

"You don't have to go anywhere, do you?" he said, suddenly, taking me by surprise and breaking the concentration with which I was standing up to him. At that point, after that truth—and truth it was—the challenge suddenly struck me as pointless, and his gaze became unendurable.

ELVIS IS A BIG FAGGOT.

"Come on," he said to me, "I'll buy you dinner. Let's go eat fish, in the open air . . ."

I noticed that he stank of cigarettes like a badly stubbed-out butt. Since I had stopped smoking, nine months before, it was a characteristic I happened to notice in people, and it really disgusted me: not for the stink as such but because it made me think that, without bothering about it, and without even being aware of it, for twenty years I too had shown up for all the most important appointments of my life stinking in the very same way (twenty Marlboros a day), including naturally the first fateful time I embraced my newborn son, which must have created in him, according to the theory of imprinting, and especially considering the following seven and a half years of equally stinking hugs, an indelible association between that stink of cigarettes and the idea of his father—in other words, me: an association against which the daily heroism I had shown in abstaining from cigarettes for nine months would count for nothing, nothing . . .

"I have to talk to you about your father," he insisted. "I have to tell you the things you don't know . . ."

Dusk. At that hour, in Viareggio, Anna would have just finished clearing the table and would be loading the dishwasher—"Don't worry, Mom, I'll see to it"—with her red rubber gloves pulled up to her elbows and a rebellious lock of hair dangling down over her forehead. In the garden, Franceschino would certainly be struggling with himself, swithering between revealing or not revealing to his grandparents that he had learned to ride his bike without the training wheels, as he waited for my father to return from the dead. And if it is true that children possess a particular sensitivity when it comes to perceiving ghosts and spirits, then in that instant Franceschino ought to have decided that yes, the time had come, his dead grandfather had returned and therefore it was time to tell everyone the great secret—since I had just decided to accept the invitation to dinner made me by an armed and stinking stranger who was going to talk to me about my father and I already wanted to hear the man talking about him, in whatever way he chose, whatever it was he had to tell me—even though, as I believed, in the end he would have tried to hit me up for cash—and I wanted to talk about him too, I wanted to remember all the details, even though my father had been the man he was, because I didn't want him to be dead, there, I've said it, and I was suffering, suffering, suffering owing to the fact that he was dead, and so I, alive, wanted to devote to him, dead, all the time I had at my disposal that evening, and all the money I had in my pocket, and I wanted to go back home drunk on him and to fall asleep thinking of him and to dream of him. And that, my son, is about as close to returning as a dead man can get.

n that car sitting next to that man once more, and of my own free will: until half an hour before I would have thought this the most improbable thing in the world.

Since we had gotten into the car the man had driven without speaking, perhaps satisfied by having managed to catch me again: He smoked a cigarette, one of those ultra slim ones, Capri Superlights, and he had taken off his jacket, revealing the famous short-sleeved shirt: it was white, with one of those stiff collars favored by petty clerks, and, excepting for the patches of sweat around the armpits, it was clean, which made me think that he must have had a good store of them. But there was no sign of the pistol. The ashtray was literally bursting with butts, whose stink was fighting a pungent battle with the scent of pine diffused throughout the car by the "Magic Pine" air freshener hanging from the rearview mirror. The wires that had been dangling from beneath the dashboard had disappeared.

"It really is hard," he began suddenly, "to redeem oneself after a false start like the one I made the other evening. I don't know what I could have been thinking of . . ."

He looked at me sidelong in order not to take his eyes off the road, which was half empty in any case, and shook his head in silence. He kept his hands on the wheel at a quarter past nine, that is, as wide open as possible, in a muscular driving style, elbows out, like a truck driver who had learned before the invention of power steering and wasn't going to change. A bit like me when I write on the computer, punching the keys hard because I'm still used to a typewriter. It means being *antiquated* . . .

"I wanted to play the nice guy," he resumed, and then shrugged, "oh well, too late to worry about that now. Ask me whatever you want, I'll explain everything."

"Weren't you supposed to tell me about my father?"

"Later. First I want to clear up a few things, because you're confused and you have a right to be. What do you want to know?"

And he smiled, again, always. Perhaps he thought this looked reassuring, but the smile on that old street urchin's face of his was not reassuring at all.

"Whose car is this?"

He hadn't been expecting that.

"Mine. Why?"

By chance, I spotted the registration protruding from the glove pocket and I took it out. Although I realize that this may have looked like a premeditated move, it wasn't: I hadn't been thinking of checking. But my move was so automatic that he was never going to believe that. Never mind. Also because the car was registered in the name of a certain Gianni Fusco, born in Molfetta, near Bari, on November 11, 1929, and resident in via del Cilianuzzo 23, Prato.

"I've just bought it and I still haven't registered the change of ownership," he explained, without being asked to.

"It's only six months old . . ."

"Correct. A bargain."

In the meantime we had taken the via Magliana, where there is always a traffic jam, always, and no one knows why.

"Where are we going?" I asked.

"To Fregene, I was thinking. Tons of restaurants there."

He lit up another one of his little cigarettes and let it dangle from his lips like Humphrey Bogart; but it was ridiculous, so slim. He took a good drag on it, and blew the smoke from his nose, accompanied by the return of the whistle in his chest, which had vanished for a while.

"Listen," I said, "the other evening, at the station, you had left the car with the engine running, and all the wires were hanging down from below the steering wheel. What happened?"

"Oh, someone had tried to steal it. Saved it by a whisker."

"Oh . . ."

"I had stopped to eat a couple of rice balls in a rotisserie, and while I was there at the counter what did I see but the car door open and an Albanian bent over under the wheel, fiddling with the wires."

He caressed his trouser pocket with one hand.

"That was one time it came in handy . . ."

So that was where he kept it, in his pocket.

"Did you shoot him?" I asked.

"Oh no," he replied, still without showing whether he had caught my sarcasm or not, "I just let him see it, and he was off like a hare. No, no, there was no shooting . . ."

But then he sniggered: the idea didn't seem to horrify him.

"Well," I said, "a pistol will go off sooner or later, won't it? In films it's a rule."

"In *American* films," he protested, "in *American* films. They're the ones that have all those little rules, climax, anticlimax, 'the pistol will go off sooner or later . . .' But the Americans aren't the only ones in the world who make movies. For example, there's a really beautiful Russian film, *Mir vchodjascemu, Peace Be to He Who Enters* it's called, in which you can see a pistol all the time, a real pistol, loaded, in the hands of some little kids who have found it in a field; you can see it all the time and you think now it's going to go off, now there's going to be a tragedy, but it never goes off."

He broke off for a moment to toss the butt out the window, then he continued:

"Wait a minute, what am I saying? it wasn't *Peace Be to He Who Enters*: it was *Outskirts. Outskirts*, that's it: I'm not sure about the director, I think it was . . . But why should I bother? You're all pro-American these days . . . ."

Now, perhaps I had made a banal remark, I can't deny it, but the point is: what made that man think he had the right to preach to me? And about cinema, at that.

"Excuse me," I shot back, "apart from the fact that I fail to see what's wrong with American cinema, do I have to take this from someone who's wearing a standard American shirt, with short sleeves and a stiff collar? Does anyone wear shirts like these in Italy? No, apart from the Mormons, and they're Americans too for that matter. But you're wearing one, and it strikes you as normal too, I bet, and you wear a jacket over it too, and do you know why? Because you've been looking at shirts like this for forty years in American films for cinema and television, that's why; worn by Hollywood actors, in stories that are always constructed with climax, anticlimax, and pistols that go off sooner or later. You saw Tom Ewell wearing one in *The Seven-Year Itch* and De Niro wearing one in *Mad Dog and Glory*; Robert Blake wearing one in all the episodes of *Baretta* and Michael Douglas wearing one in *Falling Down*; Dennis Franz wearing one in *NYPD Blue*, and Bradley Whitford wearing one in *A Perfect World* when he shoots—*shoots*—Kevin Costner (who, I recall, was unarmed, because the little boy had thrown his pistol down the well). That shirt is like the phone hanging from the kitchen wall, by now, or the basketball hoop attached to the . . ."

And at that point something strange happened, something fairly humiliating for me, something that made me shut up there and then. The man burst out laughing, heartily, complete with respiratory congestion, ever more acute pulmonary whistling, and a braying, catarrhal cough. In the meantime he looked at me, then at the road, then at me again, and then at the road again, while I observed him in silence, offended and confused.

"Sorry," he wheezed, and he was off again, coughing and laughing.

"Excuse me, but why are you laughing?"

"Sorry . . . ," he repeated, "I didn't mean to . . . ," but by that time the cough had prevailed, and he would have done well not to underestimate the turbulence with which it devoured everything else. I remained silent watching the noisy spectacle offered by his ailments, while he tried not to lose control of the car.

"I appreciate your point of view, you know," he said, once the storm had blown over. "Really, you made some *very* interesting observations," he coughed, "not to mention the way you quoted all those films from memory with effortless ease, actors and every-thing: impressive." He coughed again, then he cleared his throat. "Your father used to say you were a hard nut. But the thing is that this shirt is Bulgarian, son, pure synthetics from Plovdiv; not one single natural fiber: put a match to it and *wooof!* it burns like gasoline."

He gazed at me with those insidious eyes of his, then he switched on the light above the rearview mirror and hunched over, using one hand to turn up his shirt collar, so I could check the label.

Now, I had no interest in the label on his collar, I still felt humiliated and confused, and I didn't move an inch; but he in-sisted, he all but ripped the collar off, and had the look of some-one who was going to stay like that all night, with the wheel in one hand and the upturned collar in the other, driving through the dark waiting for me to decide whether I was going to check out his damned collar or not.

"It says 'NIKO Chic.' So?"

"You've no idea how many people wear shirts like this all over Eastern Europe," he went on. "Romania, the Ukraine, Bulgaria: as soon as summer comes they all put on shirts like this one. They're not used to the cold, in those parts. Ever been there?"

"No."

"That's bad."

There was no hope for it, that man put me in difficulty. Apart from the fact that he made me do what he wanted too often—and that included making me look like a moron too often as well—he still seemed to be too many things at once, too many opposites. Old and young, boorish and cultivated, threatening and affectionate, a gorilla's physique and an actor's voice, and then an expert in Slavonic studies, a gunman, cinéaste, thief and the victim of thieves; since the moment he had appeared before me, at the Stazione Termini, he had been disorienting me. Who was he? What did he want from me? Where was he from? How did he break his nose?

"One thing you must know about me," he said, "is that I have never been to America. Another is that Eastern Europe is practically my home. Bear these two things in mind and you'll know more or less what to expect from me."

When I was in high school, in my B.C. diary there was a brilliant cartoon strip: B.C. knocks at a cave, and when they open up he says, "Excuse me, we're doing a poll on . . ." "Telepathy?" interrupts the other guy. The last frame had no caption, and it was irresistible because of the expression on B.C.'s face: an expression that was at once idiotic and a bit dreamy, puzzled but also reminiscent, and amazed, and beaten, and admiring, which *is*, there's not much you can do about it, the expression you have when someone reads your mind. The same expression I felt I was wearing then, given that I had only *thought* my questions.

"I'm an old communist," he felt bound to add, just to confuse the issue even more, since that made his having really been a friend of my father's a complete impossibility.

In the meantime the road had narrowed, and I didn't know it. No more rabbit warrens stuffed with families, with cars parked in flagrant disregard of the law, and no more yellow streetlights, but darkness, countryside, and isolated houses. For the second time that day I found myself traveling in the opposite direction to the lines of traffic that were heading back to Rome from the seaside, and, while I was trying to get my bearings to see where we were, a large aircraft coming in to land suddenly cut across the road ahead. It was flying very, very low and was so close that you could make out the faces of the passengers behind the windows. Or maybe not, I was just imaging them, noses pressed up against the glass and expressions halfway between ecstasy for the beauty flooding into their eyes and the fear of death howling in the brain. (And, during a landing, especially at night, what an indissoluble link there is between beauty and death, ecstasy and fear: as long as you are free to enjoy the grandiose spectacle of the earth, down there, with all its shapes and its mighty veins of light, it means that your life is in danger; when, as at that moment—there, made it—the plane touched down gently, and nothing happened—in reality nothing happens *almost always*—life ceases to be in danger, but the beauty vanishes too.)

The man coughed again, and again, but less violently: more than anything else it seemed like minor tremors after the devastation of shortly before. He turned again, leaving the airport at his back, and, if my sense of direction was not deceiving me, we ought to have been running parallel to the sea: but perhaps it was deceiving me, and we were heading straight for it. In any event there was no more traffic coming the other way, only the odd car, a sign that we were on a really secondary road.

"In '91," he resumed, "I was census-taker around here. I had this whole area, Maccarese, Torrimpietra . . ."

He said this in a completely different tone of voice, as if to introduce a completely new phase in our conversation.

"I covered it inch by inch: isolated houses, small villas, farmhouses, vacation homes, small condominiums; and do you know what struck me about that experience? Do you know what I learned?"

And he fell silent, suspended in a genuinely interrogative expression. I have never been able to bear those people that ask you such questions *seriously*: in practice, they are asking you to give an answer at random so that they can then tell you what they wanted to tell you right from the start, but giving the impression that they want to correct *your* mistake, and to satisfy *your* curiosity.

"Come on, try to guess," he insisted.

"How do I know?"

"People lie," he revealed. "That's what struck me. They lie, always, on principle, even though they don't have the slightest reason to do so."

And there he fell silent, because the last phrase was pronounced in a conclusive tone. But it was a kind of mistaken emphasis, because he hadn't finished at all. And in fact he resumed:

"Naturally I knew that already, it didn't come as news to me. Yet, on seeing the proof of it in all those laboriously compiled forms, in that mass of mindless untruths about work, rights of way, and the size of the house, even after you, the enumerator, have ensured them that the data will be used exclusively for statistical purposes, well, that made an impression on me. There'd be some character living at number 212, let's say, of an unclassified road like this one. You get there and at number 212 there isn't even a doorbell anymore, not even a mailbox: the real entry, with the doorbell, the intercom and everything, has been moved to number 214, where the garage ought to be. That's where they come to open up, that's where they invite you in, and you can see the ramp that has become a flight of steps, you go down into the garage that has been transformed into a basement apartment, duly tiled, divided up by partition walls, complete with kitchenette, sofa, television, and the kid's rocking horse: in fact, you could say that that's all you see of the house, and you understand that the evacuees downstairs spend more time there than they do in the house proper, on the floor above. Then you go back to pick up the completed form and you see that the entry to the house is still given as number 212, and where it asks about 'other entries' they have unhesitatingly checked off the option 'none.' They lie with confidence, and they feel confident they will get away with it. You've no idea of how many lies of that sort I passed on to the census office, in those forms; lies that I myself, after only two visits to those houses, could have exposed. It's fascinating, don't you think? It still intrigues me to this day, come to think of it. They lie to the census. Doesn't that seem fascinating to you?"

He had done it again, he was really expecting an *answer*. Besides, I know how it works—and that's why I cannot stand that technique: he couldn't have cared less about my answer, it wasn't going to change by one iota what he was already thinking of saying. He just needed it to get underway again, like a dab on the clutch after overrevving the engine.

But I had to give him one, damn it.

"Not particularly."

"And then if you think that they lie to one another too," he was underway again, *quod erat demonstrandum,* "that is, kids lie to their parents, parents to the kids, and brothers and sisters lie to one another, husbands and wives lie to one other (almost all fibs, for heaven's sake: but sometimes, however, about important things too), then you understand that even the world you think you know best is no more than an enormous illusion, and that believing in that illusion is not a question of stupidity, but, on the contrary, of good sense; the necessary condition so that that world, the whole world, may continue to . . ."

No, this man was really a complete head case. He had interrupted himself, just like that, right at the climax of his sociological disquisition, as he brought the car to a dead stop at an intersection where the signposts said everything except Fregene—an intersection, by the way, that I had a feeling we had already passed a short time before.

"Shit," he muttered.

I had nothing to say, and so I kept quiet, but it was an odd situation. All I did was to try to bear in mind the reason why I was there, alongside that man, since it was not that there was an obvious connection between us: he was supposed to talk to me about my father, and that was why I was there. I observed him as he thought, motionless, then coughed, then became motionless again, a broad figure bothered by the lights of every car that passed. What did he have in mind? I couldn't avoid thinking that no one knew I was with him; if he were to take out his pistol and shoot me in the forehead, just for fun, and then dump my body at this intersection, I would become the murder mystery of the summer. My death would be a topic of conversation for loads of people, and my life too, and journalists I had never seen or met would recount imaginative versions of it, and every one of them, in order to talk about me, would start from that intersection, and they would come to say those unsavory absurdities that it is logical to come to say when talking about me starting from that intersection, which had nothing to do with me.

"Why have we stopped?" I asked, as politely as I could.

He looked at me. And smiled.

"It would appear that I can't find Fregene," he said.

eight

Lost . . .

It seemed impossible to get lost there, a stone's throw from Rome, on a clear June evening, in an attempt to get to Fregene—me, a Roman and son of Romans, and the strange creature beside me, who had just finished declaring that he had covered the area "inch by inch" for the census: yet that's the way it was, we were lost. I watched him rummaging about in the pockets of the door, the seats, and the dashboard, I presume in search of a map—and, even though by that time I had understood that with him everything was always very different from what it seemed, I still could not fail to mark that his way of rummaging—blind, nervous—was more that of a *thief* than the owner of the car. Anyway, he didn't find any map, granted that that was what he had really been searching for: apart from the documents I had already examined, a whole lot of other moldy garbage emerged, stale crackers, a tattered copy of a city street map (but of Genoa, not Rome), and a decomposing paperback mutilated by . . . well, it really seemed like a *bite*—I managed to read the name Clio Pizzingrilli on the cover, and a part of the title *Left At The . . . Second . . .* : not a human bite, I would have said, judging by the breadth of the mandibular arch, clean-cut, rounded, and regular throughout the thickness of the book, the way Yogi Bear bites into a sandwich in the cartoons.

"I don't believe it . . . ," he muttered.

He leaned back against the seat once more, producing a sinister creaking, then he shrugged and, with a grimace—a very expressive one, I must say, I couldn't have made it—he conveyed to me that at bottom it was completely unimportant where we were. He went back to staring at me, the whistle of his breathing reemerging from the silence, his gaze imbued with a luminous intensity, and I understood that he was about to reveal, there, at that moment, absurdly, the real reason why he had come into my life. You are free not to believe this, naturally, but I understood this before he did it: there was no logical reason why I should have seen it coming, and I can't explain how it was that I understood, but understand I did: he was about to do it. And, just as the realization sank in, he did it.

"Your father was a communist too," he said.

Hah.

"Before, I was deliberately talking about people who conceal things," he continued. "I was trying to come around to the subject, but I didn't know where to begin. But I beat around the bush a bit too long, and so it would be better to tell you clearly and brutally, in any case it doesn't make much difference. The real story of your father's life is very different from the one you know. He was a communist since he was a boy and he remained a communist until his dying day. Communism was the most important thing in his life."

A truck went past, and the shock wave of its passing rocked our jalopy.

"There's a town in Tuscany," I said, "the name escapes me right now but I could find it again, where they hold an annual challenge to see who can tell the tallest story. I don't know what the prize is, a leg of ham, I think, but one thing's for sure, if you went along and told them this . . ."

"And he wasn't just a communist," he broke in, "he was also a KGB agent."

Pause.

"A spy," he added.

I think that my reaction, at that point, is objectively important, I think that in any film I would have been in close-up then: but, just as a moment before I had felt brimful of sarcasm, so now did I feel empty, I don't know why, and there was no reaction. Nothing, no reaction at all. Unless remaining motionless and silent can be considered a reaction.

"Now," he resumed, "what I am doing is ignoble, from a certain point of view, because I'm going to break a solemn oath that your father also asked me to repeat to him the last time I saw him, two days before he died: to swear that I would never tell you anything, ever, for any reason in the world."

He coughed, then to my surprise he put the car in gear and moved off, taking without hesitation the road that led—so the sign said—to the highway.

"I swore because you can't start arguing with a dying man, but I wasn't in agreement, and he knew that, and I never thought to respect that oath for so much as one second. Because in my opinion it wasn't right that his son did not know what kind of man his father had really been. It was one thing as long as he was alive, there was no choice, but not now, I cannot respect that oath, I don't want to, because it would be a mistake, Maurizio, and you know it . . ."

He looked up to the heavens for a second, as if directly addressing my father, whose name was indeed Maurizio, even though not even Franceschino had managed to believe that he had really *gone up in the sky*; then he lowered his gaze, just in time to notice a Fiat Panda, almost at a stop and showing no lights, that we were about to run into. And I had the impression that, as he down-shifted to pass as if nothing had happened—but it had been a close shave—at the same time shaking that big head full of dandruff, that he was on the verge of tears. He did nothing in particular, like sighing or sniffing, but that was the impression I received, sudden and clear, and if he hadn't been a complete stranger, if he had been a real friend of my father's, one of those who had really been to visit him in the hospital—Attanasio, for example, or Professor Di Stefano, or General Terracina—who had been frequenting our house since my childhood and who as a consequence I had seen going gray and getting stout and wearing thicker and thicker glasses from year to year, from dinner to dinner, from bridge tournament to bridge tournament, all of my life, ending up by acquiring a kind of familiarity with them that was unwilling, passive, and cold—because I didn't exactly like them—but no less genuine for that; well, if he had been one of them I would have had no doubts, I would have said that he was *really* on the verge of tears. But I didn't know this man. Maybe I was confused, and the one on the verge of tears was me.

"And it's already cost me a lot of effort," he resumed, "to wait until today, not to take you to one side during the funeral and to tell you there, in that rain, in the middle of all those shits, those fascists. Your father wasn't like them and you have to know that: he had to pretend to be like them, and he did so, and well, all his life, but he never had anything in common with them, they were his enemies. Your father was a communist, Gianni, and he was a spy for almost fifty years, and to hell with my oath: I couldn't take this burden with me to the grave."

He fell suddenly silent, but he couldn't have finished: perhaps he had still to invent what came next, perhaps he was going to invent it on the spot, still driving with arms wide apart.

In the meantime, we were running along obscure country roads, much faster than before. Below the planes that continued to arrive, thick and fast, one after another, we skirted lighted houses, and mounds of darkness that spread out into the fields leaving a glimpse of a harsh beauty that surprised me.

"Three questions," I said. "First question: Were you really at my father's funeral?"

"Sure. If you want, I can give you all the names of the people that were there, one by one. Andreotti, General Olivetti Pratese, that prick Gramellini, the Terracinas, the Urso brothers, who came specially from Naples, and then Attanasio, Anzellotti, Scano . . ."

"Never mind. Second question: I suppose you are a spy too?"

"Yes."

We made a sharp right turn onto a wider road, lined with trees on both sides whose trunks were painted white around the base.

"On second thought, *four* questions. Third question: Weren't we lost? Where are we going now, so fast?"

"Still to Fregene. It's just that the only road I know is by the highway: maybe we were close, but I thought to turn and head for the highway, to leave it at the Fregene exit and to get there by the road I know."

"Fourth question: Sincerely, Mr. Bogliasco, do you hope that I . . ."

"Listen," he interrupted me, "can *I* ask *you* something? How about calling me Gianni?"

"What's the difference?"

"The difference is that your formality makes me feel uncomfortable. Please. You don't know it, but it's probable that at this point, with your father dead, and with the exception of your closest family, I am the person who loves you best in all the world."

"Boom."

"I'm not exaggerating, Gianni. And I'll tell you another thing that you couldn't know: it's no accident if your name is Gianni, like mine . . ."

It was certainly really difficult to deal with that man. Every time he shot a line, and one felt authorized to make a comment, he always had an even bigger one to shoot right afterward. He was like certain opponents I had come across in chess tournaments—Yugoslavs, especially—who would always set up two attacks together, sneakily, one hidden inside the other. I knew this, I expected it, but I wound up losing nonetheless.

"Okay, as you wish. Gianni. Fourth question: Do you hope that I am going to believe you?"

But the *Gianni* didn't work, it was grotesque.

"You want me to tell you what I hope?" he asked, and for a second, as he turned to look at me (why, I don't know, because in reality he was very different from him, shorter, fatter), he looked like Jack Palance. "I hope you will let me say my piece. That's what I hope. Given that I'm breaking an oath, I hope that you will at least let me break it all the way, and let me tell you this amazing story in its entirety . . ."

"Right, amazing, you can say that again . . ."

In saying "you can say that again" a little gob of white spit shot out of my mouth and landed on the dashboard in front of me, highly visible. I wiped it off with my sleeve and tried to brazen it out, but he must have seen it.

"I know," he said. "It's amazing. But if you don't even let me tell it, if you start asking questions and making comments for everything I tell you, it means that your father was right, I shouldn't have told you anything, and I shall give myself no peace . . ."

What was I to do, explode? I had something very *right* to say, so why shouldn't I do so? Why should I bottle it up?

"Now look here, Bogliasco," I said, "aren't you already telling me your amazing story? Haven't you done everything you wanted to, up to now? Have I perhaps hindered you in any way? You came into my life with your pistol in your belt and you terrorized me . . . yes, that's right, *terrorized*, telling me that business about Franceschino without so much as introducing yourself. I had to run for it in the night like a rat, you know? Upsetting my wife, handing my in-laws truckloads of bullshit, without managing to make sense of what was going on: yet here I am, listening to you telling me that my father, an army general, a practicing Catholic, a visceral anti-Communist, and a die-hard Christian Democrat, received in private audience by four popes and a friend of Andreotti (with whom, by the way, he attended mass almost every morning), as well as, according to me, but he denied this, a member of Gladio, was a *communist spy*? Have you any idea of how many questions I could ask you? A lot more than four!"

I realized that I had pronounced these last words in the severe tones of a schoolmaster, a fact that was completely beyond my control and one that sounded fairly ridiculous, given the situation: a sign that I ought to have stopped there. I know what I'm like: from then on I would do nothing but spew out a stream of verbose and useless repetitions of what I had said already, steadily losing control of the tone, then gradually of the words—and my points, which still shone out limpid and indisputable, would wind up by losing a good deal of their luster. This has always been a defect of mine, and indeed it was all but incredible that on that occasion I realized in time: that usually happens *afterward*, when it's too late.

"And in any case, Mr. Bogliasco, I can't bring myself to call you Gianni," I concluded, "so you'll just have to try to live with that . . ."

I lowered my eyes, satisfied with my sermon and even more by my having managed to interrupt it in time, but I noted with horror that, in talking, more flecks of spittle had flown out of my mouth and onto the dashboard. How was that possible? I don't spit when I talk. I would have known that, damn it; I would always have known it, and I would have had a complex about it, and I would have been maniacally careful about it, employing all those squalid devices like swallowing every three words or furtively keeping a hand in front of my mouth for as long as possible, devices that, true, are like a placard on which letters a foot high broadcast the very fact you are trying to conceal—BEWARE: I SPIT WHEN I TALK—but that at least prevent you from contaminating other people's dashboards. And as I wiped it away with another furious swipe of my forearm I became convinced that my salivation must have been temporarily altered, of course, it couldn't have been otherwise, because of the two gin and tonics drunk on an empty stomach and because of the fact that I hadn't eaten anything since nine that morning, and I was actually very hungry, conditions aggravated by the stress of that improbable evening. But the fact is that I don't spit when I talk. Fuck.

"You're right," he said, "and I apologize. But don't think that I haven't put myself in your shoes, you know, that I haven't considered things from your point of view . . ."

He lit up another cigarette, and this time I felt a sharp pang in my guts, because in that moment I could have really used a good cigarette, make no mistake. Not one of his, though, I find them disgusting, which is why I managed to resist the urge to spoil, for a Capri Superlight, all the efforts I had been making over the previous nine months. But I wondered what would have happened if he had lit up a Marlboro, if the magical red and white brand had peeped out from the tray behind the gear lever, where he kept his packet.

"After that crappy stroke I pulled the other evening, too," he resumed, "that brilliant move . . ."

He shook his head, and ran one hand over his sweaty face. In the meantime we had come to the highway. But he took the interchange that goes toward Civitavecchia, while I was almost sure that we were already beyond Fregene, and that we would therefore have to return toward Rome.

"But, you see," he continued, "your father's death shocked me, and I can't think clearly anymore. I always thought I would have died before him, because that's the way it should have been. I wasn't ready to outlive him, that's it, and to carry the burden of this business on my own . . ."

"Hey, watch out!" I yelled.

He had entered the highway without looking, the madman, and as a horn vented all its furious blaring outrage on us, in the rearview mirror I saw a VW Golf swerving sharply to the left to avoid hitting us, just as a dark-colored Saab with headlights flashing was coming up on the fast lane like a bullet. My heart shot into my throat and I had enough time to think, this is it, now we're all going to die, splattered in one of those horrendous tangled wrecks you see on television. If nothing happened it was because the Saab carried straight on without slowing down—incredibly, recklessly, but also providentially—hurtling through this sudden ambush of destiny at a hundred and eighty an hour like a fairground stunt rider taking his motorbike through a flaming hoop: the Golf, missed by a hairsbreadth, rebounded toward the right again, and then again toward the left, the horn still blaring, in one of those zigzags that made the Mercedes A class overturn during testing; but it didn't roll over, and, by the time the Golf got back into the fast lane, the Saab was a missile disappearing into the distance, and the driver managed to regain control of the situation.

Amid all this, we, the cause, carried on with the blissful indifference of Mr. Magoo: not a touch on the brakes, nor a swerve, nor a hint of apology, nothing, and perhaps it was that, even more than our maneuver, that had infuriated the driver of the Golf, who had by then pulled up alongside us to bombard us with insults through the window, still hysterically sounding his horn. Both of us turned to look at him, and we remained in a strange silence, calm, while this stranger—an ugly young man, with tufty hair and a face purple with rage, absolutely beside himself—vented on us all the adrenaline that was galloping around his brain. A bit too much, in reality, judging by the downright *hatred* he was putting into his ranting: but he accelerated and drove off with a final insult just a second before I could react—I don't exactly know how I would have reacted, probably by babbling insults myself—and, especially, before the man beside me could have reacted, as his reaction would certainly have been more formidable. And so it really seemed as if that hothead had timed things well: he was never going to know that he had been braying his insults a bare meter away from a pistol, and the recollection of how, that evening, he had been able first to avoid an accident and then insult us at his pleasure without either one of us having ventured to react would probably come in handy for him, in the future, in moments when his self-esteem was at a low ebb.

The man sitting beside me—I was still not sure what to call

him: Gianni? My father's friend? The spy?—gave the Golf driver a brief, malicious flash of the headlights, then he tossed his cigarette end out of the window, watching in the mirror as it disintegrated in a tiny, silent explosion. After which he turned toward me, and, needless to say, he smiled.

"Let's make a deal," he said. "Now I am going to concentrate on my driving and I'll take you safe and sound to Fregene, to a restaurant, to eat fish as I promised you . . ."

CERVETERI-LADISPOLI 8 KM: I was right, we had passed Fregene, and we had to turn back. But he hadn't even realized . . .

". . . and there, in front of some nice grilled king prawns, I'll tell you the whole story from the beginning. To hell with the oath. You have to know these things. Then you will decide if you believe it or not . . ."

What an absurdity, I thought. What an enormous absurdity. It was the most absurd evening of my life. And there he was driving away calmly, *concentrating*, toward Civitavecchia, convinced he was going to Fregene, and he hadn't realized. *CERVETERI-LADISPOLI 7 KM*. I couldn't believe it. I had to tell him, he hadn't realized.

And I was hungry . . .

nine

In the end, we finally got to Fregene. But not to the liveliest, best-known part, the part next to the former fishing village, which had glittered in the sixties with the reflected glory conferred upon it by migrant film stars, but to the other, on the other side of the military zone that cuts the seafront in two: the *bourgeois* part, with its monotonous and boring and dark—at night time—succession of bathing establishments drowned in nothingness, which we glided through until we found one where the restaurant was still open.

Completely by chance, therefore, we ended up in this place called the "Cutty Sark," built to resemble an ocean liner, not a clipper, with rounded corners and portholes and cement terraces and tubular handrails and enameled paintwork that shone in the darkness with a lugubrious, peeling, whitish glow. Seen from the outside it gave the impression of a big place, at least; but once we passed through the immense entry we found ourselves in a dark and surprisingly cramped passageway, where a sign saying "disco bar" made of fluorescent tubes hung from the wall and a small knot of African kids sat gazing intently at MTV; and from there, through a French window, we emerged into the open once more, beneath a fake reed matting canopy that was in reality made of lined sheet metal, and the place changed again, with the rapidity with which things are transformed only in dreams, to become a little *beach restaurant*. By that time, evidently, the old Cutty Sark had been completely forgotten.

A young girl on roller skates instantly began to hover around us, to take us to a "quiet" table, she said, alluding to the yackety-yak coming from a table full of fifty-year-olds who were in fact a bit merry, and for that reason rather pathetic, perhaps, but certainly not annoying. Short raven-black hair, very beautiful, and half naked into the bargain, all the girl was wearing was a pair of hot pants and a skimpy top that reached halfway to her navel, a top made even skimpier by a pair of impudent breasts that conferred a roller-coaster effect on the legend "Roller Betty" printed on the fabric. She skated absent-mindedly, but well, chewing gum with the air of one who regretted every single choice made in life. She set the table and handed us our menus, then she rolled off toward the phosphorescent belly of the disco bar, from which emerged a man of about forty-five, robust and flashily dressed, and, given that he bore an extraordinary resemblance to the girl, it wasn't hard to imagine that he was in some way responsible for her joylessness. While he was suggesting what we might order ("a fabulous seafood salad," "a little risotto, made on the spot"), the cell phone in the pocket of his Hawaiian shirt began to emit the theme tune from—I think—*Rambo*: he could have answered or switched it off, but he answered, and stood listening for a moment, frowning, before muttering that he was busy and would call back later. Then he apologized, but the call must have unsettled him, because he stood and waited for our order, forgetting that he had started off by suggesting it himself. Neither I nor my man reminded him, and so in the end we ordered according to intuition:

he took spaghetti in cuttlefish ink sauce, I ordered spaghetti and clams; then grilled king prawns and vegetables for two.

"And don't forget," Bogliasco said to him, "big portions, please."

After which the man went off and there we were, one facing the other, in a tactical silence that I had no intention of breaking. I was ready to let him tell his story all the way, but I sure wasn't going to ask him to do so. In fact, as far as I was concerned, if he had had second thoughts and hadn't told me anything, and had we remained stranded in that silence as we filled our bellies, and if after dinner he had taken me back to Rome, still without saying a word, to take his leave outside my house with a handshake ("See you, Gianni," "Good-bye, Mr. Bogliasco"), as if nothing had happened, and had thus gone out of my life, in a manner even more absurd than the way he had come into it, and for good, it would have been ideal. I wouldn't have asked him for any explanation.

As I looked at him I thought that if I could have hypnotized him I could have ordered him to do exactly that, and perhaps everything would have gone back to normal: but I couldn't have harnessed those electric eyes even if I had been a fakir. And so it was those eyes that darted about in search of mine, without embarrassment, a sign that all that silence hadn't discouraged him in the least, and the show was about to begin.

"Well then," he began, "I'll tell you everything from the beginning, okay? And the beginning was the end of the last war, Gianni, when the Russians . . ."

He started convulsing. "The pills . . ."

He fished a small bottle from his pocket and took out two white pills, which he fired down his throat. Since they still hadn't brought us any water, he sent them down dry, the way Oliver Hardy swallowed nails. Then he slipped the bottle back in his pocket. All without ceasing to smile, naturally.

What the pills were for, we shall never know.

"I was saying," he resumed, "that, right after the war, the Russians, as for that matter the Americans and the English, increased their intelligence effort to the maximum. It was the golden age of espionage; try to imagine, for example, what Berlin was like before they built the wall, when the city was divided into four sectors, or even Italy right after the Liberation. All the best minds, you can say, were working in espionage . . ."

The girl arrived with a bottle of water and one of wine. She opened them clumsily, especially the wine, making the cork crumble. Bogliasco paid no heed and carried on.

"First of all it was necessary to take the maximum advantage of that chaos, but it was also necessary to set things up for the future, and the future did not look rosy. It was 1945, Gianni, Europe was still smoking: amid that enormous destruction the most natural thing that a secret service could do was to prepare for the next war. And so missions of all sorts were organized, even extremely hazardous ones, with very high-level targets and with very long implementation times: missions that the Americans called *L.T., Long Term*, and the Russians, more poetically, *butylka vi morie*, 'bottles in the sea': and in fact it was just like slipping messages into bottles and leaving them in the open sea, hoping that some would get to their destination—even though, to tell the truth, not even the destination was very clear, at that time. Your father, Gianni, was one of those bottles . . ."

He grasped the bottle, of Frascati, in this case, and filled my glass, then his; and he drank, noticing the crumbs of cork in the wine only when he found them between his lips. He spat them out, as if it were the most natural thing in the world, and he looked me straight in the eye.

"Your father was Russian," he said, almost whispering, "a Cossack, to be precise."

Then he used a stubby finger to remove the crumbs left in his glass and finished drinking, heedless of my reaction. A reaction that did not occur, since I repressed it altogether, forcing myself not to bat an eyelid and—as far as I could work out—succeeding quite well too; but I have to admit that the bastard had surprised me once again—a *Cossack*, indeed.

"His real name was Arkady Fokin," he resumed. "He was a young officer with Stalin's counter-espionage service during the Second World War, and he was a sort of genius. At twenty-four he was already a major in the Red Army, he held two degrees and possessed a variety of other talents—including a flair for chess, which you, to the best of my knowledge, have inherited. He spoke three foreign languages perfectly: English, German, and Italian. He was a pilot, possessed extraordinary physical resistance, and was extremely cultivated. In short, he was one of the best men, if not the best, on which the NKGB could count at that time—in those days it was yet to become the KGB—and he was assigned to carry out one of those extremely risky missions: to transform himself into an Italian, to join the Italian military intelligence service, and to attain a position of command through a regular career.

He paused for a moment, deliberately, to check the effect of his words, and I hung on, managing not to give him the slightest satisfaction. I blinked, but it was tiredness.

"Which is what he did, Gianni," he resumed. "Because your father *accomplished* that mission; to the best of my knowledge, of all those who were assigned missions of this type, in England, in France, and in Germany, he was the only one to last the course. The only *butylka vi morie* to reach his destination . . ."

Enter Roller Betty again, zooming up with the dishes in hand to come to a noisy dead stop a few centimeters from our table. She served us the spaghetti, and they really were mega-portions. Then she filched a bowl from a nearby table and set it down in front of me, for the clam shells.

"Enjoy your meal," she said, and off she went.

Bogliasco observed his plate for a second, a mountain of spaghetti steeped in sauce as black as pitch, and it seemed as if he was working out the best way to tackle the problem. Then he unfolded his napkin and slipped it into the neck of his shirt, not by one corner but along all of one side, well tucked in, as if it were a bib.

"Bon appetit," he said. Then he rolled up a big forkful of

spaghetti, held it up to drain off the sauce, and bit into it, staining all his mouth with black. As he began to chew he wiped himself with the napkin, on which he printed a black V that looked like a swallow in flight.

"Now," he began again, still chewing, "the purpose of your father's mission was not *to spy*. It wasn't a matter of sticking his nose into filing cabinets, nor of blackmailing bigwigs into passing on information, nor of bustling about across frontiers in order to deliver it, nor of unmasking someone as a foreign spy or liquidating someone else because he was a double-agent. That wasn't the level for which a man of your father's caliber was employed—if anything that was *my* level, and it's another business altogether: by comparison, it's like *playing* at spies, if you see what I mean. How's your spaghetti?"

"Good."

"Mine isn't so hot," he said, swallowing another forkful. He cleaned his mouth with the napkin (another black smear, a cross this time) and continued:

"No, your father's mission was a radical one: the war. In the event of a war between the two blocs into which Europe was being divided—and I'm talking about a real war, Gianni, I'm talking about invasions, battles, bombing raids, get the picture?—having a man like your father inside the general staff of an enemy army would have been an incalculable advantage. Do you see? A new war breaks out, there he is, a high-ranking officer of Soviet military intelligence in the uniform of a high-ranking officer of Italian military intelligence, and at that point he goes into action. That was his mission, since 1945 . . ."

Another forkful, another wipe of the mouth, another sip of wine, and off he went again. A character actor, that's what he was. He dispatched his concoction by the large forkful and at the same time he dropped his bombshells, at his neck a napkin transformed into a picture by Franz Kline, the grimaces on his face ever exact and theatrical, the massive bulk of an old Cosa Nostra *capo*, the fat sausagelike fingers that strove not to crush the glass: and all this, it became clear to me, *characterized* him. There are people like that, I had met them before, who play themselves with the total commitment of character actors, almost as if they knew that they didn't have a very important role in life and thus felt obliged to ham it up to the limits every time they made an appearance, even at the cost of becoming heavy, as long as they left their mark.

Or he really was an actor, and I was on *Candid Camera*, which would have explained everything.

". . . extremely serious crises in Africa, Cuba, and South America," he was saying, "but the war for which your father became your father never broke out, even though almost no one knows just how close we came to it, in reality. So his masterpiece was practically of no use; he stayed under cover for fifty years and lived the strange life you knew too—strange, I say, for a man like him: going to mass every morning, making friends with fascists and reactionaries, nestled down in the bourgeois life these people lead, and arguing with his son about politics . . ."

We finished the spaghetti at practically the same time. I had eaten voraciously, because I had been really hungry, and in the meantime he must have pronounced something like a thousand words. How the devil had he done that?

"Besides, what else could he have done?" he resumed. "He could have *sold out*, of course; and he would have had some secrets to give away . . . I mean to say that had he changed sides he could have obtained several advantages; but, you see, your father was a real communist, a word that has people bursting out laughing these days, but for him it was a noble and solemn *raison d'être*, because the world was unjust, and he thought the way to improve it had been shown by Marx, period. So it never entered his head to change sides, to resign himself to the good life won in the capitalist world and to become in reality what he was pretending to be. No, he hated the life he lived here, Gianni, and his hatred did not diminish one whit in fifty years. But he had no choice, he had to carry on living that life. He was trapped in his mission."

He lit a cigarette, damn him.

"And he never even thought of going back to Russia, not even when it appeared clear that there wasn't going to be the war for which every morning he was ready to go into action—while he was going to mass with Andreotti, as you pointed out. Because in the meantime, he had found something authentic here: he had you, his family, and he loved you deeply. Despite the love and fidelity he nurtured for his country he could not abandon you, nor transport you all there. To do what, in any case? To watch the red flags burning in front of the Kremlin? To witness the defeat of everything for which he had sacrificed his life, the triumph of a capitalism even dirtier and indecent than the variety he had left here? No, he had no choice. The only choice he had was whether to tell you the truth or not, one day. And it was then, when he decided he wasn't going to tell you anything, to leave you the father you thought you had, that we parted company. Because it isn't right, I say . . ."

That's it, here we go, now I was going to react. Until then I had been able to control myself, but I suddenly felt that way no longer. It was really a physical thing, I think, a matter of nerves: my temples were pulsing, the blood was rushing violently to my brain, and I *could not* simulate any kind of calm any longer, because there was something intolerable about all that, and the intolerable cannot be tolerated.

"Excuse me!" I yelled, turning to the roller skater.

But on the other hand I couldn't even start arguing with this man, because as far as I was concerned he was a computer screen, a CD-ROM, a test of resistance, and I had to resist: it was the only sensible thing I could do, whatever the machinations that lay behind things, even if it really was a goddamned *Candid Camera* stunt.

The girl came up slowly, this time, braking delicately with the tips of her skates.

"Would you mind taking away the dishes, please?" I snarled, "We've been finished for half an hour."

It must have been five minutes, more or less. She stiffened and stared at me: I must have struck her as a real shit, but never mind, there wasn't much I could do about that—if anything, I felt better already. She stared at me, beautiful even in humiliation, and perhaps a voice inside her was roaring, come on, Roller Betty, rebel, don't let them treat you like this! React, don't content yourself with spitting in their king prawns, you're not a waitress! Upturn the table over this prick and to hell with everything, take advantage of the moment to liberate yourself at a stroke from a job and a father that prevent you from being in the discothèque with your friends, at this moment, swallowing colored pills and dancing on your skates as if you were out of your head, as you, cool lioness of Fregene, select the prick who's going to pick you up . . .

No reaction, evidently she *can't* either. She can't drop everything, she can't break the chains, she can't do anything except, as I ordered her to, take the dishes away from the table without a murmur, and slip away. We are all *acted upon*, there's no getting away from it.

"Good," I couldn't help saying. "Is your story finished? Interesting, but unfortunately I don't believe it."

He shook his head and smiled. My incapacity to maintain a silence—and therefore, control—seemed to amuse him.

"No, Gianni, it's not finished."

"Oh no? And what's missing?"

He stubbed out his cigarette in the ashtray. Bad, because the cigarette did not go out, and he had to stub it again, and still the cigarette didn't go out, and I *needed* a smoke, shit, but I couldn't even do that. I could drink, though.

"What's missing are all the questions that are buzzing around in your head and that now you have to ask me."

"But didn't you say that questions were not welcome?"

No, Gianni, no. Drop the sarcasm, he doesn't even register it, it's just not his thing.

"What's missing are all the answers I have to give you," he continued, "because for every question you ask me, I have an answer, for every objection I have an explanation . . ."

Keep quiet, Gianni. Keep quiet. Don't open your mouth.

"Listen, I have an idea," I said. "Why don't you ask these questions yourself? Ask yourself the questions and answer them, all by yourself. I'm sure it'll work better."

Yes, but get up and go though. It was the perfect line with which to ditch him there and then: it would have been enough to add "goodbye," put the napkin down on the table, and leave. Just do it . . .

But I didn't do it, and in the time I took not to do it, it emerged with ruthless clarity that I was never going to do it, because I had apparently discovered a new limitation of mine, and that is: if some character sets to telling me a lot of absurd nonsense about my father, and I decide to ignore him, and I manage for a little while but at a certain point I can't manage anymore, and then I speak up using the curt and insolent words with which I ought to ditch him there and then and go off about my own business, well, *I don't ditch him there and then*, I remain glued to my chair looking like a prize asshole. It's good to know these things.

And him? Gloating, I bet, behind an air that had become suddenly candid, the poor thing, and astonished—but this air too, I insist, was theatrical, knowing, like Lieutenant Columbo's expression when he has to speak in public.

"All right, as you wish," he chuckled. And this was fine by him all right: now it had become a game altogether . . .

"Right," he said. "First question: How did your father manage to transform himself into an Italian?"

He feigned a little embarrassment, an expression as if to say, "The things I have to do," but in reality he was perfectly at his ease: it seemed as if he had never done anything else in life except ask questions to himself.

"Your father," he replied, "became Captain Maurizio Orzan in 1945, immediately after the end of the war. Since January 1943, after the defeat at Chertkovo, there were thousands of Italians in the camps, and the Soviet secret services had procured highly detailed information on all the Italian officers who had been made prisoner. This Orzan was perfect; he was one of the very few survivors of a unit that had been practically wiped out, his mother was dead, he was unmarried, he had no brothers or sisters, and above all he was from Pola, in Istria—which, as you know, wound up as Yugoslavian territory after the armistice: therefore *he could not have gone home.*"

Roller Betty arrived with the king prawns—already peeled, and therefore frozen—and he broke off, visibly remaining in control of the situation, however, as if all he had done was to press the "pause" button: he must have been one of those people who never lose the thread, the most dangerous kind. The girl served him first, then me, then she placed the tray of vegetables in a corner of the table and went off.

"Understand?" he resumed, eating a prawn with his hands. "Orzan didn't have a place to return to, where he might find friends or relatives. For your father this was fundamental: it was fundamental, once he went back to Italy in Orzan's place, that the possibility of his being discovered was reduced to . . ."

"Sorry to interrupt you," I said, "but do you think she spat in them?"

"Pardon?"

I had thrown him off balance, finally.

"Do you think the waitress spat into my plate?"

"What for?"

"Because I treated her badly. Did you notice how she looked at me, before, with such hatred?"

He was left with a prawn in mid-air.

"Do you remember Tiberio Murgia," I continued, "the short guy, with the moustache, who played Ferribotte in *Soliti ignoti?* He wasn't an actor: he was a waiter at the '*Re degli Amici*' in via della Croce, and it was there that Monicelli saw him, and he had the idea of giving Murgia the part in the film. After the success of *Soliti ignoti*, Murgia left his job as a waiter and became a real actor, continuing to play the part of the stock Sicilian in all the Italian films, even though he wasn't even Sicilian, for that matter, but Sardinian. Anyhow, do you know what he said to Monicelli in order to express his gratitude, given that he had changed his life? Do you know what pearl of wisdom he gave him? 'In restaurants,' he told him, 'never order meatballs and never argue with the waiter.' That's what he told him."

I looked at my plate, five king prawns arranged in a wheel, the lettuce leaf garnish and the slice of lemon.

"I think she spat in it," I said. "I'm not eating them."

He ate his, heroically—but on the other hand he had already eaten one; he shrugged, and didn't waste any energy arguing the point—*how much waiters' spit have we eaten, in our lives?*—which none the less has its own grisly importance; but I was sure he was thinking about it, even though I hadn't said it, he wouldn't have been human if he hadn't been thinking about it: "The girl," he was thinking, "could have spat in my plate too."

"Sorry, I interrupted you. You were saying?" And now the game gets tougher, my friend.

I saw him nod, and cast down his eyes the way Steve McQueen used to when he was *putting up* with something. In order to raise them again he had to pry them up with his Pavlovian smile, as if it were a jack. It must have cost him some effort, then, to carry on with his story; he seemed like an elephant getting to its feet . . .

"This captain Orzan," he resumed, without preamble, "was a prisoner in a Siberian camp, one of those really tough ones, from which you didn't return. One day an NKGB delegation from Moscow arrived in that camp, with a peremptory order: to take the prisoner Orzan and transfer him to another camp. At the head of that delegation was your father, who spent four days together with Orzan, traveling across Siberia. Now you can't say that they struck up a friendship, but they got to know each other, they talked, they were two human beings who came into contact in the heart of an unspeakable tragedy; and when your father shot him in the head, one morning, at dawn, while he was sleeping, thus launching his mission, he did something that was never to give him any . . ."

"One moment," I interrupted him. "Do you know my favorite scene from a movie? My absolute favorite, I mean."

He shook his head, smiling. His gaze was of maniacal intensity, but mine was no joke either, I suppose.

"It's a scene from *La Ricotta*," I continued, "where Pasolini has Orson Welles read one of his poems from *Mamma Roma*. It's a moment in which the whole troupe is taking a break, the typical Italian lunch break, everyone chilling out in the crisp air, the scorched landscape of Cinecittà in the background, and the extras, dressed up as angels with trumpets or as Roman guards in armor, are eating sandwiches and dancing the twist. And Welles starts reading the poem to the waiter who has brought him a soft drink. Right, according to me that is the finest scene in Italian cinema. What's more, and this is something that only a few people know, Orson Welles read in Italian, but he was dubbed, and d'you know who dubbed his voice? Giorgio Bassani. Do you know who Giorgio Bassani was?"

"The writer?"

"Correct. I asked you because he has been a bit overlooked, and yet he was one of the greats. Well, he was the one who dubbed Orson Welles. And do you know something else? I know that poem by heart. 'I am a force of the Past,' I know it all, I swear, 'only in tradition is my love. I spring from the ruins, from the churches, from the altarpieces, from the abandoned towns of the Apennines or the Alpine foothills, where my brothers lived . . .' "

My voice grew louder, a few people turned to look at me.

" . . . 'I wander the Tuscolana like a madman, the Appian Way like a dog with no master. Or I gaze at the sunsets, the mornings over Rome, over the Ciociaria, over the world, like the first acts of the Afterhistory, which I witness, thanks to my birthdate, from the outer bournes of some buried age . . .' "

By that time I was actually on my feet—incredible—and my voice was even louder.

" . . . 'Monstrous is he who springs from the bowels of a dead woman. And I, adult foetus, roam, more modern than any modern man, in search of brothers . . .' "

I paused, like Orson Welles in the film.

" . . . 'who are no more.' "

By then they were all looking at me. All the fifty-year-olds in the group nearby, another pair of couples sitting in front of us, even Roller Betty: in their wary eyes, and amid the desperate silence that had suddenly descended upon all of us, I could make out the success of my sally. I had floored them all.

"After which," I sat down again, lowering my voice, "Orson Welles closes the book, takes off his glasses, and says to the waiter: 'Did you understand anything?'"

Look what I've managed to do, I thought. Who would have thought it.

"You tell me if there's a scene more beautiful than that . . . ," I concluded.

By that point I ought to have won. I was amazed at my behavior—and I wasn't the only one, because one couple was still looking at me and I smiled, raised my glass, and drank their health—but he was going to have to acknowledge my superiority over him, because, if I had done that, then there were still many other things I might have done, I had at my disposal an immense repertoire of provocative actions, which I might be capable of carrying out one after another, indefinitely, just to shut that bloody mouth of his: faced with all this he ought to have recognized that it was the end and leave off—even though I was aware that things almost never go that way, that things almost never end when the end comes.

And as a matter of fact the end hadn't come, because he was *unfair* enough to continue.

"I understand your feelings," he said. "Don't think I don't understand them. But if I have told you all this it's because I want you to know who your father was. I don't want to conceal anything from you. And your father killed that man. But even though he was the only man your father killed in his whole life, and even though he was already practically dead, the memory of that deed never ceased to torment him, because killing once is far worse than killing many times. Even in the hospital, when I went to visit him, and he was delirious, chock full of morphine, I heard him whisper: 'Poor Orzan . . . Poor Orzan.' Still, after fifty years . . ."

It was true, my father had said that, in his delirium: "Poor Orzan." But he had been referring to himself: it was so simple. The only thing was that that thought, *that thought*, was a real killer, because it meant that his brass neck was still getting the better of mine, and that no matter what attitude I struck he was going to carry on pushing me toward that point of no return in which everything would become definitively uncertain, and I would be obliged to come up with *proof* to defend something that ought not to require any kind of defense, or proof, or explanation, because it wasn't a hypothesis, damn it, it was simply reality as I had lived it all of my life: and so I hadn't won, I had lost.

"Anyway, I give up," he added. "It's all too clear that you have no intention of listening to me, so . . ."

He made a peremptory gesture in Roller Betty's direction so that she would bring us the bill.

"I can see why too," he added.

He smiled, lit another cigarette, and lowered his eyes once more, this time without resembling anyone.

Silence supervened.

So I *had* won. Hah. All he had needed to do was make one more point, just one more phrase, even, and I would have collapsed like a condemned building, because I had been asking myself his questions and how, and my brain was already irresistibly at work to substitute the sedentary, severe, *Christian Democratic* image of my father with the romantic figure of a young Soviet officer who in the heart of the leaden steppes, the war over, blew out the brains of a poor Istrian prisoner to take his place and to feel remorse about it to the end of his days. Only one more little push and I really would have begun to . . . Right, but he didn't know that. Not knowing that I had already surrendered, he surrendered. Who knows how many works of art are knocked down that way, at auction.

I looked around, I looked at all those people who, after the interlude offered by my little show, had gone back to minding their own business. The fifty-year-olds were going off in silence, by then devoid of the good cheer they had been displaying during the dinner. But it would be absurd to pretend that they had been worn down by Pasolini, of whom they were even more blissfully unaware than he would have been of them, had he been alive, and whose scandalous presence they weren't even able to scent in my outburst, as their parents would still have been able to do, thirty years before, blindly, by pure instinct, like dogs that sense the coming of an earthquake. They were tired, that's all, because it had gotten pretty late, and they were off home to put their bonhomie back in its box. Although graying, the men were sun-tanned, fit-looking, sporty types from the tennis club, whose eyes said constantly, "I'm going to take myself a nice holiday, shortly"; and their women were all beautiful enough, with that gassy beauty, however, rendered uniform by the work of the plastic surgeon, which made them more or less interchangeable. At their age my father and mother hadn't looked like that, nor did the friends they frequented: another day and age, agreed, but their ways had held a hint of austerity, of wintriness, which seemed quite alien to this new bourgeoisie. On the other hand, my father would never have patronized a restaurant like that one, so corroded by fashion, so imbued with despondency. We were fifty meters from the sea—because the black streak in front of me was the sea—and you couldn't even perceive it. No, this was not a fit place for my father, not even for *talking* about him; it had nothing to do with that idea of the solidity of bourgeois life, of immutability, which he had always wanted to surround himself with: wood, not plastic, books, not magazines, God, not the Maldives. But, there, everything had an air so transient that it made you think directly of the next change of management, when the man with the Hawaiian shirt had gone bust and the place was being restructured for the umpteenth time, and while the work was being done, in winter, amid the howling of the sirocco, Roller Betty would pass by one day, not really by chance, and she would go in, and the workers would leave off hammering and look at her, and the foreman would go up to her and say, "What are you doing here?" and Roller Betty's eyes would look for the streaks left on the floor by her roller skates but she wouldn't even find the floor, because even the floor would have been torn up in order to wipe out all trace of that past time devoid of a history whence she had come, and then she would reply, "Nothing," and she would go away.

In the meantime Bogliasco was smoking in sedate silence, in a pose that, had it not been for his appearance, would have seemed aristocratic: but when our eyes met again, his immediately began to pulsate once more, pounding out that same obsessive tattoo as when he had told me that my father was a Cossack, a bottle in the sea, a spy, and a murderer—what a fine character actor he was. No, it wasn't over. And no one had won, there was nothing to win.

"Listen," I said to him, "why did you come to tell this to me? Why not to my sister?"

"Your sister is different," he replied. "She certainly mustn't know."

"Quite. She would have called the police."

"Naturally."

"And my mother? Why say nothing to her? She married him, after all."

Roller Betty came with the bill. He didn't even look at it and handed her a credit card.

"Your mother knows, Gianni."

Gianni Costante was the name on the credit card.

ten

CHAPTER ONE

The time has come, dear boys and girls, to tell you an amazing secret. Even though he would not approve (and in fact I am breaking an oath) I have decided to tell you the truth about Pizzano Pizza. Yes, the time has come and you must know. You who have followed his adventures right from the start, as well as you who have never heard of him until they gave you this book and told you you ought to do a bit of reading instead of forever going off to play video games with Johnny (because where there are video games there is always a Johnny, there's no getting around that, and if it doesn't seem that way to you, and if you think that the friend you play video games with is called Harry or Jim or Jack or Bill or Max, or if you think you play them by yourselves, or even that you never play them, then all the more reason why the time has come to know the truth about Pizzano Pizza, since you will understand how easy it is to fool yourself, in life, about tons of things).

And so, dear boys and girls, put down this book, go into the kitchen, and prepare yourselves a snack (bread and mayonnaise, I'd advise you, and half a glass of milk), and then sit yourselves down to read in the softest armchair in your house; or lock yourselves up in your room and stretch out on the bed like a Roman emperor, that is on one side, still nibbling at your snack, and never mind if you make a few crumbs: as I have just said, what you are about to learn is the truth, and the truth has to be faced on a full stomach while the body is relaxed. Trust me, do as I say. Go. Get in the supplies. Find your little nook. I'll wait for you, I won't run away. The truth I have to tell you, about Pizzano Pizza and his secret, will not run away. In the meantime, while I'm waiting for you, I'll make you a drawing of a spaceship. Just like that, because I'm good at them, and also because later on, who can tell, it might come in handy. A spaceship taking off.

(drawing of a space ship taking off)

Well, boys and girls, we're off. Yet, now that we're off I realize how hard it is to approach these truths of ours, and I feel like talking to you about them in general for a bit, and then, in a roundabout way, I'll get to the point nice and easy. I feel like reminding you how frequent it is, and normal too, after all, for people to have secrets, and how the world is full of lies; not only bad lies, told for some sinister reason, but also of harmless, innocent, necessary lies, even good lies.

I feel like starting with Father Christmas, for example. It's a lie, you know that by now: the truth is that Father Christmas doesn't exist, flying reindeer don't exist, the sleigh doesn't exist, his house at the North Pole doesn't exist, and there's no way a fatso like him can get down chimneys.

None of these things have ever been true: your parents bought you the presents in the shopping malls at the end of November, before the rush begins, or (it depends on the parents) in the city-center shops two or three days before Christmas, when the rush is on; the same parents, you know, used to hide the pres-

ents in the back of the closet, camouflaging them between broken lamps and threadbare old carpets, and on Christmas Eve they would send you to bed early under the pretext that Father Christmas is shy and scared of being seen; and when they were quite sure you were asleep they would tiptoe off to get the presents, wrapping all the parcels up in colored paper on the kitchen table before putting them under the tree. And the next morning they would go through the usual farce, "Let's sneak up really quietly," "I wonder if he came," "Hmm, I have a horrible feeling," and along the hall the more fanatical ones would try to put the wind up you with dark hints about behavior not having been good enough and maybe Santa had decided not to come. And that's how it has always been, more or less all over the world, because Father Christmas doesn't exist. Yet there are no children to whom this lie has not been told, and not only by their parents, but also by schoolteachers, by the television, by all their relatives, and even by their daft uncle, the one who tickles them until they can't stand it any more and when mommy isn't there jumps on the bed until he breaks the springs.

So what is it, then, a plot?

No, it's just an example of those lies I was telling you about, the good and innocent ones that make the world go around. Perhaps the world might even go around without them, I won't deny it, but these lies are here to stay and there's a lot of them, and if you think about it a moment you know this very well because you tell a good few of them yourselves. Just as I'm sure you have secrets too. Well, Pizzano Pizza's secret is simply a bit more sensational, amazing, and breathtaking than yours are, protected by lies like the ones that protect Father Christmas, a bit more complicated than yours.

For, you see (I've finally gotten to the point), the truth is that Pizzano Pizza is not a little boy as I have led you to believe. He is a Martian. And his name is not Pizzano Pizza, but Qlxxzw'kvsfqz (there are no vowels on Mars). And he isn't nine years old, but seventy-six—and the years on Mars, as we know, are much longer than the years on Earth, because Mars is farther *away from the sun and takes much longer to go around it, and so he is really quite a respectable age.*

But that's not all, listen to this: Pizzano Pizza is not even an ordinary Martian. He is a Martian secret agent on a mission to the Earth. A spy.

Now, that's left you flabbergasted, I'll bet. And you also suspect that this is the lie, I know, and that the liar is me. But, think about it: why should I tell you a lie like that? What's in it for me? It's really hard for me to tell you what I am telling you now; it would be much easier to carry on telling you his adventures as if nothing had happened: why on earth should I complicate my life like this? And what's more, you know me, at least those of you who have read some other Pizzano Pizza book know who I am, and I like to think I have earned your trust, by now. If I were a menacing-looking stranger, if I had suddenly pounced on you, at night, maybe armed with a pistol, scaring you to death, only to tell you something like that, I'd understand: but it's me, and even though you have never seen me we have spent a good bit of time together, and by now there's a certain familiarity between us. Also, if it helps you to dispel all your doubts, I can even give you an idea of the way I look. Here's my self-portrait:

(self-portrait of the author with a swollen cheek)

Yes, this is me (while eating a chestnut, and that explains the swollen cheek). Do I look like the kind of person who gets up in the morning and imagines that people are Martians on secret missions?

No, resign yourselves: Pizzano Pizza is a Martian sent to the Earth on a super-secret mission, and to carry out this mission he has transformed himself into a nine-year-old Earthling boy. It's the honest truth.

Now I know that thousands of questions will be buzzing around in your head, and believe me when I tell you that I consider myself duty-bound to answer them all. Only, since this is a story, you'll have to give me time, let me tell the story,

*and you'll see that one by one your curiosities will be sat-
isfied.*

*Right then. Let's start from the beginning. Or rather, let's
recap, as they say. Pizzano Pizza, the boy who travels through
time sitting on his stool, looks like this:*

(drawing of Pizzano Pizza)

*But Qlxxzw'kvsfqz, the Martian spy sent to the Earth on a
super-secret mission, looks like this:*

(drawing of a Martian)

*As you can see, there is no resemblance between the two. Yet
they are the same being. And it's not that all the adventures you
read about in the previous books are not true: it all happened
exactly the way I told you, except that inside the nine-year-old
boy that had them there was the adult Martian who was carrying out his incredibly important secret mission.*

*But what was it about this mission, you will be wondering,
that was so important and so secret that it had to be hidden from
you for a good two books?*

*The answer is: Pizzano Pizza's secret mission was to let no
one know he was on a secret mission.*

*And now, I'll bet, you will be wondering: so how come we
can know now but we couldn't before? What has changed?*

*And that is a good question, boys and girls, a very good ques-
tion: so good that it is the ideal question with which to close this
first chapter. Not that I don't want to give you an answer, but as I
have already said, this is a story, and it's a good rule, in stories,
not to answer too many questions right away. Believe me, it's
better to let the others wait for a bit. So trust me, carry on reading, and when the right time comes you'll know the answer to
this question too. But for now let me tell the true story of Pizzano Pizza from its true beginning . . .*

eleven

First curse. Second curse. Third curse. Pause. Madonna. God. Madonna. Pause. And so on.

The sun was slowly setting over the Janiculum, and the muezzin of abuse had struck up the same litany as the day before, with the same desperation as the day before. It is extraordinary how quickly you get used to things: on the lounger on the terrace again, drinking gin and tonic on an empty stomach again, more or less at the same time. The curses howled by that poor kid already struck me as a part of the landscape, no more mysterious than the bellowing of the traffic in the street below, or than the calling of the swallows wheeling in the sky. I had to make an effort of will to find in it the same unknown quantities that had disquieted me the evening before: Who was shouting? Why was he suffering? Why were there not other voices, apart from his, or other sounds? Could he really be tied to the bed?

I got up and went to the parapet to take a look, through the mesh of the child safety netting.

Like the day before, more than the day before, the surrounding windowsills were crowded with an audience of little heads: elderly people, mostly, scandalized and perhaps frightened by the arcane voice that continued to rage: Madonna. God. Madonna—at full volume. They gesticulated and murmured from windowsill to windowsill, with a worried air, planning heaven only knows what collective exorcism (the revenge of the peace on suffering); but they looked excited, and they hadn't hesitated to abandon the quiz shows that were still baying from their living rooms. Just as I had done the day before, I beat a retreat: it's in moments like this that people give the worst of themselves, better not to see it.

I went back to the lounger and stretched out. I was enjoying a strange calm, unimaginable until the previous day, and I didn't want to spoil it. Yet I had done none of the things I should have done: the list of things to do drawn up with such care was still there, intact, under the telephone, and the Vespa—flooded, if I recall aright—on which I ought to have been skipping through the traffic to get them done had spent the whole day chained to the one-way street sign on the pavement outside the house. I simply hadn't had the time. I had to *work*, because that morning I had been visited by a state of grace I had not known for some time, and whose absence had been wearing me down. Now, I am well aware that the word *inspiration* may sound ridiculous in the mouth of a writer of children's fiction, but I really wouldn't know any other way to define what had assailed me on my awakening that morning. I suddenly knew what to write: the doldrums of the previous months had been overcome, and I couldn't wait to get started. The matter had taken me by surprise, naturally, since I had fallen asleep in the womb of a rambling question mark and it seemed entirely likely that I would spend the following day trying to free myself of its immense bulk. But I had woken up and the cloudburst that had fallen on me the evening before immediately flowed in the one direction that could have permitted what was a problem, or disturbance, or anxiety state to be transformed into a solution, and before I knew it I found myself sitting at the computer, carried away on the dear old roller-coaster of words that slip out by themselves. A feeling of rare buoyancy accompanied me all day long, as the pages began to mount up and I rediscovered the desire to write that I had lost—writing without stopping to answer the telephone, to eat, or to think about my own affairs, without worrying about anything other than carrying on reeling in the big fish that had finally bitten. And the fact that all this did not concern a work of great literary importance but merely a book for children is, as they say, my business, in the sense that it is a matter bound up with my destiny: a destiny, I want to make it quite clear, that I accept without reservations. Kafka wrote *Metamorphosis* in the grip of inspiration, I was writing *The Secret of Pizzano Pizza*: so what? I have never even dreamed of becoming great, I have no ambitions to glory or immortality: it's enough for me to come up with a few decent ideas that allow my fingers to bang away at my damned keyboard in order to earn an honest living for my family: no more than that, for God's sake, but no less either. I willingly leave creative crises to the geniuses.

Of course, I realize that putting it this way sounds atrociously cynical: a stranger breaks an oath and reveals to you that your recently deceased father was a spy, obliging you to see things, albeit for only a moment, from an amazing standpoint that makes every single instant of your past life no more than a painstakingly created cover story; and you, the following morning, even before you take the trouble to recapitulate the thousands of reasons that make this story simply ridiculous, dive off to the computer to recycle the whole thing as a book for children, transforming it into entertainment—not to mention *product*, given that you are a professional—thereby overcoming *your* case of writer's block. What a horrendous world, we are all beyond redemption. But doing this was not so terrible, really; and in any case I had done it by then, and had even found relief in it—and if this isn't very nice, then I say that it's not very nice to spend whole afternoons playing solitaire on the computer either, or filling the screen with "Gianni Orzan Tough Blighter Horse Soldier and Injun Fighter" repeated hundreds of times in dozens of different fonts; and

I also say that, whatever the case may be, having started to write again made me a better man, even if only a little better, even if no one noticed, and even if, as was possible, on rereading the next day what I had written the day before I had found it ugly and deleted it—because this is simply my duty: to write, to delete, to write again, and to improve by struggling every day with the white whale that is the blank page.

No, I hadn't done anything wrong. I had only kept faith with my commitment. I took an idea from something that had happened to me and I began to write. Where's the harm in that? All writers do that, and the feelings of guilt that were trying to gnaw at me were wholly misplaced. Besides, I had them before, even when I couldn't manage to write one line, and that was worse.

What's more it wasn't even true that I had been neglecting everything. During the day I had fielded two phone calls, I had devoted a little time to the others. The first call had been from the mother of the little boy in a coma. I didn't recognize her right away, because when the answering machine had responded she called herself "Matteo's mother," and when I dashed to lift the phone she was already saying good-bye. I was glad to catch her before she hung up, and I think that had I not made it in time my day would have been a very different one (how many variables, really, influence our lives), because I would have launched into a dizzying round of phone calls, to the organizers of the prize, to the local journalist, to the outgoing mayor and to the mayor designate, and to the hospital of that town, in an attempt to get hold of her number and call her back; but there was no need, so much the better. After thanking me again, the woman told me that she was coming to Rome the following day, to consult with a certain luminary regarding the advisability of transferring the child to a specialty clinic in Austria, and that she would like to meet me, before she left. As on the evening of the prize-giving, she spoke of her tragedy in detached tones, devoid of anguish, uttering without betraying any emotion fatal words like *irreversible* and *final attempt*. I told her I would be very happy to meet her and we agreed to meet at eleven on the following morning. When I asked her what part of the city was easiest for her she said that it was all the same to her— as long as, she added, it was in the open air. And so off the top of my head all I could think of was the café in front of Porta San Paolo, near my house, and we agreed on there: but not because it was handy for me, let it be perfectly clear.

After hanging up it took me a bit to get back to work: I started thinking about the exemplary nature of that woman's battle against medical science, which considered the survival of her "laurel hedgerow" pointless, which defined as "therapeutic implacability" the functioning of the machine that was keeping it alive, and sat waiting with the patience of vultures for the moment in which this mother too, as happens to all mothers in her situation— exhausted, discouraged, and abandoned by all—would resign herself to considering her own child for what he is in our wretched society, that is to say, a mere carcass to be carefully stripped of all reusable organs and buried with a solemn funeral service held by the bishop. I thought that, in her place, I would have behaved exactly the way she did, and I was reminded of a story by Raymond Carver in which at a certain point the narrator begs his wife, if ever he happened to go into a coma, not to pull the plug on him, ever, for any reason. I went to search for it among my books. I found it, reread it, and copied the passage in question (already carefully underlined) into my notebook, because I had suddenly decided to give that book to the woman, the following day, and if I didn't have time to buy her a new copy, or if I couldn't find one, I would give her mine. The passage goes like this:

No. Don't unplug me. I don't want to be unplugged. Leave me hooked up just as long as possible. Who's going to object? Are you going to object? Will I be offending anybody? As long as people can stand the sight of me, just so long as they don't start howling, don't unplug anything. Let me keep going, okay? Right to the bitter end. Invite my friends in to say good-bye. Don't do anything rash.

The second call was from Franceschino—that is, after a whirl-wind of endearments from Anna. Although, obviously, I was expecting the call, it caught me by surprise just the same, and I didn't manage to tell her anything about the previous evening. As I had not yet spent so much as a minute trying to find the right words with which to tackle such an absurd story, I simply couldn't find any, and I was reticent as a child, and I reassured her in that spare, generic way that, usually, does not sound reassuring at all. I didn't even tell her about my fit of creativity, but I was frank about not having done a single one of the things I was supposed to have done, including phoning Francesco's school to inform them of his absence during the last days of the school year. And I was expect-ing Anna to protest about that, given that she had been very insis-tent on this, on account of a certain musical show in which he was to have played an important part: all I was supposed to do was to let the teachers know that he couldn't take part in it, so that they would have had time to redistribute the roles. Anna was a member of the parent-teacher committee and she was very scrupulous about this kind of thing; I thought she would have objected, seeing that I actually could have made the telephone call, but instead, to my surprise, she didn't say a word. She too was laconic, even curt, and all in all it was a strange telephone call: but I was too taken by my own conspiracy of silence to notice anything. It was only as I hung up that I realized that she was still coming to grips with the mysterious armed lunatic who had shown that he knew everything about our son: a threat that had disappeared from my life, but not from *hers*, and, together with the tenderness you feel for those who continue to see what has been erased from your own con-sciousness—J. D. Salinger was the poet of this—I also felt the bur-den of a similar gap between us two, and the duty to bridge it by telling her everything as soon as possible. Something I was going to do that very evening, as soon as I had found the words with which to do so. As soon as I had once more shouldered the respon-sibilities from which, in order to go back to being a writer, I had dispensed myself for a whole day . . .

And that's when the Voice stopped. Just like the day before, suddenly there was no more cursing, and like the day before it seemed that something was missing from the warm June sky and the encroaching twilight. For a long moment everything seemed suspended, waiting to discover whether it was only a longer pause or whether, simply, that was it for today and tune in tomorrow at the same time. And that's obviously how it was, because over those two days the Voice had made things clear: shorter or longer pauses did not exist; it was either *that* pause or nothing. But a few minutes had to pass before the World, down there, would bow to the inevitable and begin turning normally once more, dusting off its arid capacity to do without everything. And I, who had been suspended for the day from all my duties bar one, and from all my responsibilities bar one, saw that suspension as a gift because it unburdened me even more, and it finished emptying my gaze, allowing it to roam pure and free over the horizon as if I were Elagabalus. The rooftops. The trees. The red and white antenna on top of Monte Mario. Three quarters of the dome of St. Peter's. The Pyramid. The gasometer, which for some mysterious reason Franceschino calls the "Postal Coliseum."

Soaring, silent, the absolute master of his flight, a seagull was heading toward me, really, ever more unequivocally, until he alighted—incredible—on the windowsill right in front of me. He sat there looking at me, breast puffed up, with his predatory frown and his hooked beak, moving his head from one side to the other to fix me first with the right eye then with the left, as if there were a difference between the two gazes—and actually there probably is. The bird was looking at me with such power that for a long golden moment I was nothing but the vague and irrelevant thing looked at by him, and I felt an absolute, perfect peace, which I would like to remember always; then he went off, suddenly, letting himself drop into the void and disappearing beneath the line of the windowsill to reappear already a good distance away, already oblivious to me, headed elsewhere.

I finished the gin and tonic in one long last draft and lay down again. The sun was setting, the day was over. I had to think about what to do. I had to call Anna. I had to eat because I was hungry. Awareness suddenly returned, and with it the flow of thoughts, stimuli, duties, and recollections that are mine and mine alone. All things once more began to pulse with that Principle of Individuation that nailed me anew to myself and repeated obsessively—but without ever explaining *why*—that I am I and I am not what that seagull had seen, and above all that I am not that seagull; that this is my terrace and not a gray point in the blue where you can alight to take a breather; and that what was ringing was my doorbell, that's it, end of interlude, it really was my doorbell, and it was ringing, and whoever was ringing was looking for me, that me I had managed not to be entirely for the whole day, and a short time before, for one fantastic moment, I had not been at all, but that I inexorably am and know I am.

And I was afraid that I knew who the person ringing the doorbell was too.

twelve

There is a spyhole, in the door. We never use it but it's there.

Deformed in the fish-eye lens that gives a view of the whole landing, Gianni Bogliasco/Fusco/Costante was waiting, planted as solid as a fire hydrant, holding a bulging plastic bag spiky with sharp edges. I don't think he thought he was being observed, yet he was smiling as usual. It really must have been a kind of conditioned reflex. What to do, open up or not?

I opened up.

"I've brought something to eat," he began, as if it were the most natural thing in the world. I didn't ask him in, but I didn't prevent him from doing so either, and he came in. He looked around for a bit, nodding.

"Nice place."

Then, since he was the lord of all creation, and could always do what he wanted, he started inspecting the house. He went into

Francesco's room; he came out again; he went into my study; stayed there a little longer; he came out again; he disappeared into our bedroom; out he popped again. Nodding and smiling the whole time. I was still standing in the same place, I hadn't even closed the door.

"Well done," he decreed. "Simple but welcoming. You can see that you both have taste."

Then he waved the bulging plastic bag, which dangled slowly: it must have weighed a good bit.

"Where shall we sit?" he asked. "This stuff is hot."

"Make yourself at home."

"Thanks."

As had already happened several times the day before, he didn't seem to notice my sarcasm in the slightest. He was invulnerable. (Or maybe I'm just no good at sarcasm?) Perhaps, for a second or two, he was waiting for me to lead the way, but even if that had been the case he didn't even leave me the time to decide, and he went into the living room, disappearing once more. And now I was going to find out if this really was the first time he had set foot in here, by the way, or if his tour of inspection had merely been play-acting—anything was possible, with him. Because if it was the first time he had seen my house, then I knew what was going to happen: it always happens, when someone goes into my living room for the first time . . .

"Wow, what a great terrace!" I heard him yell.

Anna and I had had the same reaction, when the guy from the agency had taken us to view the apartment. The fact is that the house is small, the building is in poor repair, and the terrace is at the back, invisible from the road and absolutely unimaginable until you enter the living room and find it in front of you, wide and bright, with Rome spread out beneath it. It's a real surprise, all right.

"Fantastic," I heard him say, in a lower voice. "Who would have expected this?"

I joined him. He was at the windowsill, hanging on to the netting, ravished by the sunset.

"Fantastic," he repeated, "you can see St. Peter's too." Then he spun around. "Look, you won't find many balconies with a view like this, in Rome. Is the house yours?"

"No, it's rented."

"Oh. And does it cost a lot?"

"Well . . ."

I don't know what the glance I shot him must have looked like, but he immediately felt obliged to add:

"If I'm not being indiscreet, that is . . ."

Which, I realize, is not "Forget it, it's none of my business," but it was still better than nothing.

"A million four," I replied.

"And you're complaining?"

"I'm not complaining at all."

"Hang on to it, mark my words, a landlord who asks you for a million four for a house with a terrace like this one! Who is he, a friend of yours?"

"No."

"Oh no? So who is he?"

I tried to look at him the way I had done a moment before, but this time it didn't work, and he didn't add anything.

"No one in particular," I replied. "I found him through an agency."

"Then you're a lucky boy, let me tell you." He shook his head. "A million four . . ."

Boy. I am not a boy.

"Come on, let's eat, before it goes cold."

He pulled out a number of packages from the bag and placed them on the table—grease-laden wrappers and aluminum foil trays, plus two cans of beer and two plastic cups that immediately began to sway in the westerly breeze, and if something wasn't done about that soon they would fly away. Then he started unwrapping the packets, one by one, to reveal riceballs of various types, mozzarella and bread fried in batter, olives stuffed with meat and then fried in breadcrumbs, potato patties and other fried stuff. There was enough to feed a school trip.

"Here at the Pyramid there's one of the best rotisseries in Rome: did you know that?"

"Which, Di Pietro's?"

"Right. D'you ever go?"

"I pick up a roast chicken when I'm on my own."

I caught one of the plastic cups that was about to take off, and I filled it with beer. Then I filled the other one, and attacked the roast potatoes piled majestically in a tray. I was hungry.

"As a matter of fact," he went on, "since they cleaned it all up it's gone downhill a bit: now it looks like an ordinary pizzeria, respectable, even welcoming, while a real rotisserie has to be filthy, cramped, and smelly: just the way Di Pietro's used to be. But, despite the aspirations to gentility, it's still great for certain things. Try one of these . . ."

He proffered me a kind of slab with a menacingly oily look: it was the last thing I would have chosen of my own free will, but I was well aware, with him in action, that this was a detail devoid of importance. He waited until I had taken the slab and taken a bite of it, and, as I began to chew, he enlightened me:

"Sandwich done in the oven: new one on you?"

I shook my head, while I tried not to burn my tongue on the scalding hot interior.

"Brilliant, don't you find?"

In fact the taste was good. The fried pizza crust was filled with cheese, and boiled ham, I think. But what gave you the willies, if anything, was the squirt of oil that gushed into the mouth as you chewed . . .

"It's a bit oily . . . ," I said.

"*You can say that again*," he shot back, in an implausible Roman accent, with the vowels wide open, the way Celentano spoke in *Rugantino*.

"That's why it's good," he went on, biting into one himself. Then, still chewing, he carried on talking:

"You see, I don't know about you, but I am a rotisserie fan. I've even written a book about them: *Under 10*, it's called: a guide to the rotisseries of Italy, where you can eat—where you *used to* be able to eat, the prices have gone up now—on less than ten thousand lire. Maybe I'll bring you a copy the next time . . ."

Great. A writer too.

"The fact is," he continued, "that I have always eaten in rotisseries. I have seen them come and go, and change, in Rome, Genoa, Livorno, Naples, and in Milan, where they have now become a rich man's thing, but until twenty years ago, believe me, there were some great ones. I have tested at least three generations of Italian rotisseries, my friend . . ."

He seized a riceball, and, rather than eat it he *sucked* it, the way Gassman did with crème caramel. I carried on digging into the tray of potatoes—extremely greasy, browned to the maximum, saturated in garlic and rosemary, and so, effectively, lethally good.

"And d'you know what I say? When I'm abroad, rotisseries are the thing I miss the most about Italy. Not Italian art, not the Italian climate, and not Italian restaurants, which are all over the place by now: the rotisseries. You don't find those anywhere else. Probably it's because I've never had a mother's home cooking, not even as a kid, but when I go into a real rotisserie, one of those that is still the way it was forty years ago, with feeble lighting and the smell of frying that impregnates your clothes, I feel at home. It's sheer poetry, for me: those burly men with dirty aprons and perennially greasy hands, those washed-out-looking women who have spent a lifetime at the cash register, the brusque way they give you the change, pretending that they know you really well even though it's the first time they have seen you . . ."

He downed the rest of his beer, and he too fished a potato out of the tray, and then another. And another.

"The pills," I said.

"What's that?"

"You're forgetting to take the pills."

He stiffened.

"Oh, right," he said, and, shaking his head, he rummaged in his pocket.

He found the bottle and repeated the operation of the other evening, swallowing the two pills without washing them down with a drink, getting them down with only a jerk of the head.

"Well," he said, looking at me, "you've got a good spirit of observation . . ."

He swallowed a second time—the pills must have gotten stuck halfway down—and plunged back avidly into the tray of potatoes as if he wanted to scoff the lot before I could take another one.

"And then there's the flavor . . . ," he resumed. "*These* are perfect flavors, according to me. Try a rice ball . . ."

He bit into a rice ball, and I did the same: it was good, sure enough. He finished it in two mouthfuls, then he drained his glass of beer before tackling the fried mozzarella—a tricky task requiring both hands. The thing was running copiously with oil and, after the first bite, also with a white cheesy serum, which obliged him to hunch over in that reflex typical of the hamburger eater, shoving himself as far back as possible into the seat and craning his neck in order to channel all the liquids into an empty tray on the table.

"They're heavy, all right," he resumed, with his mouth too full and his voice suddenly guttural, "but you won't find any modern fads, another *American* thing: fat-free cooking," he said, adding in English, "cholesterol free . . ."

He had to fall silent in order to swallow, otherwise he was going to drown. His English pronunciation, however, was perfect.

"But it's a war in there," he said, and his voice was back to normal, "and the rotisserie chef is a soldier in the trenches, fighting all day long to give pleasure to those who can afford only to satisfy their hunger . . ."

He finished the mozzarella and attacked a potato patty. As on the previous evening, he was extremely fast, despite the fact that he was talking and eating at the same time. There must be a specific technique.

"Because with truffles it's easy to produce cuisine with flavor, or with mushrooms and balsamic vinegar that costs two million the liter, anyone can do that: but try doing it with rice, bread, potatoes, using cheap seed oil. It's really like making war with rifles and bayonets, it's heroism. And *that's* where the difference lies . . ."

He finished off the last potato, which was floating in brownish oil. I would have willingly eaten it myself.

"Mmmm," he moaned, "will you taste that? Here we are at the extreme limits of taste. A little farther and it becomes mere chow, swill, and the rotisserie chef's art lies precisely in his capacity to get as close as possible to that limit without ever exceeding it. Do you understand the difficulty, the *greatness*? To load you with calories for only a little money, to satisfy your hunger, but also to give you the maximum possible pleasure, and all without poisoning you. But in restaurants they give you these things as appetizers, just like that, for fun, and the intention is to transform them into refined stuff: they fry them for you on the spot, and massacre them with diminutives, 'a couple of dainty little croquettes,' 'two little olives,' 'a little mozzarella' . . . Then they slip you some mussels that have gone bad and you get hepatitis."

It was strange, but I agreed with him. Perhaps it might have pleased him to know this, but I didn't want to make the same mistake I had made the evening before, I didn't want to say anything. I still believe that, sooner or later, faced with a stubborn and impenetrable silence, even the most garrulous of talkers ends up by feeling uncomfortable. And that is exactly what I would have liked: to make him feel uncomfortable, just for once. But he was right about the rotisseries, they're great places.

In the meantime the food was almost gone, and the hunger with it. I had already stopped eating, he was still nibbling at the stuffed olives, but you could see from his look that he was sated, and that he was doing it more out of a sense of duty than anything else: in fact another thing I think we agreed on was that rotisserie leftovers become instantly unbearable. So either it all gets finished or it has to be gotten rid of in a hurry. And when I saw that he too had finished eating, and, after draining his beer in one long swallow, was lighting—ouch—a cigarette, I got up and started collecting the stuff.

"Want a hand?" he asked, without even *hinting* at moving.

"Doesn't matter."

Then came the disgusting part, which has to be done in a hurry. The leftovers dripping one onto the other, the empty trays piled unsteadily one on top of the other, the crumpled balls of paper: holding my breath, I gathered up this greasy mess and took it into the kitchen, where I threw it immediately into the garbage. Then I washed my hands, which had been greased to death in the course of the operation, and before returning to the terrace I took two cans of beer from the fridge, because I was still thirsty, and probably he was too. I found him on his feet again, close to the netting: I handed him one of the two cans, he nodded at me as if to say "good idea," opened it, and took a long pull, a lit cigarette between his fingers. His interest seemed centered on the swallows, which were wheeling and circling madly in front of us. His jacket was open, and beneath the short-sleeved Bulgarian shirt his belly bulged over his belt. The shirt was the same one as the day before, this time dirty and wrinkled. No sign of the pistol, no bulge in his pockets: could it be that he had done me the courtesy of coming unarmed?

"They call them swallows but they're wrong," he said. "Swallows are bigger, and they live in the country. These are *chimney swifts* . . ."

He lingered a little longer to observe the swallows (I'd never heard of these chimney swifts), then he sat down and dragged the seat over to where I was sitting.

"Not exactly an orator, this evening, are we?" he said.

Stretching out on the lounger, I put my hands behind the nape of my neck.

"Nope."

I was dying to smoke, damn it. He was probing about in his mouth with his tongue, making those little sucking noises that scandalize Anna so much, getting the stuff out from between his teeth.

"Look how beautiful it is . . ."

In fact it was a moment of great beauty: the sky was an illogical metallic blue color, and the wind kept it burnished as enamel. It was hot, and the jasmine on my terrace was sending out an almost unbearable scent. The lights of Rome shone out everywhere, even the monuments were glittering. It all seemed to be saying that there is a right way to sink into the night of a decadent metropolis full of history, and that this was it.

"Listen, Bogliasco," I said suddenly. "Why have you come here?"

Here we go again, why had I spoken? The silence was working, it had been troubling him. Why had I spoken?

He shrugged. "Because I felt like having a little chat with you."

"What if I hadn't been in? Or if I had had guests?"

"I'd have gone away again."

He shifted his gaze toward the sky, to follow an airplane that was shaping its winking course right above us.

"Listen, I don't believe your story," I said.

His gaze returned to me, and he affected an air of surprise.

"What story?"

"The one about my father. I don't believe it."

"What's that got to do with what's happening now?"

"It's the reason why you came here, that's what it's got to do with."

"No. I only wanted a little chat."

"A little chat, right . . ."

"Right, a little chat. Why, is that so strange?"

"And what is it that we are supposed to talk about, in this little chat?"

"There are lots of things we could chat about . . ."

"Oh yes? For example?"

"Oh, goodness knows. Lots of things . . . we could talk about the cinema . . ."

He emitted a long, silent belch, and a whiff of beer-laden breath reached my nose.

"Lots of things . . . ," he repeated, and he went back to looking at the sky.

What was I to do? I wanted to free myself of this man: what was I to do? The previous evening I had allowed myself to get involved, I had fought, I had tried to show him just how objectively ridiculous the things he had wanted to convince me of were, but it hadn't worked, and he had gotten what he wanted: he wanted to tell his story, and he had told it. This time he had taken a more roundabout route, and I was managing to resist, I had almost humiliated him with my silence, but there he was, unabashed, enjoying the cool air on my terrace and belching as he waited for the right moment to begin. He was certainly feeling better than me, even as things stood then. But there still had to be a way of getting rid of him, I would find the words with which to explain to him that his efforts were in vain, and that he could torment me for the rest of my life but that he would never convince me that my father had been a Russian spy, because my father had *not* been a Russian spy.

"Listen," I began, but I was already on the wrong track, because I always begin with "listen," it's a kind of pet phrase that infests my speech, I know, but even though I am aware of it, it always slips out, which means that I do not have total control over my words, not even at that very moment, when a conclusive remark came to mind.

"Now hear me out, please," I continued. "Pay close attention to what I have to say to you . . ."

I fell silent for a moment, to see if he intended to let me speak or not. He fell silent too. He looked at me and said nothing, a sign that—according to his concept that conversations are like games of American pool, in which a player holds the table until he makes a mistake, at which point he stands aside to let the other player have his turn—he had recognized that my turn had come. Here we go then . . .

thirteen

I don't believe your story," I said, but naturally this wasn't the conclusive remark I had thought of moments before: the thing was that, in a flash, it had gone the same way it had come. It had to do, I recall, with a certain power that we sometimes feel come over us, a power that permits us to let things happen without our putting up any resistance to them, letting it seem that we have been overwhelmed even though this is not so, we are just curious to see these things happen; which would have been tantamount to explaining to him—but generally speaking, which is always better—why I had let him into my house and why I had given him all that rope and why he was free to lord it over my terrace; and for a moment all this had taken a splendidly convincing but, alas, evidently ephemeral form in my head, and before I managed to fix it with a discourse it had vanished: later, I already knew, it would have returned to mind, but by that time it would no longer have been of any use. What's more, he too was left disappointed, almost disconcerted, by my vacuity: he carried on staring at me in silence, and it was as if he couldn't bring himself to believe that there was no more to it than that, it was as if he suspected some trap. I recall that same expression in the eyes of certain opponents—when I had been a candidate chess master and everyone expected great things of me—at the climax of extremely badly played, slipshod, defeatist games, when I finally decided to attempt a combination: I *deluded* them into thinking I could put them in difficulty, but then I would retire two moves later. They were almost more disappointed than I . . .

"So thanks for the dinner," I floundered, "in fact for the dinners, yesterday's and today's, but if you want to carry on talking to me you're going to have to point your pistol at me, because I, if I am to have any say in the matter, have no intention of . . ."

The telephone rang.

"Anna!" I said.

I looked at my watch: half past nine, and I still hadn't called her. I leaped to my feet and ran to answer before the machine cut in, leaving him sitting there like a dummy—which at the end of the day was more conclusive than any words could have been.

"Hello?"

"Daddy?"

Franceschino. How marvelous it was to hear his voice, then. What a relief to think that he was really there, and that it wasn't a question of belief or disbelief. How marvelous to hear him start off with a quickfire burst, as usual ("What are you doing?" "What's Pizzano Pizza up to?" "When are you coming?") and then, suddenly, but still as usual, to seize up and become reticent, beginning to respond with a grudging "yes" or a "no" to my questions ("Have you been swimming, little fish?" "Did you go to the pine wood?"), as if he had suddenly lost all interest in me, or as if I had disturbed him in the middle of some fantastical game that continued without him; whereas this is what happens with all children, it's well known, it's a question of a reduction in the attention span owing to the fact that the telephone, for example, and technology in general, belongs to the world of adults, and, for this very reason, just as that world attracts them at first, so it bores them immediately afterward, with all its insane fragility and monotony and rules to be obeyed—and this is the only reason, let this be quite clear, and not because he didn't want to speak to his father, that Franceschino hastily got rid of me, passing me Anna. It's the *means*, damn it, that doesn't suit him . . .

"Gianni?" Anna's voice was hesitant, as if she had just woken up.

"Hi. Everything all right?"

"I'm sorry, you know. Franceschino called you on his own initiative," were her strange words.

"So? What's wrong with that?"

"Well, nothing, maybe you were busy . . ."

Anna was cold, distant.

"What's the matter?" I said. "Are you angry?"

"No . . ."

"Is there some problem?"

"No, no," she repeated. But there was a problem, of course there was: she still thought we were all in danger . . .

"Listen," I said to her. "I was about to call you, because it's all sorted out: no one was threatening us, you know, the other evening was merely a misunderstanding, that man wasn't a stranger at all."

"Oh," she said. "And who was he?"

"He was . . . an old aide of my father's," I ventured, "a person who thought I had recognized him. A good man, he brought my bag back and we cleared everything up. It was all a colossal misunderstanding, really. We don't need to worry about a thing: no one wants to hurt us, everything is as it was before."

"Thank God," she said, introducing a strange pause. Strange because at that point she ought to have laughed, made fun of me, or, were she still not satisfied—and she would have had every right—asked me for further explanations, bombarding me with questions. But she remained silent.

"It did seem odd to me . . . ," she concluded, but after a good bit; and the tone of her voice was still embarrassed and cold, as if that had not been the problem. But if that was the case, then things were not right at all, because that *had* been the problem; what else?

"It was probably a touch of paranoia on my part," I said, "but I assure you that it wasn't easy to understand at the time, what with that pistol in his belt and especially because he hadn't told me who he was. And in fact he realized that too and he . . ."

And that's when matters began to get complicated, because Bogliasco came into the living room holding his bag, the same one he had brought the fried food in, which still wasn't entirely empty because he took a videotape cassette out of it and showed it to me. Then he gestured at me as if inviting me to carry on with the phone call and not to mind him, before heading menacingly toward the videocassette recorder, and that was no good either. ". . . apologized to me . . . ," I continued, gesturing at him to stop, and *not to touch anything*, but all I received in exchange was another of those reassuring nods of his that didn't reassure me in the slightest.

"Well," said Anna, "the main thing is that you sorted things out . . ."

"He's here with me now . . . ," I whispered, awkwardly, so that he would not hear me as he was fiddling about near the television, the cassette in his hand.

"Oh . . ."

What was going on? It was impossible to be so detached when faced with the prospect of liberation, since that was what my words ought to have meant for her, liberation from the distress of being threatened without knowing why.

"Anna," I said, "what's the matter?"

"Nothing."

In the meantime the man had switched on the television, turned off the volume, and was fiddling about with the remote control for the VCR. He had donned a surprising pair of reading glasses—surprising on him—small, elegant, with ultra lightweight metal rims that gleamed in the light. My father had had a pair like that too.

"Listen," I said, "tomorrow I'll come to Viareggio and I'll explain everything to you, but the main thing was that you knew. In fact, I'll call you later, if you want . . . Okay?"

"No, it doesn't matter."

"Are you sure? Would you prefer if we talked about it right away?"

Despite my whispering, he could hear perfectly well, and he raised his arms as if authorizing me, *much obliged, I'm sure!*, to send him away whenever I wanted so that I could talk to my wife. In the meantime, however, he did not go away, and he slipped the cassette into the machine.

"No, no," said Anna. "We can talk tomorrow . . ."

"All right, but don't worry, please . . ."

"Yes. Good night."

I hung up and, had I been alone, I would have sat there for lord knows how long, motionless, mulling things over and worrying, because Anna had been really strange. But I wasn't alone, I had that man underfoot, and once more he was laying claims to my time and my attention . . .

A roar. I don't know how, but he had set the volume of the television to maximum power, transforming the pop song it was transmitting into a deafening blast. I leaped to my feet to intervene, but he instantly found the control and turned the sound down.

"Sorry," he said, "I inadvertently . . ."

"What the hell are you up to, eh?"

"Nothing," he said. "Everything's under control. I only wanted to show you something. We're already at the right place, it'll only take a second . . ."

He didn't even let me say "all right" (I would have said "all right" in any case), and he pressed the "play" button on the VCR remote control. I heard the usual sound of levers and mechanisms laboriously coming into action. It was the beginning of that necessary start-up time that magnetic tape image reproduction systems have never managed to eliminate: two deadly seconds that come to think of it are really unbearable, because they remind us of the failure of the utopia of absolute progress and ruthlessly reveal the limitations of technology: a direct flight from Rome to New York takes the same eight hours it took twenty years ago, while the most sophisticated of the latest generation of internal combustion engines produces and wastes the same exorbitant quantity of heat as the engine in Laurel and Hardy's car. Two seconds that, now, were the cause of a certain sudden trepidation on my part, really, regarding what I was about to see, because it really could have been anything, considering the person who was showing it to me, and if it turned out to be something I didn't want to see—blood and guts, let's say, which I can't stand, or some little film shot for the purposes of blackmail—I would not have been free to refuse to watch, since at that point I would have already seen it. A gratuitous trepidation that grew steadily greater—my father doing something embarrassing? *Me* doing something embarrassing? Those were two very long seconds, in reality—until the tape finally decided to get underway and on the screen there appeared a medium close-up of Clint Eastwood standing in the middle of a field, wearing a cowboy hat and a policeman's uniform and saying "*All right.*"

A few meters away, Kevin Costner, bleeding and in pain, is kneeling down to talk to a little boy. "'*I want to give you something,*" he says.

It was the end of *A Perfect World*, I recognized it right away; I glanced at my man, to see what he wanted from me, and he gestured at me to carry on watching.

In the distance, on the far side of the field, ranks of policemen keep Kevin Costner in their sights, because they don't know he's unarmed. "*Watch him,*" says the one with the binoculars. "*If he so much as moves . . . ,*" says Bradley Whitford, with rifle pointed.

Laura Dern, also with binoculars, breaks in: "*No. Just another second!*"

Again Kevin Costner kneeling in the field, saying to the boy:

"*Maybe you'll go there, one day . . .* ," and he puts his hand in the hip pocket of his jeans.

"*He's going for his gun!*" says the cop with the binoculars.

Kevin Costner pulls a postcard of Alaska out of his pocket, and Clint Eastwood turns toward his colleagues, shaking his head, because he has understood what is about to happen; but Bradley Whitford, with his high-precision rifle aimed . . .

Click: Bogliasco, using my remote control, had decided for some reason that the tape was to stop on that frame: a close-up on the hands of Bradley Whitford holding the rifle, the index finger on the point of pulling the trigger, the watch gleaming at his wrist, the shirt cuff protruding from the sleeve of his . . .

I couldn't believe it.

The shirt cuff protruded from the sleeve of his jacket. In other words his shirt did not have short sleeves. In other words this man noted everything I said, and then went to check out everything I said—*he* was checking *me* out—and he noted down the mistakes I made, and then he came to my house to rub salt in the wound, using my television, my VCR, while I should have been talking on the telephone to my wife, who had a problem . . .

"Now don't go thinking that I went to check this out on purpose," he said, "only to come here and show you that you were wrong: I'm not that much of a prick. The fact is that I was struck when you mentioned this film yesterday, because I really liked it too, you know, even though it's an American film, especially the part where the outlaw says that he didn't know what he would have done to those Negroes he had bound and gagged, if the boy had not shot him, because *that's the way it is*," he said, waxing fervent, "criminals don't have the slightest idea of what they're going to do, before they do it: they have a pistol, okay, they point it at people, okay, but they never really think of shooting before they do so, and if someone interrupts them, as happens in this film, they will never know if they would have done it or not. And it is precisely this business of keeping good and evil on a level of perfect equivalence that is, I think, the real essence of criminality, in the sense that it is more than enough to make a man a delinquent, without any need for him to *know* it, whereas in American films the criminals are always so aware that they are bad, always so self-satisfied . . ."

He broke off, as if awaking from a dream.

"Anyhow, this was just to say that yesterday you mentioned a film I really liked . . ." His voice recovered that calm it had lost when he had gone off on a tangent, " . . . and so I felt like watching it again, and today I rented a cassette, and I began to watch it, and when I came to the scene you mentioned, you see, *this* scene, I could hardly help noticing that the shirt worn by . . . what's the actor's name?"

"Bradley Whitford . . ."

He made a grimace of admiration, and remained silent. I was simply stunned, by then, because this man was mad all right, he was an insane paranoid solipsist mythomaniac, and he was in full swing, and he had two hands that could have crushed a brick to powder, and he was half a meter away from me—which was why it might have been a good idea to start being afraid again. But the fact remained that those cuffs were sensationally visible: how the devil had I managed to . . .

"All I want to tell you," he resumed, "is that things can be different from what we think, or from our recollections. That's all. If it had just been a matter of contradicting you I could have done so yesterday evening, when you recited that scene from *La Ricotta*: because Orson Welles does not read the poem to a waiter, as you said, but to a journalist, and I could remember that without any need to . . ."

Here we go again: a bigger bombshell hot on the heels of one that was *already* big.

"What was it I said?"

I had fallen for it, there was nothing I could do about that.

"Forget it . . ."

"No, I'm not going to forget it. What did I say?"

"Nothing, come on, it's nothing . . ."

"It is *not* nothing. What am I supposed to have said?"

He made a grimace, camouflaging his malignity as embarrassment, with millimetric precision.

" . . . You said that Orson Welles reads the poem to a waiter, but in reality he reads it to a . . . Come on, it's got nothing to do with anything, I was wrong to mention it . . ."

To a journalist, of course, an idiotic journalist that wanted to interview him. But I had said to a *waiter*, it was true, I recalled that perfectly well. Why? How could I have been mistaken about that scene in particular, I who know it by heart. Perhaps because we were in a restaurant (but there was no waiter, there was that girl on roller skates), and I had just been told that my father had killed a man, and perhaps—or rather, not perhaps, *certainly*—I was very upset; or, more simply, perhaps the famous one million neurons that everyone loses every day, from the age of thirty onward, having well and truly eroded the entire periphery (how many variants of the Nimzo-Indiana defense was I able to recall in that moment? Seven? Eight? Nine? What were the names of the noncoms that used to punish me in military college? Sabella or Savella? Schillaci or Schillace? Or Squillace?) were beginning to attack the active nucleus of the memory, the one we rely on every day, and dip into it automatically without suspecting that long sleeves can be transformed into short sleeves, or journalists into waiters, because otherwise we would never . . .

"What I wanted to say to you," he resumed, "is that sometimes we are absolutely certain of something, we would bet our life on it, whereas in reality that something was never that way. Because we don't remember well, or because that thing has always manifested itself to us in a certain way, but in reality was different . . ."

I sat down on the sofa—in fact, to be precise I slumped into it like a dead weight. I didn't want all this: I didn't want things to be different. I didn't want to recall them vaguely . . .

He sat down beside me and put one hand on my shoulder.

I didn't want this man to touch me . . .

"Try to put yourself in my place, Gianni. You have a certainty, and I come along to contradict it with an incredible story. What do you think, that I don't realize?" He took his paw off me. "And do you think I don't know that I look . . . well . . . not very reliable, let's say? I know, I don't look good, but what can I do about that? That's the way I am, I've always been like this, and it's a problem I've never even had to pose myself: no friends, apart from your father, no girlfriends, wives, children, and zero social life. Only whores, secrets, and hideouts, always pretending not to know what I knew, and to know what I didn't know . . . Not that I have any regrets, let's be quite clear about that, but after a life like mine how can I be reliable? I shouldn't even be alive, in theory, with the life I have led . . ."

He gave a chortle.

"To tell the truth, I was even dead, once, in '72; dead and buried. I have a plot, really, in Livorno cemetery, with my name on it and everything: only it's occupied by a man from Luxembourg. When I happen by there I always take some flowers, and while I'm at it I arrange them in the little vase . . . well, it's pathetic, I know, but that moves me . . . because I think that when I really die there won't be any Luxemburger to do the same thing for my grave, and there won't even be a grave, for the simple reason that I have no one anywhere in the world. And for a good bit, by now, when I stand there at my grave thinking about these things, I occasionally start crying like an idiot . . ."

He shook his head, disconsolate.

"On the other hand, it's normal," he added, sniffing, "it's old age . . ."

My head was beginning to ache, this man had worn me out. I looked at him: how was it possible that not one of the things he had said could be believed without an act of faith? Where was this old age that he was talking about? Certainly not in his eyes, which were still as mendacious and shifty as those of a small child, or in the stamina he had shown in demolishing me, a mere thirty-seven-year-old. Not in discourse, not in language or manner of speaking, and not even in appearance: massive and intimidating, the build of a sixty-year-old, a sixty-five-year-old at most, a bit overweight if you like, but in good health—apart from the whistle in the lungs that moreover had not been in evidence so far. Why did he not say at least one thing, any thing, which was not violently at odds with the evidence?

I threw myself back and closed my eyes, while he ranted on.

" . . . and I wasn't ready to become old, and I was even less ready to tackle a situation like this one. Because, you see . . . all the secrets I have known, in my life (and there are lots of them, take it from me, *lots*), did not interest me, at bottom. It was only information, for me, a means of exchange, it was my job . . . The so-called "invisible Italy," Gianni, the country in which an airliner plunges into the sea and some people *know perfectly well* what happened, and those responsible immediately get to work so that the parents of the victims, the press, you, never come to know it, well, that Italy was my place of work. I was in my element there, and the only way to be in your element there is to become callused, because that's the way of the world and that's precisely why there are spies in the world: I had a goal, you know, and that goal redeemed me. But now it's different. For the first time I cannot bear the burden of a secret, because I think of you, of the memories of your father that you would have, and then I think of the man your father really was, and I feel responsible . . . The only thing is, how can I convince you? I cannot bring proof, that's obvious, because if your father had left even a scrap of evidence it would have been a . . ."

Suddenly, the sound of the television program crackled back into life, and he fell silent. Of course: the videocassette's resistance to the freeze-frame command had timed out; here too, zero progress in the last twenty years. I worked in television once, and I noticed that even professional equipment has this limitation: a few minutes on freeze-frame, and then it lets go.

I reopened my eyes. The television was showing an ad in which a famous TV personality gives his shoes to the little green man at the traffic lights at the crosswalk so that he may try them out. So comfortable are they that the little green man steals them, leaving the personality shoeless on the pavement. The usual concept that some adman had lifted from the cinema, from Kasdan's film to be exact, what's it called, the one about Los Angeles, and the title is the name of a place, two words, like "Bay Area," only it's not "Bay Area," with Steve Martin playing a psychoanalyst, and someone kneecaps him and he rediscovers the meaning of life, and there are a whole lot of other intertwining stories, but in any case the best story is the one with Steve Martin, and he's the one who talks to the little green man at the crosswalk, oh shit, what was the title? The name of a place, two words, I can't have forgotten that as well . . .

Nothing. I couldn't remember. I reached out for the remote control and switched off. Bogliasco gave me an approving nod. He was no longer wearing the glasses.

"Do you remember," he said, "when your father took you all on that tour of Europe in the Fiat 1500, in the summer of '68?"

And there he was back on the attack. But I knew him by then, he always used the same tactic: he would skirt around a subject, play dumb, digress, with patience and cunning, and then suddenly attack. Boom: the trip around Europe with the 1500. How could I even feign indifference, if he spoke to me about that?

"Do you remember that on the first night you stopped at Stresa," he continued, "on Lake Maggiore, to watch the final of the European Championship on television? What game was it?"

Play for time a bit, pretend not to know certain things, ask me them, just to draw me into the action, to involve me . . .

"Italy-Yugoslavia . . ."

"Right," a swig of beer, "but it ended up a draw, and in those days it wasn't the way it is now, there were no penalties: drawn matches were replayed three days later, and you couldn't watch the replay because you would have been abroad. And you and your father had a fight, eh? Because you wanted to stay in Italy, to watch the match . . ."

Then, a quick counterattack and the first serious thrust to let you know that while you were still wondering what he was leading up to, he was leading up to it. This phase has to leave its mark, it has to strike home, you have to wonder about it, irresistibly, you have to ask yourself how the devil he knew these things . . .

"Apart from anything else, it was better that way, in my opinion: if a match ended in a draw it was replayed, what is this invention of penalties that always lets the weaker team win? Is that supposed to be football? There are teams, today, that even aim to . . ."

Then, by surprise, a *digression*—and this a really subtle touch: to simulate a weak point, leaving you to believe that by setting out to dispute an irrelevant point ("no, penalties are thrilling, spectacular . . . ," etc.) you can contain him, send him off the track. Something that would never happen, and in fact the one who would come out of it weakened would be you, distracted by a meaningless argument that you would never otherwise have thought of engaging in . . .

" . . . let the stronger side win. And in short you argued, and you were dragged along on that trip, remember? Germany, Belgium, Holland, without being able to see the match, poor kid . . . And now I've come to the point: do you remember that in Amsterdam you had an accident, because your father mistakenly took a one-way street along a canal in the wrong direction, and you scraped the fender of a Volkswagen? Do you remember that the driver of the Volkswagen picked you up in his arms, after he and your father had signed the insurance papers?"

Here we go, the final combination was about to be unleashed . . .

"Do you remember that you burst into tears and you wanted to get down right away, and then you said to your father that you didn't like that man?"

And when everything has been duly set up, shoot a big line. A really big one . . .

"That man was you," I beat him to it.

There was a flash of surprise in his eyes—he hadn't been expecting it—then he nodded, lowering his eyelids.

"Exactly."

I burst out laughing, and it was a spontaneous laugh, this time, a genuine one, a real tonic, because I hadn't expected it either, basically: bulls-eye.

"Don't you believe even this?" he said.

"Do you remember what Totò used to say?" I blurted out, " *'Pull the other leg, will you!'* "

The imitation came out awful, but it didn't matter: I was getting to the bottom of this man. I could predict his moves . . .

"Do you think it's normal for me to know these things?"

He smiled, imperturbable.

"Listen Mr. Bogliasco," I said, "you possess some highly detailed information on my account, I can't deny it. And maybe you really are a spy, and had contacts with my father, for a certain period, certainly in connection with confidential, military matters, or whatever. But, believe me, despite everything, you *don't know* how things really were. It's not enough to be well informed in order to tell people their life story. For example, you brought up that touring holiday, and you were accurate about places and episodes, but you are convinced that I went on that trip against my will, which is not true. I thought that was a wonderful holiday, and if anyone asked me what the happiest period of my entire childhood was, I would say 'the trip around Europe in the 1500.' And my father knew that perfectly well. Sure, I was upset when I found out there was going to be a replay and that we would not be able to see it because we had no idea where we would have been on the day. That final was important for me, football was the stuff of my dreams, and there was nothing I wanted more than to see Italy win the European Championship. But I was a *kid*, damn it, and by the very next day, when we were traveling through the heart of Germany, and we stopped to eat some of those fantastic giant frankfurters, to watch the deer in the Black Forest, or to sleep all in the same room in the fragrant inns of Mainz or Freiburg, I was happy, and I had forgotten all about the match: I didn't need anything anymore, I was happy the way things were, in that whirl of picnics on the grass, foreign winds, monorails, dykes, Gothic cathedrals, barges on the rivers, Friesian cows, windmills, absurd number plates, and color televisions. And when that Italian waiter popped up, in Amsterdam, to be precise, and told us that Italy had won, and started telling us about Riva's and Anastasi's goals, even miming them, and Facchetti holding up the cup, and Valcareggi being carried shoulder-high in triumph, I didn't feel any happier than I was already feeling for the very fact of being there. Understand?"

He wore a puzzled expression, as if to say, "What has this got to do with anything?"

"And don't go thinking I don't remember the man in the Volkswagen," I continued, "for while it's true that I cried, when he lifted me up, it was only because I was overexcited—*an accident in Amsterdam, a Dutchman who lifted me up*; and afterward I certainly did not say that I hadn't liked that man, quite the opposite, I liked him very much, and that is precisely why I remember him so well. He was tall, smelled of aftershave, and he had this really fine hair that was ruffled by the wind, *blond* hair, and above all he was not you."

I was lying, damn it, I did not remember that man at all. I had a clear recollection of the accident, the sun glittering on the windshield, the Volkswagen hitting us, the dull sound of the fenders as they met. I remember my father and that man bent over the hood of the car filling in the forms for the notification of an accident, the wind making the sheets of paper flutter, and then Mom holding my sister by the arm, the people driving by without paying any attention to us, the barge that passed by at a certain point, floating down the canal in prodigious silence; but it wasn't true that I recalled the appearance of that man, nor if he was tall or blond. I didn't remember saying that I didn't like him either, but in any case I was sure of one thing: it hadn't been Bogliasco.

"It was me," he insisted.

"Pray tell me," I said, and for some reason it came out in a strange Milanese accent, "do you really think you can intrude so easily into people's recollections?"

"It was me . . ."

"Do you really think I will cease to trust in my memory only because I mistook a journalist for a waiter?"

"It was me, Gianni. The accident was a sham, a pretext that enabled us to do a *Ka Tri*, a K3, in other words is a contact made in a public place with an exchange of material."

"Hah . . ."

"It was a K3," he insisted, "where K stands for *Kontàkt*, in point of fact. There were only three types of contacts allowed between undercover agents, like your father, and agents with no cover, like me: that was the third type, the riskiest. Precisely because it was in a public place: it was only used in case of emergency . . ."

"That wasn't an emergency," I said, "it was a holiday."

He lit one of his little cigarettes and took two long pulls on it. He coughed.

"Do you remember," he said, "General Di Lorenzo? Does that name ring a bell with you?"

"No."

"Well, he was a Fascist general, even though he was officially a monarchist, who four years before, in '64, had organized a coup d'état: he was discovered, but they didn't do anything to him, in fact they sentenced those who had denounced him. Well, that year, with Europe in revolt, and while the Lombardi commission was busy exonerating him, he was organizing another one, through a clandestine network that was far more secret and dangerous than the notorious 'Gladio,' which in case you didn't know was merely a decoy. You father *knew*, naturally, and he wanted to give me the names of the journalists and parliamentarians connected with the new plot, so that I could pass them on to Moscow in my turn. There's your emergency. That's why there was that accident, in Amsterdam: he wrote down the names on the insurance claim forms, instead of the insurance data. The Novosti press agency published the list, the Italians rebutted it, but the plot was aborted. That's why he couldn't let you have your way, about the football match: otherwise he would have done so . . ."

"He would never have done that," I shot back. "He would never have scrapped the itinerary he had meticulously prepared with Mom, with his red marker pens and his road maps spread out on the table in the dining room—the same table, by the way, that a few years later he was to bash in with a punch during an argument in which he accused me of being a communist . . ."

He leaned his head back, smiling.

"Yes," he said, "I remember that period, when the pair of you used to argue every day. He was very proud of your being a communist. Still a bit too *bourgeois,* he used to say, but at bottom that was his fault . . ."

"I was *not* a communist. I have never been a communist. It was a fixation of his . . ."

"But *you* were the one who used to say . . ."

"*He* used to say, and I let him believe it to piss him off. Because he was a bigot, and the idea of having a communist for a son used to piss him off . . ."

"A bigot . . . ," he chuckled.

He crushed the cigarette out in the ashtray, energetically, then he took a last swig from the can, wiping his mouth with his hand.

"Your father a bigot . . ."

"Yes, a bigot."

He belched and shook his head, his smile broadening.

"You didn't know him . . ."

"Sure I knew him. He was the most bigoted person I ever met."

"He was faking it."

"He was not faking it, he *was* a bigot."

"Your father was not a bigot, Gianni."

"*With me* he was a bigot."

I shouldn't have said that. It was a mistake, it was like admitting that my father might not have been a bigot, with the others, whereas he was that way with everyone. Once he left the table during a Christmas dinner down at the bridge club, because a woman had come with an overgenerous décolleté. He *was* a bigot. But the mistake had been made, and he stared at me with a radiant, triumphant smirk. It was the way a pyromaniac must look at the fire he has just lit.

"Right . . . ," he said.

He got laboriously to his feet, went to the door of the terrace, and began to look outside, nodding imperceptibly.

Silence.

Silence.

Silence.

Silence.

An unexpected, benevolent silence.

I threw myself back and closed my eyes once more. From the depths of that Roman evening, outside, the friendly sounds that Bogliasco's harassing voice had obliterated began to reemerge: an ambulance siren, warped by the Doppler effect, the monstrous roar of an accelerating motorcycle in via Marco Polo, all the sounds of the indifference with which Rome puts up with itself and keeps the show going, sounds that end up by seeming to be— and perhaps even by being—silence.

I felt sleepy, and this gave me new heart, because sleep offered me an unexpected escape route. He was still silent, and from the depths of his respiratory apparatus the whistle began to make itself heard again. All it needed was for him to keep silent for a minute or two more and I—besieged, tired, defeated—could still outflank him: of course I could fall asleep, thereby encroaching on the terrain occupied by so-called "metasolutions," just like Franceschino does when he's losing at cards and scatters the deck. At bottom that too is a way to solve problems. I remember that in my chess-playing days there was a Russian—a real Russian, called Victor Balanda—who earned my total admiration, as well as a legendary lifetime disqualification, for his tendency to resolve difficult situations with a lusty metasolution: laying out his opponent with a punch in the face—a move that to this day, I believe, is known as the "Balanda variant" . . .

Yes, old Balanda. The brightest meteor to cross the chess firmament of the seventies: no one knew how old he was, where he lived, or how he kept himself, he appeared from nowhere and began to rack up victories at an impressive rate, and in fact he seemed well on the way to the famous Candidates' Tournament, in which they

designate the challenger for the world title. Then, one day, in Aca-
pulco, he found himself in serious difficulty against a Mexican out-
sider, and, after having used up almost all his time in a search for
the move that might spare him the ignominy of his first defeat, he
got to his feet and gave his opponent a punch right in the mouth,
sending him to the hospital. He was disqualified, expelled from the
tournament, and later banned from all official competition (not
without a grotesque debate during a sitting of the Disciplinary
Committee of the International Federation, since the rules did not
even contemplate the eventuality of players resorting to physical
violence), and he disappeared from circulation. But one and a half
years later, on the occasion of the World Championships, there was
an amnesty, and Victor Balanda was able to take advantage of that
to return to competition. And my memory of him, clear-cut and
accurate, dates precisely from the time of his reappearance on the
scene, in Palma de Majorca, in 1979: he was crossing the foyer of
the Consolat del Mar wearing his usual brown corduroy suit, heedless of the looks that fixed upon him from all sides—because,
despite the presence of a couple of international grand masters, he
was the attraction of the tournament; I can still see his long,
bearded face, his aquiline nose, his scaly skin, the frank gaze
beneath metal-rimmed spectacles. It was a Swiss format tournament, in which every competitor takes on the player immediately
below him in the rankings after every round, and so Balanda, after
a run of four straight victories, found himself dueling with the
strongest players. More victories, a couple of draws, and there he
was in the final match, by then ranking second, sitting opposite a
grand master and fellow Russian who was half a point ahead of
him: in order to beat him and mark his return with a triumph,
Balanda had to win, while if he lost or drew he would have been
overtaken by many others. I can barely recall his opponent, a fairly
ordinary person enveloped in the mists of oblivion, as is his name
for that matter, since even though he was the strongest player in the
tournament, and that tournament was one of the last in which I
took part, what was about to happen left him eternally blurred in

my memory. I was in the front row; I had forfeited my last match in order to have that seat, because Balanda was my idol; in my twenty-year-old's pantheon he had taken the place of Bobby Fischer, and I wouldn't have missed his match for all the tea in China. The game was a classic Ruy-Lopez, Balanda's favorite, and around the table there reigned an unreal, fabulous silence, two or three hundred people motionless and intent upon the greenish, vaguely submarine icon—greenish because of the lighting—of those two Russians competing beneath an enormous ceiling fan. The other player had white and was obviously playing for a draw, and Balanda had used up a bit too much time in trying to smoke him out; but he could still have pulled it off, he held a promising position on the Queen's side and his rooks were slightly better placed. He wasn't losing, he wasn't in trouble, and even if in the end he had had to accept a draw he would have been unbeaten. Yet, something inside him had snapped: I was the only one to notice it, I'm positive, and I couldn't even say how it was that I had this certainty, nor on what it was based, but I had it. Something snapped inside Victor Balanda and suddenly the chessboard, the pieces, and the position, became irrelevant, because the solution had been shifted elsewhere, beyond that table, beyond the rules that suddenly made this rite of the intellect—apparently sacred until a moment before—look ridiculous. He began to waste time: he slipped off his glasses, cleaned them, put them back on, then he turned to look at the spectators, almost all of whom were gray middle-class mono-maniacs whose imagination had not the slightest outlet over and beyond those sixty-four squares, unable even to conceive of what was about to happen, even though it had already happened once and even though that was basically why they were there. His clock still running, Victor Balanda got slowly to his feet, as he had already done other times during the match in order to concentrate, wandering about with lowered head, but this time his concentra-tion was different, it was that of the leopard in the middle of the savannah, calculating the direction of the wind, the distance from the prey, the speed required to reach it . . . His opponent, this

Cartesian fog full of calculations and matches consigned to memory, was sitting composedly, pensive, his chin resting on the backs of his hands, elbows leaning on the table. He hadn't understood anything either, he was not afraid, did not suspect, did not see the hard reality that was taking shape before his eyes: perhaps he saw an irrational combination of moves that, in a future that that match no longer had, might have brought him a pawn, but he did not see the punch coming, a phenomenal hook that took him right in the face, between nose and mouth, and put out all his lights: he collapsed, poleaxed, making a lugubrious thud on the floor, moving straight from the rational and satisfying future foreseen by his calculations to the confused and swollen one he encountered on coming to inside the ambulance ("Where am I? What happened?"), in which the doctor advised him not to get agitated. That was that: Balanda sat down, moved a pawn forward, and stopped his clock. He smiled, while all hell broke loose all around him, and, jostled, insulted, and threatened, he sat motionless in his seat while attempts were made to bring his opponent around, because despite everything the Balanda variant had still to be consummated: it required that his opponent did not get up again, the referee had to be obliged to suspend the match without being able to write in his report that Balanda had retired, lost, or drawn, no, he had to rack his brains and search his wooden bureaucratic vocabulary for the words that might explain the occurrence (". . . struck his opponent in the face with brutal violence, causing him to lose his senses and thereby making it impossible for him to continue the match, before going on to make move 41, . . . H5-H4").

An absolutely inconceivable event in the little world to which he belonged, yet absolutely simple, and *normal*, in the big world to which Balanda belonged.

And still his opponent did not get up, did not get up, did not get up . . .

fourteen

I opened my eyes abruptly: I was panting, things were going at an absurd speed, my heart was racing like mad to keep up with them . . .

I sat up. I looked around. The room was empty, the television was off, the lights were off. I was wrapped in the light blue cloth that was normally used to cover the armchair so that it didn't get soiled. A little breeze was coming in from the terrace window to chill the sweat on my neck. How long had I been asleep? And where was Bogliasco?

On the table there were three cans of beer, all empty.

Suddenly, a green flash lit up the darkness, followed by a burst of explosions. So that was what had made me wake up with a start.

I got up and went out onto the terrace, but he wasn't there either. I had a good look all over—absurdly, since the terrace offers no hiding place. None whatsoever. Another stunningly beautiful firework described an enormous red umbrella in the sky above the Janiculum, right in front of me. I looked at my watch: twenty past midnight. I stood there gazing blankly at the fireworks, which still thrill me the way they did when I was a child, but rather than comfort me they increased my anxiety, because I would have liked Franceschino to be there, asleep in his bed, so that I could wake him as I had done the year before, and carry him on my shoulders to the terrace, and stand him on the table so he could enjoy the show, which seemed made specially for him, for us—in the meantime Anna would certainly have joined us, and she would have stood on sentry duty close to the table, to cover even that 0.0001 percent risk that Franceschino might elude my grasp and, still half asleep, tumble off the table. And I felt a piercing, sinister yearning for all this, as if I had lost it forever, as if my marriage had fallen apart and that little picture would never again be reconstructed. I didn't even want to think about it. I don't understand how people with children can divorce: and yet they divorce. I can manage to understand how you can resign yourself to tragedies, like the mother of that little boy in a coma—misfortunes that happen with pitiless exactitude to you, and you can't do anything to avoid them—but I cannot imagine how you can start up and fuel day by day and ultimately carry out the complex succession of deliberate acts that lead to the ruin of a family. It is precisely at moments like these, when the mirage of an alternative emerges—be it ever so vaguely—that one ought to think: okay, you are attracted to this girl, you could see her again, get to know her better, discover that she is marvelous and so on, and she too could fall in love with you, you could be made for each other, why not? and together attain a happiness that you had never even dreamed of in all your life, sexual rapport and everything; but know that one summer evening you will find yourself on a terrace looking at a shower of fireworks, and the utterly banal thing that you would like to do most—to wake up your son to watch them together—will no longer be possible, and not because he is at the seaside or in a coma or has become a man and you an old man, but only because it's not one of the two weekends a month in which you are permitted to stay with him. This is a thought I always bear in mind, like an emergency telephone number, which guides me in the day-to-day maintenance of my marriage and occasionally regales me with moments of a great, solitary peace— the kind I call the "peace of the landing," precisely because it comes to me on the landing, immediately after having gone out, perhaps after saying to Anna, "I have to go to such and such a place, I don't really feel like it, I'll be as quick as I can," and as soon as I get down the first flight of stairs I stop, lean against the wall, look at the front door that has just closed, and I feel at peace: because I am *really* going to such and such a place, I *really* don't feel like it, and I *really* will be as quick as I can. Only those who have experienced this sensation can understand the beauty of time spent like that, leaning against the wall of the landing of your own home (before, I also used to light a cigarette, but not anymore), contemplating how far one is from the morass of the conjugal lie, of sex with guilt, and the famous court order that sooner or later crops up to tell you how many hours a week you may spend with your son.

Boom, boom, boom: the three final explosions, dull and violent like the beating of a big drum. For a few moments the white fumes lingered snaking in the blurry sky, then they dispersed, and I didn't feel at all well. I had a lump in my throat, a kind of cold, hard clot lodged in my chest, which hurt me as if it were a knife blade. My head was spinning: Anna, Franceschino, where are you? What's happening to me? Why am I suffering like this?

I stretched out on the lounger and breathed deeply: the pain in my chest diminished. Everything's all right, I repeated to myself, everything's all right. It wasn't a heart attack, I wasn't about to die. And it wasn't even a panic attack—I'm not that fashionable, I have always suffered from old-fashioned maladies: acetonaemia as a child, Osgood-Schlatter disease as a boy, backache as an adult. We might also add memory blanks, but it ought to be borne in mind that I have a *formidable* memory, damn it, far higher than average, which probably no one could have kept intact for all that long. In all my life I have never been afraid of being alone, and what's more I was not alone, and never have been.

I stayed the way I was for a bit, looking at the sky and breathing in the scent of the jasmine, and I felt better. The clot was gradually dissolving, and the pain in my chest had vanished. Gingerly, I got up, and my legs were solid, everything seemed to be back in working order again. It must have been a drop in blood pressure, I thought, or indigestion, what with all the fried stuff I had eaten. Then there was that sudden awakening, that fright: one should always be woken up gently, that's the point.

I went back inside. The man was gone all right—good—thank God for metasolutions—even the cassette of *A Perfect World* was gone. Just for once he had done something normal: he had seen me sleeping like a little angel, drank himself a couple more beers, and when it had gotten late he had taken himself off along with his story—but how difficult it was, and even embarrassing, to imagine him coming to grips with the tenderness that had prompted him, before slipping away, to drape me with the blue armchair cover so that I wouldn't be cold . . .

I sat down on the sofa and began to toy with the idea of calling Anna: Hi, sorry to call so late but I wanted to talk a bit with you . . . There was nothing wrong with that, after all, I had lots of things to tell her; and I was about to do it, I was about to pick up the telephone, when I became aware of a strange sensation that filled my mind: a kind of alarm that had been ignored, something that had been begging to be noticed for some time. There had been no sound, nothing unusual had happened, yet there I was nervous as a coyote again. I went into the kitchen, and everything was normal; the same thing in the bathroom, in my study, and in Franceschino's room; that left my bedroom, whose half-open door filled me with a sudden, irrational fear. I went up to it and listened, my heart beginning to thump again.

Silence . . .

I flung the door wide open with a sudden heave, more to give myself courage than to frighten or surprise *the other*—and then, let's be serious, the other who?—but I put too much muscle into it, and the handle banged into the wall, leaving a nice dent in it: the fact was that I really didn't know the correct amount of muscle required to fling doors wide open with a sudden heave—who had ever had to do so, before then?

The room was in order, or rather, it was in disorder, but the right disorder, the kind I had left: open window, unmade bed, jacket on the chair, underwear scattered over the floor. There, too, all was normal. So it was like I said, everything was all right: that man had gone, Anna and Francesco were in Viareggio and I could join them whenever I wished. There was no reason to get agitated.

I went back into the living room, still determined to make that phone call—yes, a long, languid long-distance call to my wife—but my eyes blatantly disobeyed me, because instead of alighting on the telephone they pounced of their own accord on a highly specific point in the room, with the voracity of a dog springing on a slice of roast—onto the television cart, they pounced, next to the remote control, where Bogliasco had forgotten his lighter and the pack of Superlights. And immediately after that something unpleasant happened. It happened that I wanted to take one and light it, I wanted it so much that I did it: I took a cigarette and I lit it.

That was that, I had started smoking again. I sat down in the armchair and voraciously inhaled from the filter of that ridiculous cigarette, in an absurd attempt to make it become stronger—but, I realized, it was already strong enough to give me the old whack in the throat that I had missed so much.

I had started smoking again. That was what that feeling had been: *I had already seen* the pack, probably it was the first thing I had seen upon reawakening, but my willpower, which had allowed me to resist temptation for nine months, must have estimated that this time the risk of giving in was too high—alone, anxious, with a pack of cigarettes at my disposal—and it must have instantly fallen back on an apparently less difficult task, and that was *to deny the existence* of that packet, to prevent me from taking its presence into consideration . . .

Besides, I had always known I was not safe, I even did a *course*, down at the Alcoholics Anonymous association in piazzetta del Velabro: a course intended not to help one stop smoking but to prevent one from starting again. It was a precise method, in reality, complete with a name that escapes me at present, English, something like Smythson—but which Smythson? Smythson is the brand of my diary—and it worked, it worked, I can well say that, because since I took the course I hadn't smoked again. It is a course based on awareness, in which they teach you everything that happens inside you when you stop smoking, they explain the physiological and psychological mechanisms of nicotine dependency, so that you have a profound knowledge of the enemy, and you know in advance what you have to do to get the better of him. I knew, for example—they had explained this to us very well— that you must never pretend not to see packs of cigarettes within reach, on the contrary you have to look at them, challenge them, and beat them, mentally repeating all the reasons why you decided to stop smoking. And I had been taught to tell the difference between the simple *nostalgia for smoke*, which is eternal—like all forms of nostalgia—but results in no serious consequences—like all forms of nostalgia—and the so-called *fatal impulse*—that was the rather melodramatic term they used in the course—in other words, that sudden and fiercely powerful stimulus that continues to strike you from time to time, and that can have you smoking again even years afterward. I had successfully mastered it on many occasions, precisely because I recognized it and knew that it would last from twenty to thirty seconds, that it was exclusively psychological in nature and that, therefore, it was not by any means irresistible: all I had to do was to get rid of it by means of any gesture—by biting into an apple, kissing my wife, taking a series of deep breaths—all I had to do was to hang on for that wretched half minute, and it would go away, like all unpleasant things. It was sufficient to know this, and I knew it, they had taught me; yet there I was: after having struggled so hard and won, I had started smoking again without even having struggled and lost. I had caved in for a Capri Superlights: how could it have happened?

In the meantime the cigarette was already finished. I put it out, slim and red-hot, with trembling hands, my brain woozy—for a Capri!—and in my mouth, I noticed, there was the taste of the first cigarette I had ever smoked—Virginia tobacco, I recall, stolen from the silver cigarette case in the living room, and hastily smoked in the garage, hidden behind a pile of wickerwork baskets, with the same bitter taste in my mouth, the same fabulous palpitations, the same diabolical feelings of guilt as I was feeling now. It was in 1972, just after the massacre at the Munich Olympic Games . . .

Grand Canyon. That was the title of the Kasdan film I hadn't been able to remember earlier, the one where Steve Martin talks with the little green man at the pedestrian crossing. *Grand Canyon*. Wouldn't it be funny if there was a connection, in my intoxicated organism, between the ingestion of nicotine and the capacity to remember the . . .

No! Judging by what they said in that course, now I absolutely had to avoid finding justifications for my capitulation. I had to react, right away: throw away the tempting pack and drink lots of water, lots of water, sure, because nicotine is water soluble and I had to get it out of my system as quickly as possible. I took the pack of cigarettes, went into the kitchen, and threw it into the garbage—furiously, I'd say—then I opened the fridge and pulled out the bottle of mineral water. I drank more than half of it in one long draft that left me breathless. Then I drank again, and again, even though I was no longer thirsty and my throat had closed up.

A bit muzzy, I went into the bedroom and lay down on the bed. I had to relax, I had to regain lucidity. One cigarette, they had explained to me in that course, can be tolerated, as long as the reaction is determined. The basic thing was that it had to be only one. Furthermore, I knew what was going to happen, I had been trained: on the next day and in the days that followed, more or less at that time, I would feel more *fatal impulses*, made even stronger by the weakness I had just shown, and it was going to be vital to resist them. I had to get into the best possible condition to do that—therefore, for example, I had to leave this house, where the misdeed had occurred, and I had make sure that, when the impulse came, I would not be alone. I would go to Viareggio, of course: basically it was also what I wanted to do. I would carry on drinking water and urinating as much as possible, and when the nicotine I had ingested with that Capri had been completely expelled I would be out of danger, in other words I would be able to go back to winning my battle day by day as I had been doing over those nine months.

If, on the contrary, I did not do it, if I were to smoke only one more cigarette, thereby doubling the quantity of bastard nicotine in my blood, I would be in for a long period in which I would struggle furiously to stay at one cigarette a day, then at two, at three, under the pious illusion that I could stop at any moment whereas I would continue to smoke more, steadily, inexorably, because my system, faced once more with the substance that had intoxicated it, would continue to demand more and more until I had gone back to the daily dose it had once been accustomed to, and only at that point would it be satisfied. I would lie, pretend, and smoke furtively for months, until I was caught at it like a kid, because my fingers, my hair, and my breath would have begun to stink again. Or I would be caught red-handed, by Anna, in my pajamas, at night, on the terrace, when the cold weather had already returned and I would have even run the risk of catching my death: "Gianni! What in heaven's name are you doing? . . ."

Yes, I knew exactly how to go about things, and I was going to make the most of that, but in the meantime I was back in the kitchen—*how the devil had I wound up there?*—rummaging through the rubbish like a tramp, in order to salvage the pack of Capri Superlights—*when had I decided to do that?*—and I lit another, from the gas ring, obsessed by a consideration that was wretched, perhaps, but scientifically irrefutable: since those slender little American tubes are specially designed to make people smoke less, then one of them is barely worth half of a normal cigarette, which gave me the perfect right to smoke two. Otherwise it couldn't be said that I had really smoked a cigarette. And I smoked, again, I smoked. No more palpitations this time, or guilt feelings, or the thrill of transgression: I had already gone back to the pragmatic logic of the habitual smoker. How the devil do these things manage to change so quickly?

The cigarette was finished in a flash—I had sucked this one down too. I stubbed it out in the ashtray, doubly disgusted because I had smoked it and because it hadn't been good. My head began to spin again, while the taste of smoke in my mouth had become intolerable. In the course they had taught us to concentrate on these things, and never to forget them: the bad taste, the stink, the disgust for butts . . .

And then I was suddenly fighting back: my hands tying up the yellow handles of the garbage bag, extracting the bag from the container—laboriously, because it was bulging full—and I was out of the house in a flash, remembering at the last moment to take the keys, luckily, otherwise things would have gotten far more complicated—the fire department? the domestic help line? Or a hotel?—and things were already in a pretty mess, moreover, since I suddenly realized, right there on the landing where I cultivate my sense of daily peace, that I hadn't thrown the cigarettes back into the garbage bag, of course not, I had merely taken it for granted that I had done so, but I hadn't, which was why I went very slowly back up the stairs, humiliated, and at the same time relieved by the fact that no one had seen me, no one would ever know about this amazing series of screw-ups.

I went back into the house, returned to the kitchen, and there were the cigarettes, on the marble countertop next to the stove; I tried to untie the knot I had only just made in the handles of the garbage bag, but it was no good, I had put too much anger into the job, too much desire to make the knot inextricable, and so I had to cut it with the scissors. I took the pack—there were still six cigarettes left—and I threw it inside, thrusting it down deep, soiling my hand, until it definitively, irreversibly vanished into that morass of rotisserie leftovers, crumpled plastic bottles, and empty cans. I don't bother about sorting recyclables, because in any case I know that at the end of the day they burn everything just the same.

I washed my dirty hand, dried it, then I took the bag by the handles that, after my handiwork with the scissors, had become more like strings, but strings too short to be tied up again. Calmly, this time, I took the keys, went out of the house, and headed off down the stairs, careful not to lose my grip on the bag, in order to avoid at least the comic finale, in other words, spilling my garbage in front of some other tenant's front door.

And as I was about to take the last flight of steps, my mind already on the dumpster down in the street, where I was going to deposit my bag with the devil inside, I heard the creak of a door opening, footsteps taking the stairs, and the slam of the door closing again. Who could it be? And with what smile could I face whoever it was, as I went downstairs to throw away the garbage at that hour, past one in the morning, a sure sign that there was something really horrendous in my bag?

It was Confalone, the tenant on the first floor, the only person with whom, for a certain time, I had had relations that went farther than the famous "good morning and good evening," more specifically, the occasional dinner with the wives and kids on our terrace. This was before his marriage had gone to shit, leaving him alone in the first-floor apartment he used to share with his wife and the twins, who were Francesco's age. After that, relations had cooled.

"Hi," he said.

"Hi."

I carried straight on—let him think what he wished—and went through the main door without looking back. I crossed the yard where Francesco had learned to ride his bicycle, went out into the street and—finally—dumped my garbage in the fetid refuse container. There you go: my damned duty was done.

But there was to be no rest for the wicked, that night, it really seemed as if I could not free myself of apprehension: because now I couldn't stop thinking about Confalone, it was easier said than done, to carry straight on as if everything were perfectly normal. I looked up and caught a glimpse of the flickering, bluish light of the television coming out of his window: that man was there, I thought, alone, on the sofa, pretending to be watching *The Late Show*, certainly stalked by the desire to caress the twins as they slept, something he couldn't do. And I had seen things I shouldn't have seen, regarding his misfortune, I had thought things I shouldn't have thought, and I had known things I shouldn't have known: no wonder relations had cooled. I had been a witness to the most appalling moment of his separation, very early one Saturday morning, as I was leaving for the airport: I saw the moving van as they were filling it with tea chests full of frighteningly familiar things, and I greeted his wife through the wide-open door, asking her, as she was removing two little plaques from the front door: "What's up, are you moving?" The question instantly sounded obscene, the kind of blunder people come out with when trying to wriggle out of some intolerably distressing situation—like saying "How's it going?" to someone who is terminally ill—but by that time I had said it; and she punished me: she could have pretended not to have heard, she could have smiled and left me to go off and bite my tongue, but instead she replied "only us," pitilessly, nodding at the twins who were hanging about looking lost on the landing, their eyes full of shame. And then I had thought, that day, during the first-class flight to New York—the only time I ever flew first-class in all my life—I thought that the business wasn't really at all surprising, because I had never really liked that Confalone, and would never have socialized with him had it not been for the fact that he lived in the same condo: ultra sporty, a motorbike fanatic, with an irritatingly well-groomed look, and with a job—advertising sales—that dragged him down into an endless round of business trips up and down the country, at bottom he was really the kind who sets himself up with a mistress within the firm and then—until disas-

ter strikes—lives a double life based on secret cell phones and
phony business trips; while his wife was a brilliant endocrinolo-
gist at the Policlinico Gemelli, sweet and maternal but attractive
too, in her plump way, who loved Roxy Music and the novels of
Graham Greene. And I had talked about all this, later: I had pon-
tificated about it to my publisher, who was traveling on the plane
with me, and then to Anna too, on the telephone, as soon as I got
to the hotel, when I informed her from a distance of six thousand
kilometers about the vicissitudes of the lady doctor on the first
floor. Then, seven days later, in the VIP lounge of JFK airport,
waiting for the return flight to Rome, as I was intent on guzzling
my way through the luxuries of first-class travel (cocktails, cham-
pagne, smoked salmon), I found out *for sure*: Confalone's wife
came in, together with a much older man, sun-tanned, athletic,
who embraced her with nonchalance while talking in an excessively loud voice about a certain swamp around Bombay airport.
The *consultant*, damn it, that legend I had thought to be old hat,
at least from a sexual standpoint, and that evidently continued to
reap its victims: *she had ditched her husband for the consultant*.
They were in the company of another equally ill-assorted couple
(he a mature type with an international look, she young and sub-
missive), evidently on their way back from a sumptuous conference on some glandular dysfunction or other, financed by some
pharmaceuticals multinational in order to consolidate relations
with the West's most distinguished doctors so that, after having
spent four enjoyable all-expenses-paid days in New York with
their paramours, they would continue to prescribe a certain drug
on which hinged the two-point-two percent of increased market
share and the eight-point-seven increase in turnover decreed for
the following three years by some fucking board of directors.

The frigid greeting that I exchanged with that woman in that
haven of privilege at New York airport also marked an irreversible
cooling in my relations with her husband. And now that some
time had passed, and she was also free to walk around Rome arm-
in-arm with that dirty old man, and maybe even lived with him

and he was the one who could caress the twins whenever he felt like doing so with his expensive freckle-covered hands, I was just waiting to see Confalone come home with a woman, one evening, any woman, beautiful or ugly, young or old, it would have made no difference, who one might be able to think had been around before, who had always been around, and who was the real cause of everything, like Camilla Parker-Bowles: but he continued to return alone, tired and alone, and so I am nothing better than an obtuse gossip, who had found out too much about a matter that he had never really known anything about, and who had thought and talked about it out of turn from one side of the ocean to the other instead of minding his own bloody business. It was going to be tough, the day I picked up the intercom to hear myself defined that way; but if the voice were Confalone's I would have little to wax indignant about.

I went back into the house thinking that at bottom it was true, no one knows what we really are, because we conceal it, and if we don't conceal it deliberately we do so instinctively. Once, a woman friend of mine was really shocked because she unexpectedly discovered, after five years of marriage, that her husband was allergic to chicken. Agreed, there was an explanation, given that they lived above her parents' restaurant and they almost always dined there, where he limited himself to not ordering chicken, while on the few occasions they had eaten at home, until then, she had simply never happened to cook chicken; when it eventually happened, he told her he was allergic to chicken. On a technical level, my friend accepted this explanation, but how could I gainsay her when she protested that in any case a wife ought to know things like that about her own husband, and if *she* didn't know them then lord knows how many other things she didn't know about him . . . Then, as the humorous side of the story had not escaped her, she set to imagining the face her daughter would have made, on the day she brought home her intended and she asked him to state right away the foods he was allergic to or forever to hold his peace; but in the meantime, unlike before, she found herself paying a certain attention to all the things her husband *didn't* do, the things he *didn't* order at the bar and that he *didn't* read before going to sleep: and that wasn't such a natural thing to do. They didn't break up, though, and that was already something.

I made up my mind, I was going to bed. I closed the window, undressed, and threw myself onto the bed without even washing; but I wasn't really sleepy, and so I resigned myself, because my tribulations were not yet over for that day. I was going to lie there for goodness knows how long, I knew that, with eyes closed, adrift in doubt and melancholy. Very well, so be it. Better to think about certain things when awake than to dream of them asleep.

After all, it had not been a negative day: I had started writing again. But I had also started smoking again. That pack of Superlights, and how it had gotten the better of me. The fireworks. Confalone. The mysterious cursing. That seagull, and the power with which it had looked at me. *I am a force of the past, only in tradition is my love.* The perfect trap that Bogliasco had set for me, the immense weakness it had pounced upon: how could I have taken the journalist for a waiter? How was it I could remember the name of an insignificant actor like Bradley Whitford and not remember the cuffs of his shirt? Why is memory so complex? Why is it that it takes up all that space and then fails to respond to the simplest questions? Had the Dutchman of the accident been dark or fair? How did Burt Lancaster fan his guns in *Vera Cruz*, backward or forward? How many legs has an ant, six or eight? On which side does Francesco usually sleep, left or right? And if I were a spy pretending to be an author of children's books, and if I were mysteriously killed that night, *pffft,* with a silencer, what would Franceschino remember, of me?

I opened my eyes and stared at the ceiling, at the point in which for years I have been saying I would like to install a fan, and why I hadn't done so is another mystery.

That I was an author of children's books, that's what he would remember.

fifteen

I sat up bolt upright in bed: a quarter to eleven. That woman. I had an appointment with that woman. I couldn't be late with her of all people.

Still befuddled with sleep I went into the bathroom. The cold water completely defused the dream that had been tormenting me—a waiter was going into the hotel room where Anna was sleeping, but he wasn't a waiter, I caught up with him and faced him, Anna was pregnant, he was armed—with the result that I definitely gave in to my haste to make the appointment on time. I couldn't make her wait, damn it, that woman deserved punctuality.

I looked at myself in the mirror, and I saw a face that I would have preferred not to see, vaguely criminal: a heavy stubble, puffy eyes, hair in mad disorder. I couldn't show up like that, that woman also deserved a well-groomed appearance, a minimum of elegance. She merited this even more than punctuality, if a choice had to be made; which was why I determined to forget haste and to prepare myself suitably, without keeping an eye on the clock. *Let every man do what he must. May life carry on as normal . . .*

As I shaved I thought over the night just past with feelings of sincere relief, for the simple reason that it was in fact past. Besides, we all know how these things go: you get off to a bad start and things go from bad to worse, it is not humanly possible to fall asleep in a state of anxiety. I drank and pissed an infinity of times, every time convinced that it would be the last, but every time, in reality, annulling the only mechanism capable of defeating insomnia—time. The heavy morning sleep that had finally overtaken me could not restore me but could only lead to my spoiling the following day, and it was my good fortune, I told myself, that I had an appointment for which I could arrive a little bit—a *little* bit—late, because it was more than probable that the damage would be limited exclusively to that: given the subject we would be talking about, the meeting with that woman would be a kind of new paragraph, after which I would no longer be able to dare so much as to *conceive* of ill humor. In fact, it would give me the energy of a coiled spring, launching me once more down the highway toward Viareggio, and by mid-afternoon I would already be in the pinewood, with Anna, watching Francesco bounding about on the springy grass, madly thanking the Principle of Individuation that made him who he was and not another, there and not in an intensive care unit.

After shaving I got dressed, hastily but with discernment, selecting the items of dress one by one, something I almost never do: clean shirt, light-colored trousers, dark socks, boat shoes, and a jacket, really, even though it would probably be hot and I would sweat. In reality my favorite jacket—gray, in lightweight wool, a present from my sister, who has taste—having been worn on the evening of the prize-giving ceremony, then on the train journey back to Rome, then in the car during the flight to Viareggio, then last Sunday on the return journey, and after that having been left draped across the back of a chair, abandoned to its creases without even the charity of a coat hanger, was decidedly crumpled: but it was still my favorite jacket, even so, and I was going to wear it all the same.

Before going out I took the book by Carver that I was going to give to the woman, as well as the keys of the Vespa and the house keys, and carefully switched off all the lights, and only at that point, in a ridiculous but significant—for me, at that moment—demonstration of self-discipline, I allowed myself to glance at my watch: two minutes to eleven. How much time would I have gained had I given in to haste? How many things would I have forgotten or, worse still, as in that magisterial passage in *Alice in Wonderland*, would I have done in the wrong order? The Emperor of Japan was a wise man, no doubt about that. And as I went down the stairs I decided that I wouldn't even take the Vespa: I would go on foot, yes, I would look at the bushes like Marcovaldo, I would breathe deeply of the air of Rome despite the smog, and I would get to the bar in the park slightly—only slightly—late.

Out in the street the light was dazzling: amid the grainy glare that was dazzling me I could make out a sizeable group of people in front of the main door of the building next to mine, and an ambulance on the other side of the street, with its doors wide open and lights flashing. A short distance behind that, inside a police car, an officer was talking into a radio. His colleague had his work cut out trying to keep the entrance to the building clear. The crowd was made up of practically the whole neighborhood: shopkeepers, doorkeepers, kids, old folks, passersby, the glazier, the tobacconist, the upholsterer, all gathered in a semicircle around the wide-open door. Some, on seeing me, said hello, and it was simply unthinkable, I realized, for me to go about my business without stopping to take a look: it was as if they were saying "Come on, there's something here that concerns the entire community, something that concerns you too . . ."

In reality they were saying other things. They were saying:

"*Poor woman . . .*"

They were saying:

"*It's the cross she has to bear . . .*"

They were saying:

"*She couldn't take it any longer . . .*"

A woman emerged from the main door, weeping. It was Anita, a nurse at San Camillo's, an energetic and taciturn woman who always came to our house when we needed injections, in whose superiority over medicines taken orally our doctor had a passionate belief. She was walking backward and weeping, her hands over her mouth and her gaze trained on the entry to the building.

"*But she didn't call the ambulance . . .*"

"*No?*"

"*No, it was Father Furio . . .*"

The stretcher emerged, pushed by two gnarled stretcher-bearers who struggled to make their way through the crowd of people. On the stretcher, bound with straps like Hannibal the Cannibal, there was Anita's son—Italo, if I'm not mistaken—a big lad with light blue eyes and a lantern jaw, who when he first came to this district, ten years ago, had been a promising midfielder with the AC Roma Colts. He would practice his ball skills for whole evenings against the wall of his block, in summer, and sometimes I used to watch him from the window. He had class.

"*Father Furio? But he was the one who found the boy a place in the rehabilitation center . . .*"

"*Look, the kid's been swearing his head off every evening for five days . . .*"

So he was the one who had been doing the swearing.

He wasn't hurt, nor had he fainted: he kept his head still and slowly rolled his eyes, to look at the spectacle of the people looking at him, but the impression was that he could have done much more than that, had he wished to. He didn't seem to have been overcome, despite the belts. I was struck by the absolute absence of languor in his gaze, or of shame, or of suffering: on the contrary it held a threatening bravado, as if recourse to the fervent and mystical power of blasphemy had led him exactly where he wanted to go, and everything was going according to plan.

And it's curious how reserve can lead you off the track. When his mother came to give us injections—Bentelan for my backache, Buscopan for Anna's menstrual pains, Cortigen B6 and Epargriseovit for Franceschino, at five-thousand-lire the injection—I always used to think of that boy and his talented feet, but she was so taciturn that I never asked her how he was getting on, and all that noninquiry had led to my indulging in a lot of unrestrained guesswork regarding his destiny, which I wound up really believing in. That destiny spoke the coarse dialect of some small town in central Italy—Teramo, Viterbo, Chieti—where I imagined the boy had run aground in the course of a dusty apprenticeship in the minor leagues: a local wife met at the disco, a sturdy baby son in the stroller, the captain's armband, and under his boots fields that were always short on grass and long on holes, fields on which it was impossible to show what he could do . . . I imagined a man who hadn't made it, that's it, with regrets and all, but only because at a certain point in his life a good number of people had led him to overdo it with the dreams; in reality I imagined a tranquil life, like many others, perhaps even better than many others. But there he was, trapped and carried off like a mangy dog before the eyes of the whole neighborhood: it would have sufficed to have asked Anita only once about how he was getting on, after an injection, and from the way in which she would have shaken her head, with the syringe in hand—a syringe, right—I would have understood that his destiny had taken a very different turn. Because this really looked like something that had been going on for a good bit, and that naturally was not going to end there. And that explained, perhaps, the bravado that still galloped in the boy's eyes: he knew perfectly well that this was not the end; he knew that the end would be much worse, much tougher and more squalid, and more desperate, and without witnesses, the way he liked it . . .

Suddenly things went incredibly quiet. Before disappearing into the dark maw of the ambulance the boy took a last scything, gyroscopic look around. He could have also fired off a parting curse of farewell, a last savage bellow aimed at that priest, if he had really been the one who had had him taken away: but he let himself be swallowed up, quiet as a mouse. His mother disappeared after him, but a second later she peeped out from the open doors, a further dismay in her eyes.

"The bag!" she yelled.

The doorkeeper of her block vanished into the vestibule and immediately emerged with a Q8 bag, one of those rubber ones they hand out at service stations when you have an oil change. Relieved, the woman took it, smiling and thanking the doorkeeper, and the importance suddenly conferred upon that bag touched me deeply, it really moved me: hastily filled with stubbornly everyday articles as the stretcher bearers were binding the young man to the stretcher—pajamas, slippers, socks, toothbrush, toothpaste, razor—that bag had suddenly become the last bastion of the one hope that that mother still had the right to cherish: that things would not turn out the way her son was envisaging. With its neutral, absolutely ordinary contents, it had not been forgotten beside the elevator, on the floor of the vestibule, where it would have become the most genuinely tragic detail of that sorrowful morning (oh, the unbearable sadness of luggage abandoned in airports, still going around and around on the conveyor belt after the owners have committed suicide, been arrested, or been stricken by a heart attack): in fact the bag was where it had to be, in the mother's vigilant hands, alongside her straitjacketed boy, and she would make sure that it stayed there all the time, through changes of ward and treatment, ready to ignite its powerful charge of normality the moment in which, once the worst was over, he should feel a rekindled desire to spruce himself up . . .

Slam! The doors were closed. The ambulance left, slowly, making its way with difficulty through the crowd, and slipped away silently, perhaps even toward San Camillo's, where the mother had only recently clocked out, or would shortly be clocking in again: no siren, only the flashing lights revolving, to tell the people, as soon as it turned the corner, to tell all the unknowing people who would see it going by in the midst of the morning traffic, that it wasn't a serious matter, after all, and that there was no need to make the sign of the cross.

The cops lingered to write something down on a sheet of paper, then they got into the car and they left too. I looked at my watch: ten past eleven. Now I really was late: I could no longer go on foot, it would have taken me ten minutes, ten plus ten, twenty, and I would no longer be slightly late. I was obliged to take the Vespa: there she was, worn out by the years and despoiled of her fenders (I have always wondered why people steal them), chained to the post of the one-way street sign, and dirtied by the *sand* that had fallen with the rain the week before—a wind from the Sahara, they said. As the crowd dispersed in small groups, each one wrapped in a little cloud of comments, I held my breath and carried out all the operations necessary in order to leave. It wasn't so simple: I had to remove the chain, open the pannier, take the rag to clean my hands with (the chain was very dirty), get out my helmet, put the chain in the pannier, clean my hands again, lay the rag over the chain, put Carver's book on top of that, close the pannier again, put on the helmet, open the gas . . . and open the choke, because I suddenly remembered that the Vespa was flooded, damn it—and that was why I hadn't used it for a bit, because it ought to have been taken down to the garage. I tried to start it all the same, one, two, three, four attempts with all of my weight on the twisted kick-start pedal (nor have I ever understood why people twist kick-start pedals), until, on the fifth attempt, that confounded old kickback whacked into my foot. The pain that transfixed me was a familiar one, an old acquaintance, reminiscent of adolescence: I would go back to Rome after whole trimesters at college—in Trieste, Florence, Naples—and my Vespa would be flooded, and wouldn't start, and invariably, before resigning myself to pushing it, I would try the kick-start again and again like a madman, until the kickback came along and made me see stars. It is one of those things from my earlier life that I haven't managed to throw off, and in fact it is pointless, and it hurts.

I started to push. Lots of people watched me as I limped about the little square under the pitiless sun: I got up a bit of speed, then I leaped onto the saddle and engaged second gear—nothing—then the desperate attempt to exploit the remaining momentum by engaging first: nothing. I persisted, I got stubborn, I repeated that useless maneuver three, four times, only to wind up where I had started but, panting, soaked in sweat, and later than ever.

And I realized that I hadn't even shut off the choke, before starting to push, and so the Vespa must have been flooded even more.

This left me with one chance. To drag myself over to a very steep slope that was nearby, and launch myself down the hill in a last-ditch attempt to get underway, a maneuver made more complicated by the fact that I would have to launch myself in the wrong direction, since the road in question was an uphill one-way street. It was dangerous, I shouldn't have done it, but I had no alternative, the time was passing and that woman was waiting for me, and so I was going to do it: I arrived at the top of the slope, waited for a van (Francia brand mozzarella) to come puffing up the hill and I presumed, really, suddenly turning into a misguided sixteen-year-old reprobate, that for the next thirty seconds no one would come up the hill. I went for it, really, and the Vespa immediately picked up speed, because it is a really steep, and straight, slope, and I engaged third, then second, and I was already halfway down the hill but the scooter still wouldn't start, and, despite the engine braking effect, it was still going too fast for me to drop down into first, and the junction with via Marco Polo was getting closer and closer, and if someone had come up the hill then it would have been bad news for me, but no one was coming, luckily, and in any case in a few moments I was going to stop because I was almost at the bottom—when, at the last useful moment, after which I would have become a chap pushing a broken-down scooter along a fast road, it came to life. A white puff expelled the air that was flooding the carburetor, the engine caught, accelerated, and I had to brake immediately so as not to shoot straight into the wide road where the traffic was racing by at seventy an hour, but I had to keep the revs up at the same time, so that it wouldn't cut out, sawing away at the throttle, the brakes, and the clutch like a maniac, and the rear end gave a wiggle, and I managed to control it, and the exhaust carried on spitting out its white pestilence, and I braked harder, but progressively so as not to skid again, and I stopped right at the junction with the main road, safe and sound with the engine going. Done it. Now I could go into neutral and rev up as much as I liked to flush out the engine, and it is hard to explain the pleasure I got out of this simple operation. Only then did a car turn and take the road up the hill: it was a white Fiat Uno belonging to the driving school, no less—a frequent sight, into the bargain, on this road, much favored by examiners for the hill start part of the driving test. The learner was a very short girl who was hanging on to the wheel the way a shipwreck victim clings to a piece of wreckage. She seemed decidedly scared by the trial before her, but her fright was as nothing compared to what she would have experienced had she taken the road up the hill fifteen seconds before—a maniac plunging straight for her in the wrong direction—and she would never know.

I took via Marco Polo, and the breeze at forty miles an hour caressed my sweating flesh. This old, popular, profoundly Italian balm is the exact reciprocal of the kickback of a few minutes before, and is compensation for it. Seen through that caress, with a full tank, the sunshine, and an entire metropolis at my disposal, even my adolescence no longer seemed so bad. After all, it had given me many moments like this one. And seeing that I had begun to forget things, let's say that within ten seconds I was going to forget the bad night that had just ended—*zot*—the sinister awakening, the capture of that boy, the kickback. Let's say that my day was going to begin here, with this wind in my face, with this unexpected good humor . . .

sixteen

"Oh, hello."

The woman held out her hand, and her beauty took my breath away. I hadn't remembered it at all—in fact, come to think about it, I didn't remember absolutely anything about her, almost as if she weren't made of flesh but existed only within her tragedy. But there, outside my tired and unreliable memory, in the brute objectivity of quarter past eleven in the morning, her beauty seemed clear-cut and imperious, flamboyant, brazen, Mexican, and, I noticed, as if intensified by an amazing resemblance, a sort of cross between Florinda Bolkan and Tony Musante that made her absolutely unreal. It was exactly like that, she looked like *both of them*, in an amazing somatic crasis that seemed to have been achieved, after hundreds of monstrous results, by some Dr. Frankenstein with an obsession about *Anonimo Veneziano*.

Her lightweight outfit followed the contours of a splendidly abundant figure, maternal but decidedly firm and supple, set off by a dark and lustrous skin that made you think of the interiors of luxury motor cars. The hand I shook was large, soft, well-manicured, and adorned with glittering rings. Her black hair shone like cat's fur, the mole on her cheekbone seemed to have been placed there by some precise mathematical equation, while the center of her face was marked by a mouth as large and red as a blazing sunset.

"Sorry I'm late," I said.

She smelled of smoke, but also of the sea, in the same fantastic way as the emporia in the Tuscan Riviera of my childhood, where my mother used to buy face cream and I used to get one of those plastic balls with photos of famous cyclists in them. A scent I hadn't come across since, because these days those shops smell only of plastic.

"Oh, don't worry," her teeth gleamed, "I was in good company . . ."

She motioned with her chin at the coffee ice, already half finished, in the glass on the table. Between ordering it, waiting for it, and eating it a quarter of an hour must have gone by.

"They make the best coffee ice in all of Rome here, you know," I said.

"Oh really? In fact it's very good."

"Oh it's good all right. Thing is, it took me years to find that out, and I live just around the corner. Whereas you come to Rome one morning, someone makes a date to meet you here, and you discover it right away."

"I don't know about you," she added, "but I have a sweet tooth. I make Matteo all the snacks you suggest in your books, but I eat them too."

She was using the present tense, typical.

"They are the snacks of my childhood. Ricotta cheese with cocoa powder; bread, butter, and sugar; chocolate spread with pears. And d'you know something? I had forgotten all about them. If it hadn't been for you, I think I would never have eaten them again. These days children only ask for those ready-made junk food snacks . . ."

She ate a spoonful of her ice—the last one, I would have said—and as she swallowed it she closed her eyes, like a little girl.

The waiter came and I ordered a coffee.

"On the other hand," she resumed, "everything is like that in your books. That's why I like them. You tell stories to the children of today, but the references are to the childhood of their parents, yours, ours. That's true, isn't it?"

"It's true."

"You explain to our children what we adults are like when we dream. Because by now, when we dream, all we are doing is remembering."

She carefully scraped together the remains of the ice in the glass, managing to invent herself a last spoonful, which she sent down gracefully, but without closing her eyes again.

"Yes, you are a really good children's writer," she continued, "because it seems to me you don't write, you *translate*. You fish around in places where children don't go, and then you translate into their language the fine things that don't concern them. Our memories, the cinema, Leopardi, rock music . . . Isn't that so?"

I was struck. A very beautiful woman with a son in a coma compliments me on my books and at the same time reveals that she has understood the trick: a cheap little trick, which was there, before everyone's eyes, but that no one had ever noticed. Because it's true, I have never invented anything, I merely copied, I merely recycled all the things I liked in life. Rock, Shakespeare, Beckett, American films, psychedelia, Leopardi—precisely—even Pasolini, are inexhaustible mines for the writing of children's books: even though she says I translate them, in reality I plunder them. Children cannot notice this, but I put my money on the fact that publishers, reviewers, or adult readers wouldn't notice either, and that's how it went. Do we or don't we live in a superficial society? Once a Catholic magazine awarded me a prize for the best line of the year found in a children's book: *The devil finds work for idle hands*. And I accepted it, what was I to do? I could hardly stand there and tell them that it was an English proverb that I had come across in a song by the Smiths, and that I had lifted it wholesale for *The Adventures of Pizzano Pizza*.

Then along comes this woman, and for her, on the contrary, it was all obvious.

"Well, yes, actually," I admitted, "even though on hearing it said it sounds like an accusation of plagiarism."

"Oh no . . . ," she blushed: she was one of those women who blushed. "It was meant to be a compliment, I would never dream of . . ."

"In any event," I tried to make a nice smile, heaven knows how it came out. "Until now no one has ever noticed. Not as far as I know, at least. So, all you have to do is refrain from writing it, and I'll be able to carry on . . ."

"Oh," she broke in, "but I *have* written it . . ."

She opened the handbag sitting on the chair next to hers, and took out a sheaf of papers, which she proffered me.

"Here it is. It's a piece of foolishness, naturally, the fact is that . . ."

The fact was that before she closed the bag again I thought I saw inside—*again*—a pistol.

" . . . primary school teacher," she was saying, "and in our school we do this little magazine, pupils and teachers together. I write the book reviews, and I really wanted to . . ."

What the devil was going on? It was a pistol, I saw it perfectly well. It wasn't normal for a pistol to be in there. Or was it? Since when have people been going around armed?

" . . . even though, as you will see, I have definitely copied your style. Now *that* is plagiarism . . ."

The waiter came with my coffee, and I drank it in little sips as I pretended—*pretended*—to read the magazine: in reality all I was doing was trying to make sense of that pistol, to reconcile it with this surprising woman, who looked like a couple of actors, and who had unmasked me in the school magazine, and began her sentences with a sigh; while trying to reconcile the result, already pretty incongruous in itself—I'd never suspected that women like this existed—with the reason for our meeting, which was not, damn it, the secret of my literary cuisine . . .

I looked up from the sheets of paper as she opened the bag once more. The pistol was still there, and it was still a pistol. Small, silver-plated—no way it was a toy.

"Do you smoke?" she said. A pack of Marlboro Lights and a gold lighter had appeared between her jeweled hands.

"No, thanks," I replied, "I've stopped."

"Oh, then it would be better if I didn't smoke under your nose . . ."

"I'm used to it."

"Really? How long have you been off them?"

"Nine months."

"Oh, then you've made it. Sure it won't bother you?"

"Sure."

She looked at me intensely, as if she intended to rid herself, before granting me her admiration for that too, of the suspicion that maybe ten hours previously I had been raking through the rubbish in search of a Capri Superlight. Then she lit the cigarette, and took a long pull on it with those gorgeous lips of hers.

"I had stopped too," she said, "ten years ago, when I was pregnant with Matteo. I started again not long ago, after the accident . . ."

And now it was getting tougher. How had she managed to broach the subject so rapidly? She was still looking me right in the eye, with a gaze that had been difficult to meet before and that was now boring holes in me. I lowered my eyes. Why was she looking at me like that? What could I say to her? And what if, on talking, I were to spit the way I had done the other evening? Could I muddle through simply by giving her Carver's book? And, above all, was I still sure I should give it to her, seeing that she had sussed me and seeing that I had copied a good bit from Carver too?

"What have you done to your face?" she asked.

Instinctively I brought my hand up to my cheek, and she shook her head, smiling, to indicate that I had touched the wrong place. Then, beating me to it, she reached a hand out to my other cheek, letting her fingertips slip down to the jaw, in a chaste, velvety caress—exactly the kind it must be most beautiful to give to her, starting from her mole.

Then she showed me her fingertips, and they were stained with blood.

"You cut yourself shaving . . ."

"I hadn't noticed," I said.

"Uh-huh . . ."

She immersed the paper napkin in the glass of water standing next to the one with the ice cream, and then she delicately cleaned my cheek.

"Sting?"

"A bit."

So for all that time I had had a bloody face. That was why she had been staring at me that way. And so I must have been bleeding outside the house too, among all those people, while they were taking away Anita's son.

"Oh, it's nothing," she said, as if I were her son, "just a little scrape . . ."

She finished the operation leaving the wet napkin stuck to my cheek, and smiled, visibly amused by the fact that it stayed up by itself. Anna laughs at things that remain stuck to other things too.

"Thanks," I said, and I detached the napkin from my cheek. I looked at it: the blood was so diluted it looked like alcohol-free bitters. She picked up the cigarette she had left in the ashtray—in which, I noticed, there were another two butts—took a puff, and then suddenly darkened, as if a cloud had passed over her.

"Listen," she said, "I don't think I thanked you enough, the other evening. Your generosity completely overwhelmed me and I was unable to express all my . . ."

For a second her voice broke, and it looked as if copious tears were about to overflow from that crack. But by then she must have been used to not bursting into tears, and it took very little for her to regain full control of herself. In this case, another puff on her Marlboro Light.

"Above all," she resumed, "I wanted to explain to you why I accepted your money, and what I will do with it."

"It wasn't my money," I said.

"Oh, it was yours all right, and how. And if I accepted it, it was only because . . ."

She broke off once more, and with a lunging movement that scared me she wet a second napkin and applied it to my cheek.

"You're still bleeding," she said. "Perhaps you ought to leave it on for a bit . . ."

Again she left it, and it stayed up on its own, and she smiled. But I held it on with one hand: less ridiculous.

Another puff of smoke, slow, rounded.

"You see," she resumed, "the Austrian clinic where I have decided to take Matteo is the only possibility in Europe for a cure. I have just met the professor who founded it, and he is the only specialist who has not said 'zero chance' to me. He said 'not much chance,' but he also said that in his *House of Reawakenings*, which is what the clinic is called, the word *resignation* does not exist: there is no political bickering, no one is breathing down your neck waiting for the intensive care unit occupied by your son to become free, or hoping that you will agree to the removal of his organs to save some other life . . ."

She took a last drag on the cigarette, with a violence that suddenly reminded me of Visintin, a classmate in college who always asked for a drag on other people's cigarettes, and handed them back incandescent, so hard did he pull on them.

Then she stubbed it out in the ashtray, in one go.

"But I don't want to save another person's life," she said, "I want to save my son's life. And in that clinic I shall be able to try to do so without feeling guilty."

Mechanically, her hands extracted another cigarette from the packet, brought it to her mouth, and lit it. In that course I had followed they taught us how to deal with certain highly stressful situations that could drive one to start smoking again—losing one's job, moving, getting separated etc.—but they had never dreamed of considering the eventuality of having a child in a coma.

"The only thing is that it's very expensive," she continued, "and there's no knowing how long he might have to stay there. That's why I accepted your money: for Matteo it could mean an extra ten days of treatment, and in those ten days he could regain consciousness. I shall put it aside, in the bank, and, when I have used up my other money, I'll spend it, and all the time that Marco survives from that moment onward, and everything that happens during that time, will be a present from his friend Pizzano Pizza . . ."

Again, her voice cracked; and again a puff on her cigarette instantly repaired the damage.

"But if," she resumed, "alas, it were not needed, I will give it back to you."

She fell suddenly silent, and the noisy Roman silence immediately reemerged all around us. Here too, what could I say? The only things that came to mind were questions: why did she never mention her husband, given that she was wearing a wedding ring? Why did she keep a pistol in her handbag? Why, during the prize-giving ceremony, had she addressed the local dignitaries with such passion, if she had already decided to send the child to that clinic in Austria? And if she had still to make up her mind—as I believe—if this business of the Austrian clinic had come along *after* her outburst, perhaps even as a consequence of it, and in fact she had met with the luminary only shortly before, then why should she lie, now, illogically, about the reasons why she had accepted the money, and to me—who had not asked her for anything? But, on the other hand, what price logic, for a person stricken by such a terrible misfortune?

I looked again at the damp napkin I was holding to my cheek, and the blood/bitters had almost disappeared. She spruced up her hair, smoked, lowered her eyes, then opened her handbag for the third time—there was a pistol inside, for the third time—took out her wallet, opened that too, and made as if to take out money, which gave me a providential opportunity to say something, a way out, given that I couldn't have borne that silence for one second longer.

"No, no, allow me," I said.

I took the two sodden receipts from beneath the water glasses, and reached for my wallet at the same time, trying to make the gesture look natural, but also assertive, as if it were the irrevocable act of the gallant and resolute man I shall never be. She didn't object, but I noted that she was *immensely* surprised—open-mouthed, even—and was gazing at me with a vacant, shocked stare, devoid of expression, as if she didn't understand, as if she didn't know that on the receipts was written the price of our order, and that someone had to pay it, and that it was with that money that the café owner earned his living. It was as if she knew nothing about the world anymore, and in that dead stare her beauty abruptly vanished, torn by some phenomenal inner gust from lineaments that were left naked, frighteningly stark. No more Florinda Bolkan, no more Tony Musante; no more anything: for a long terrible moment that paralyzed me too she really seemed to have joined her son in the gelid space that held him prisoner.

"The bill," I stammered, showing the slips.

"Oh," she gave a start, "Thank you . . . ," as if she had realized only now.

Very well, I thought, all this is passing strange, at least as strange as the pistol in her handbag, but there again this was a woman close to the breaking point, and it was already something if she wasn't completely off her head, which was why there was no sense in my expecting to understand the things she did. The only thing was that, while I was taking out the money, and laying it on the table under the glass, still forcing myself to look natural, assertive, etc., she was still rummaging about in her handbag. Why?

"But there's one last thing I have to ask you," she said, and blushed again. Blushing much more than before, to tell the truth: I don't think I've ever seen a person blush so much. Why?

"What can I do for you?" I said, and again I forced myself to smile, but this time I really couldn't manage, because from her wallet she took out a check, a check already made out that, damn it, was not just any check . . .

"Really, I hate to be a nuisance but . . ."

. . . it was *the* check, it really was, and so evident was this that I recognized it right away, there was no doubt, even though in reality I had never seen it, given that when they had handed it to me it was in an envelope . . .

"Would you mind endorsing it for me?"

Oh, no, *no*.

O plate of the Society for the Prevention of Accidents, to whom all eyes turn in elevators to avoid looking at the ogre that is upon us, to avoid meeting the oxyacetylene gaze of the stranger, O Goddess of Embarrassment, to whom by dint of turning to Thee, we have learned by heart the prayer that accompanies Thee (*Stigler Otis / Maximum Capacity 4 Persons / Maximum Load 360 Kg / Category A / The Use of the Elevator by Unaccompanied Minors of Under Twelve Years Is Prohibited . . .*), save me, send one of Thy angels, here, quickly, upon whom my gaze may be fixed, so that I may bear this unbearable moment . . .

The coffee cup, yes. The logo of the coffee company, *Morganti il caffè d'autore*, to be stared at as hard as possible, to be scrutinized, analyzed: brown, with a gilt rim and slipshod, pretentious graphics in a taste so ephemeral that it must have been out of fashion even before they had finished the sketch, a little drawing supposedly meant to represent the outline of a Haitian, I presume, or a Haitian woman, or in any case a native of the Caribbean in a skirt made of banana leaves (or was it an African native? And in this case what would he or she have to do with coffee?), but sitting in a typically Indian pose, alas, like the Goddess Kalì, with the disastrous result that . . .

No way out, the check crept up to the point on which my gaze was fixed, followed by a gold Parker, a probable birthday present, from the days when that woman still celebrated birthdays; and I looked at it, I couldn't avoid it; I screwed up my courage, grasped the pen, and looked at that rectangle of watermarked paper that didn't bear looking at (Banca del Fucino), with all its flatulence of zeros and below them that excessive and offensive safety measure, the transliteration of the sum into letters (*Fifteen million #*, where the purpose of the crosshatching was to prevent the payee Gianni Orzan, after he had found a pen of the same type and color, after he had practiced the handwriting of whoever had made out the check, and after he had effortlessly transformed into nines all the zeros of the figure in numbers, from adding in his own prize-winning writer's hand a nice nine hundred and ninety-nine thousand nine hundred and ninety-nine); creased, dog-eared, exhausted by six long days spent in the company of grubby small banknotes, expired season tickets, and crumpled receipts that took the mickey ("*You're not worth shit, that prick didn't endorse you . . .*"), it was like one of those fortunate souls that are miraculously pulled out of the rubble a week after the earthquake; unlike them, however, it was not silent, befuddled by the light and amazement, but protested, furious, with the last vestiges of its dying strength. "*You,*" it bawled, "*wretched weekend do-gooders, who do things without knowing what you're doing, who donate and don't endorse, and oblige the mother of a child in a coma to make appointments, to take trains, taxis, and coffee ices, and to face up to blood-curdling situations, blood-curdling I say, to make up for your bloody superficiality! My curse on you, you rats!*"

Yet, despite its pitiable state, all it took was a signature, and we were pals again. There you go. And so the mortified, illegible scrawl to which I attribute the meaning "Gianni Orzan," and which I humbly applied to the back of that incredible piece of paper, was sufficient to reanimate something that, before its fall from grace, had been a prize and then, albeit only for a few seconds, a catamaran, a trip to Disneyland, and/or a loft, and transformed it once more, this time definitively, into ten days of vegetable life for a little boy. (And, just by the way, how can a civilization in which *this* is possible fail to dominate the world?) "No hard feelings, old boy," the check said to me, before returning to the wallet whence it had come—a wallet in which the small fry that had mocked it before was going to get some tough shit.

"Thank you," said the woman's voice.

Morganti il caffè d'autore.

What now? I was obliged to look up. But was I able to do so? Now I knew that, right from the first moment, in the woman's big dark eyes there had been written "You have to endorse checks before you give them to people, you *prick!*": how could I look into them again? Damn it, why hadn't someone taken me to one side, after my handsome gesture—the outgoing mayor, his successor, the journalist—to tell me the check would have to be endorsed? Why hadn't this woman forged my signature, rather than take a train and come all the way here to face up to a scene as distressing as this? Was she not suffering enough already, perhaps?

The waiter arrived, took the money, and while he was giving me my change my eyes climbed up his slim figure, all the way to his face: uniform slightly grubby, earring, flat top, goatee beard, he must have been about twenty, right, and he must have had a cat too, judging by the scratches lining the backs of his hands. He tore the receipts, slipped the change under the glass, thanked me, and went off toward the kiosk with a light, sinuous step: he must have been gay. And how I envied him the simple thoughts he must have had in his head—love, money, the desire to have fun . . .

"May I leave you my number?" said the woman, still voice off—"I'd be glad if you called me, sometime . . ."

And finally I did it. I turned toward her, what would be would be. Luckily she wasn't looking at me: she had taken a cell phone out of her handbag—she had everything, in there, it was Eega Beeva's magic pocket—and she began to fiddle about with it, her head bowed and her eyes intent on the keypad.

"Excuse me," she said, "I haven't had it for very long, and I don't remember the number . . ."

Beep, beep, beep, she was pressing buttons, shaking her head . . .

"Ah, here it is . . ."

She looked up, and, that chilling moment having passed, her beauty slipped over her again, escorted by the two stars of *Anonimo Veneziano.*

"Do you have something to write on?"

I slipped my hand into my pocket, but my little diary wasn't there. There was a ballpoint without a cap, but no diary—and in fact I had taken it out of my jacket the other evening, of course, to read the phrase by the Emperor of Japan that I had noted down, and I had laid it on the desk, I remember perfectly well, without putting it back in its place.

"Just a moment . . . ," I mumbled.

So, this woman's number: where could I write it down? I was never going to call her, not after what had happened with the check; nor did she, I was sure, really expect me to do so—but I was going to have to write it down, seeing that she wanted to give it to me. I could have written it on the school magazine, but I felt that that would have been a bit insensitive; on Carver's book, seeing that I really didn't think I was going to give it to her now—but who knows, I might have changed my mind at the last moment; or I could have written it on my hand, but that would have been an excessively sensual gesture, and there had been enough misunderstandings already. I rummaged in my jacket pocket and found a slip of paper; or rather, when I pulled it out, I realized it was an envelope, a crumpled, unsealed envelope, with nothing written on it, but full. What was it? But that was a secondary problem, at that point, in the meantime I had to find somewhere to write down the number.

"Okay."

"0335," she intoned, "5348318. They tell me I can receive calls even in Austria. You know, that's where I'll be from next Monday onward."

I diligently wrote down the number, and I felt a bit better.

"Where, exactly?" I even managed to ask her.

"Innsbruck."

Yes, the worst was over, was almost over. That woman didn't hate me anymore, she smiled at me, so beautiful once more that it hurt; and at bottom it was not even necessarily true that she had ever hated me—on the contrary, she admired me, she had said so herself. After all I was a kind of angel, in her eyes, who told stories to her little boy to make him fall asleep, and now that he had fallen asleep too deeply I was giving her a hand to try to wake him up. Perhaps she would even appreciate Carver's book, if I gave it to her, perhaps she would read it, and that underlined passage might help her not to give in, with all that she was going through. Yes, overlooking the terrible detail of the unendorsed check—very Carverian, what's more—she had had nothing but good from me. Why should she hate me?

"Well," she said, "perhaps I'd better go now. Do you know a taxi number, by any chance?"

"3570."

"Thanks."

She set to fiddling with the telephone once more, and she really wasn't expert, you could see that perfectly well. Then she put it to her ear.

"Where are we?" she asked me.

"Porta San Paolo."

She remained silent for a bit, with a sweet and bewildered air that did a lot for her.

"The lines are busy," she said, and I encouraged her, with a grimace, to trust in the syrupy taped voice that was asking her to hold the line. She complied, and waited. Then, suddenly, she stiffened.

"Good morning, a taxi in Porta San Paolo, please . . ."

A *pigeon* landed on the arm of an empty seat, next to mine.

"Oh, just a second . . . ," said the woman.

She moved the phone from her ear and pointed at the envelope on which I had just written down her number. The pigeon flew off.

"Sorry, what's my number?" and she blushed again.

"Say that you're calling from a cell phone," said I, the man of the world.

She did so, then nodded with a grateful expression to let me know I had had her do the right thing. No, she didn't hate me. And I don't even think she would speak badly of me when walking past intercoms.

While she was waiting for them to assign her a taxi, so beautiful, with her telephone to her ear, she looked like an ad for the phone company. When she lit another cigarette—that made five—she looked like an ad for Marlboro Lights. And I cannot say that I felt the *fatal impulse*, that, no; but nor did I feel the solid, compassionate disgust that I ought to have felt if I was to say that I was out of danger: therefore the time had come to do something, according to what they had taught me in the course, if possible a pleasing gesture, or at least a useful one, in short, a deliberate gesture with its own precise dynamic, to keep the devil far—as the saying goes—from my idle hands.

One gesture I would have liked to make was to take that woman's hand and to guide it, ape-fashion, in another caress down my cheek, the way Christopher Lambert does in *Greystoke* with the hand of his dead grandfather. But I couldn't do that.

Another gesture I would have liked to make was to take that pistol out of her handbag, touch it, and ask her if it was loaded and why she carried it. But the gesture I did make was to open the envelope I had in my pocket and to take out the contents, a lined page from a "Batman" notebook folded into four. I opened out the sheet of paper, which bore writing on only one side in Anna's hand—tiny, neat, unmistakable: *Dear Gianni . . .*

"Cuba 22," said the woman, "in four minutes."

I looked at her, smiling, but my eyes immediately went back to the sheet of paper.

Dear Gianni, there's something I have to tell you. You say you don't like writing letters. I never wrote any, except during that period we both know about, when I used to write you one a day, but for what I have to tell you there is no other way, given that—

"So I'll say good-bye, then," said the woman.

I looked up again. She had gotten to her feet, and was sticking cigarettes and cell phone into her handbag. I got up too, and I forced myself to look at her, but by then that sheet of paper was everywhere.

given that I couldn't manage to tell you face-to-face. The fact is that

"Thanks again," stammered the woman. "I shall always be in your debt, I know, but . . ."

And then I hushed her. I put my hand on her mouth, I did that. I raised my hand, really, and I touched those lips of red sponge, brazenly, with my fingers, *me*. And I know why I did it.

"Hang in there," I whispered to her.

And I also know because immediately after I said that to her, pronouncing the words so intimately, so *well*, that they triggered the impulse that catapulted her into my arms in a real, carnal embrace, so that her hands were clinging to my back, her breasts flattened against my chest, her perfume redolent of lost emporiums erupting under my nose, as her suddenly sobbing face buried itself in the hollow of my neck. Yes, I know exactly why I caused all that.

The fact is that the other night

I did it because that way, camouflaged in that embrace, I could raise the hand clutching the sheet of paper

when we were in the car

behind her back

and you asked me

and carry on reading

if I had ever had

while my other hand returned her embrace

an affair

but in reality I was the one leaning on her,

and I told you
so that I wouldn't collapse
that I hadn't
because by then I had realized
I lied to you.
—I was all washed-up.

seventeen

Dear Gianni,

There's something I have to tell you. You say you don't like writing letters. I never wrote any, except during that period we both know about, when I used to write you one a day, but for what I have to tell you there is no other way, given that I couldn't manage to tell you face-to-face.

The fact is that the other night when we were in the car and you asked me if I had ever had an affair, and I told you that I hadn't, I lied to you.

I have had an affair, Gianni. I have broken it off, because I love you and I can't bear the idea of betraying you. But I did have an affair. It was the most despicable thing I have ever done in all my life, and I was ashamed of myself right from the first moment, but I did it. And the other evening, after having lied to you, after having seen how readily you believed me, I had the terrifying feeling that the fact of having broken it off would count for nothing until I succeeded in having you judge me. I saw that until such time as I managed to tell you I couldn't really say I had stopped betraying you.

I know that this is the worst possible moment in which to tell you, and I also know I am running a terrible risk, given that I simply cannot imagine your reaction, but it is right, it is right, it is right that you know.

Now I have told you, and my life is in your hands. Depending upon how you react, I can go back to being happy with you and Francesco, or I shall end up unable even to conceive of happiness, and the fault will be mine.

Forgive me for the pain I have given you, Gianni. I feel awful too, even though I know that this does not diminish my responsibility. And whatever happens, know that I love you.

Anna

eighteen

And so my marriage is dying in the arms of a woman exactly the way I have always tried not to let it die day after day for years struggling and toiling to learn the painstaking art of diminution and acquiring the clinical capacity to peel other women of all their charms as if they were onions and blindly asserting the untenable dogma according to which they cannot have charms period and everything that glitters around them is to be considered illusory period and ought to be forgotten instantly on principle period or better still not noticed in an immense and sullen injustice that I manage to commit by now out of sheer habit and in fact I have also committed it with this woman who is propping me up in an embrace that is interminable and languid and soft and impetuous and incandescent and almost obscene in the way it incinerates the fabric of clothes to aim straight at the flesh a woman would you believe to whom I had donated the equivalent of one sixth of my annual income without even noticing how beautiful she was but I wonder if I really hadn't noticed and will it emerge one day that I gave her the check precisely because she is beautiful and could it be like last night with the pack of cigarettes or even with this deadly letter I have been carrying around for days stubbornly refusing to find it even though its effects have become tangible all around me no wonder Anna was glacial over the telephone no wonder I had done nothing recently but note other people's suffering as if there were nothing else around me when instead there was all of creation pistol-packing bellies roller skaters blasphemers seagulls neighbors nurses mothers of comatose little boys all trying compassionately to warn me so that I might waste no more time and realize once and for all simply by putting my hand in my pocket that *the one doing the suffering was me* and in the end I understood and my marriage is dying and this woman will not stop weeping and I carry on caressing the warm nape of her neck mechanically and desperately and perhaps that is why she cannot stop weeping perhaps I am making her cry yes and she is crying for me too and although it is clear that it is precisely the weeping that is gluing her to my body and I am aware that an embrace like this is the most powerful anesthetic that a man who has been hurt can find God only knows why I stop caressing her and it is like releasing a button because she immediately stops sobbing after which it is only a catastrophic domino effect that I no longer have the time to interrupt and in fact our bodies are already separated and she says good-bye and she has already gone off with a rather wooden gait and to tell the truth she was better immobile and she doesn't even turn to wave nor do I run after her to catch up with her and her taxi has already arrived and she is already inside it and both of them are already vanishing one confused in the other and both confused in the midday traffic and I know the taxi was called Cuba 22 but I don't know her name really neither her name nor surname she had never said all she had said was Matteo's mother and above all how alone I am now without her how forlorn with that letter in my hand I reread *Dear Gianni* no I cannot and then again it's not as if rereading it is going to change anything and my eyes are on fire my belly is on fire my chest is on fire and now where am I to go and what am I to do *there's something I have to tell you* the woman did not turn back like in films *I have had an affair* and in fact what did she care about me all that mattered to her was that I endorsed the check *my life is in your hands* sure it is sure now it was going to emerge that I am the shit and my blood is boiling in my veins it really is and I want to smoke vomit howl with the desire to smash something but not something at random I want to smash something beautiful and precious that I will not be able to pay for afterward like a work of art for example *The Last Supper* by Jacopo Bassano yes in the Galleria Borghese my favorite picture because it is fucking *realistic* and the apostles are all portrayed blind drunk which was the way it really must have been on those sacred evenings Jesus abstemious preaching and the apostles soused with wine nodding yes well said master words of wisdom and belching away and Simon with the hiccups hic and Thomas passing out yes it must have been exactly like in that picture at bottom they were only fishermen they were poor coarse drunken fishermen and in fact it wasn't that you could trust them that far they were prepared to repudiate to doubt to betray the first chance they got no they were not to be trusted unless you *wanted* to end up nailed to the cross and Jesus wanted that yes *he* wanted to be betrayed but not me shit not me and now I know where to go or better I know where I'm going given that I'm starting the Vespa *vrooom* and this time I manage first kick and take off like a rocket first second third and I've forgotten to put on the helmet and I've left Carver's book on the table and who cares because there is a dog in that picture and he's pissed, too, curled up under the table near an empty bowl and you can understand very well that he has just emptied it he has a sated look and inside the bowl there certainly hadn't been water because there is not the slightest trace of water in that picture there is an orange I think and a ghastly lamb's head on a tray and bread and knives and wine wine wine everywhere but no water because unlike wine water was scarce in Palestine and in short the dog is drunk too and the drunken dog is the really formidable thing about that painting because he is the only innocent in the whole crew the apostles certainly aren't innocent and not even Jesus with his advance knowledge of everything is innocent and not even the lamb's head is innocent a whole lamb might have been but a lamb's head on a tray is merely disgusting no the only innocent is the dog that the apostles have gotten drunk because drunks like everyone to get drunk and it was right there on the dog that I wanted to deface the picture with the screwdriver I have in the rear toolbox and in fact I'm going there now and I'm going to deface it so it's off to Galleria Borghese quick but where the fuck am I going these days you need to book it's no longer possible to feel like going to see a picture in a museum and then go to see it you have to book a week before you have to know things in advance like Jesus to foresee that on such and such a day at such and such a time you will feel like seeing or defacing such and such a picture and when we went Anna made the booking she called that number and booked two tickets and in short she took me given that I went on and on about going but never never managed to remember to make the booking and maybe that day as she was taking me to the Galleria Borghese Anna was already having her what had she called it an affair in fact no maybes she was certainly having one and she had made the booking between one call and another full of sweet nothings for her fancy man is he there no he's not here but he's about to come back see you tomorrow at the usual place yes love bye and you hang up first no you no you no you no you no you and coochie-coo and I'd like to know who this bastard is I'd like to see him face-to-face I'd like to smash his face in yes who can he be someone I know or someone I have never seen or worse still someone I barely glimpsed some time without imagining for a second that he was screwing my wife for example one of those smart-aleck dads who go to pick up the kids from school all well dressed with jacket and tie to let you know that sure they have come to pick up the kid sure they have but they have been working because they have a real job and no fucking around but they still manage to find the time to share domestic duties with their wives and they go to pick up the kids from school and load the dishwasher and attend the parent-teacher meetings where they ogle the little mommies who always go alone like Anna coming to the conclusion that they must be unhappy and neglected by their husbands and working things so they can linger there alone in the school parking lot at dusk while the children play a bit farther away and the traffic light is red and I have to brake and let's see where am I the Baths of Caracalla and where to now and what am I going to do now and what's this repugnant old shit got to stare at look at your own ugly face in the mirror of your Mazda you ass-hole for two cents I'll take it out on him I'll beat him to a pulp blood blood blood an unheard-of ferocity if you can't deface an innocent in a picture then you can always deface one at a red light but it's gone green and he's gone too go on get going if you know what's good for you and I shoot off too first second third and I overtake him bye-bye you old bastard I wouldn't know what to do with your stupid scalp anyway unless you are him maybe it's a doctor one of those specialists with a plum in his mouth that Anna is forever taking Franceschino to and it's hard to understand the reason why seeing that Franceschino is sound as a bell but in any case the insurance reimburses us and I really want to know who he is it can't be the Belgian damn it the dashing beau from the days when she ran around Viareggio with a leather squaw head-band and two bloody tribal scabs on her calves caused by the red hot exhaust pipes of that prick's motorbike and he had also deflowered her I know that for sure because she had told me and yes yes yes yes it had to be him I remember that Anna had even talked about him to me one time last summer she talked about him to me because they had met again after many years and she told me he had lost almost all of his hair the poor thing and was going through a bad patch working as a photographer for scandal sheets like *Novella 2000* and the lord knows I couldn't have given a damn about that but what Anna had really been telling me was that she had been to bed with him and no shitting me or that she

was about to do so and how could I have failed to see how could I
have not doubted her for so much as a second because I remember
it all very well I didn't doubt her for so much as a second how
could I have left her alone all of August that's certainly when it
happened no doubt about that me in Rome writing *The New
Adventures of Pizzano Pizza* and her in Viareggio enjoying entire
romantic afternoons Franceschino at her mother's while she went
to the beautician's to the hairdresser's to the little American market in Livorno and to Montignoso to visit such and such a girlfriend or to Lucca to meet up with such and such a girlfriend for
the first time in years but in reality always going exclusively to
screw with the Belgian in some seedy dump that he called a studio
impregnated with the stink of developing acids and the walls plastered with photos of sports stars and actors Alberto Tomba Luca
Barbareschi Max Biaggi or the politician Pierferdinando Casini on
his yacht with his dick hanging out and ashamed of herself of
course but after when she went back home and Franceschino
leaped on her neck and together they would phone me in Rome
and how are you and is it hot and when are you coming but clearly
not ashamed of herself *during* and here we are talking about real
sex here there are some hard words flying about like *cock in mouth*
and stuff like that and what's this piece of shit in the Golf up to
are you going to turn or not fuck off you shit yes I'm talking to
you I'll bust your ass yes that's it off you go go on get out of it if
you know what's good for you and let's see where am I *surprise* I'm
back at the Pyramid that's to say almost at the little bar where I
left Carver's book and what better occasion to go to get it back
given that it's mine and it's also rare so now I'll go there and take it
back in any case I don't know what to do or where to go and I bet
it's the Belgian it can only be him of course it happened in
Viareggio not before my eyes but while she was at the seaside with
hubby in the city like in one of Edwige Fenech's sexy films then
maybe they billed and cooed over the telephone all through the
winter and that's why Anna got a cell phone the cheap two-timing
malignant liarrrr I thought it was odd she said it was so she could

be reached in case they called her from Franceschino's school when she wasn't at home but that was a real load of bullshit because I am almost always at home and there too how could I have failed to have doubts dumb asshole that I am and then maybe they met that weekend last December when she went to Viareggio when I was in New York and dived back into that hole for a screw in the cold this time and forever hurrying and scurrying about with the pretext of going to do the shopping in the supermarket you've no idea of how crowded it was there Mom and then the shame and you know what I'm going to do now I'm going to look for that son of a bitch and when I find him I'm going to kill him I swear I'll do it oh fuck the streetcar sorry driver I didn't see you and you keep your fuck-ing hair on you faggoty piece of shit I said I was sorry that's right yes get out of the way if you know what's good for you and fuck you and your stressful job and I'll stop here I get off leave the engine running and I can already see the book down there still lying on the table where I had left it the faggoty waiter still hadn't taken it yes I swear I'll flush him out and I'll kill him I'm not jok-ing and you know how I'll play it I'll play it so that just as soon as fatguts with the pistol shows up again because he certainly will show up I'll get on first name terms since that's so important for him and I'll say well Gianni the time has come for you to do some-thing for me you said you loved me and that I am almost a son to you etcetera and now the time has come for you to prove this to me because I need you to help me give a bastard a lesson and you cannot refuse me what the hell do you care you're an outlaw you steal cars you have false documents false surnames false credit cards you have nothing to lose and then it seems to me he is sincere when he says he loves me and he even put the blanket over me after I had fallen asleep and so off we go together in the Daihatsu Feroza and we get to the Belgian's studio in Viareggio or wherever the fuck it is *ding-dong* and as he opens the door and even if he only opens his fucking door by so much as a crack the fun begins I and fatguts with the pistol a couple of salty dudes and first we'll have a little fun à la Quentin Tarantino with questions like do you know by any chance how much an eight-year-old kid grows in one

week come on have a guess or has your tongue gone all dry how
much taller does a kid grow in a week you sure don't know you
don't know shit about life and without saying a word fatguts with
that ischemic smile of his will let him have a bullet in the knee
boom so I'll tell you because I know the Americans have made a
study of it and it so happens that I have studied their research an
eight-year-old kid grows on the average 0.133 (repeating decimal)
centimeters a week which means watch out don't lose your concentration don't look at your knee it's had it in any case which
means that if a separated father can see his eight-year-old son only
two weekends a month because he threw his wife out of the house
and his wife went back to her little hometown what else could she
do with the child because in any case the judges always award cus-
tody of the kids to the mothers even when they are at fault and
here *boom* fatguts lets him have another round just like that for no
reason this time in the ankle of the other leg and this father pay
attention to me now and please don't groan *this father* for reasons
of *force majeure* a banal appendix operation let's say is obliged to
miss two straight weekends in which he had the right to stay with
his son and so he sees him again after a total of six weeks don't try
to make the calculations trust me if he misses two and it's his turn
every two this make six weeks without seeing him well in the
meantime his son will have grown 0.799 (repeating decimal) centimeters get it that is almost a centimeter which for an individual
roughly one meter thirty tall you'll acknowledge is a good measure
but especially and here's the point it's a measure you can see with
the naked eye listen don't cry I haven't finished and so this father
who up to a certain point hadn't noticed that his son was growing
because he saw him every day suddenly finds that he has grown by
almost a centimeter and I don't know about you but I don't like
this no I don't like it one little bit and the worse thing for you is
that it doesn't go down well with my friend here either who as you
have seen cannot even bear to hear it said without *boom boom
boom boom* and fatguts at this point fires off a rapid burst with a
Capri Superlight hanging from his lip and with the pistol held
with the butt parallel to the ground the first to do this was John

Woo in *The Killer* boom boom boom boom elbow shoulder hip
wrist the other knee the other ankle he's a pro and he shoots him
in all his agonized joints one by one before the final shot to the
temple that not by chance is known as the *coup de grace* and the
blood spurts all over blood blood blood but what am I thinking of
am I really thinking this crap at midday holding a book by Carver
in my hand in front of the Cestia Pyramid I have to calm down I
must breathe deeply ooooooone twooooo oooooone twooooo I
have to get back in control may life carry on as normal let every
man do his duty I have to put the book back in the pannier I must
put on my helmet there you go and set off nice and slowly right
but what am I going to do where can I go I don't have any friends
there was always Paolo but I can't go to his place after years of
talking to each other only of football and politics and then I up
and start telling him my own fucking business and I'd be embarrassed what can I tell him I no longer have anyone to talk to this is
the truth these days I only have Anna and now I don't even have
Anna anymore and anyway let's make no bones about this Anna
must have gone mad she must have gone completely off her rocker
not only has she betrayed me and this is already indecent but let's
also take account of *when she told me* the moment she chose right
after the death of my father she went and told me and right in the
middle of a sinister and mysterious event that had obliged us to
flee like evacuees in the middle of the night and inexplicably
threatened us now let's leave aside the fact that it wasn't true but
while she was writing that letter we thought we were in grave danger and therefore we *were* in grave danger and what does she do
when I heroically return to Rome to face the unknown she slips
this time bomb into my pocket she had waited for lord knows how
long she had let pass lord knows how many moments in which I
would have been better able to take the blow and in the worst
period of my whole life when if anything I could have used a
strong hand to cling to she brought the blow crashing down *blam*
like those wretched women who give their fiancés the push when
they're away on military service or as happened to me when I was

in military college Ilaria Ortoni her name was may God damn her and this was not like Anna as for that matter betraying me was not like Anna and in short now Anna is no longer Anna and this is the really terrible thing I no longer know the woman I married and so my marriage is dead it's dead it's dead distress lawyers movers tea chests that's all the future holds and now I am calm now I am no longer thinking of killing anyone and I wish to stress that I am not even going to scream fuck off at this sonofabitch who is squeezing me up against the guard rail with his clapped out Panda and he looks like my brother-in-law shit he's identical I would like to point out that I am not getting upset I slow down a bit and let him through on your way and may the Lord be with you I am extremely calm but in this state of calm I can have nothing to do with this Anna of the letter I cannot even manage to conceive of it because she is not the Anna I love she's a woman I don't know and I don't love a woman I don't know I don't love a woman who gives blow jobs to her old flames if she has done it she can do it again if I forgive her I'll have to forgive her again and again and again every day I'll have to forgive her continuously and I don't want to live like that and what's this taxi up to is it slowing down or is it not slowing down *it's not slowing down* but it's coming from the left I say he's crazy he's not slowing down he's not so much as hinting at giving way he's got people on board too and so I'm going to smack right into him fuck or he's going to smack right into me and the fact is we're going to crash fuck we're going to crash even with the brakes full on the rear wheel has locked the Vespa begins to slide broadside on but the momentum is still driving it on there's nothing to be done about it now we're going to crash I'm going to hit him yes we're crashing luckily I put the helmet back on *crash badaboom* this would be the sound I've just had an accident I've hit him full on I have staved in his door the window has shattered I am falling to the ground I have fallen to the ground I am alive I was right I was coming from the right Anna has betrayed me that's all I know.

ook where we are . . .
   When Franceschino was one year old, in the mornings I used to go to the newsstand in San Saba to buy
the papers. One morning I noticed that from here (that is to say
not from that exact point, in other words not from the center of
the junction where I was lying, certainly injured, after the knock I
had taken, but alert, conscious, and so far without any pain, but
from the steps, that's it, exactly from there, near the colonnade in
white stone from where two people were coming, presumably to
help me) you could see the terrace of my house. It was pretty far
away, the Ardeatine walls are in the middle, as well as tall trees full
of leaves and several ranks of buildings, but you could see it. It
was late spring, we had just put up the wire netting on the parapet
of the terrace because Franceschino was learning to walk, and I
could see the green of the netting, through which you could make
out Anna dressed in white. When I got back home it took me a bit

to reverse the field of what I had seen, but thanks to the little stone colonnade I managed to pinpoint the exact spot from where I had seen our terrace, and I showed it to Anna. So, from the morning after that, when I went out to the newsstand she would stand on the terrace with Franceschino in her arms and, once I got to the colonnade, I would wave the newspapers in greeting. Anna would see me, wave back, and we were happy. I cannot even say just how happy we were, or at least—okay, let's go easy about this—*how happy I was*: all I know is that I had never imagined that you could be so happy, so intensely happy, about a trifling matter like waving to each other from a distance. I was so happy that I remember very well, one of those mornings, being struck by an extremely simple and sad thought, as devastating as a storm in a rose garden: one day, I thought, things will not be like this any longer. One day, I thought, these mornings and this happiness will seem remote and unrepeatable to me, and I shall be moved on remembering them. I thought of the possible causes of this happening, the result being a series of grim and relentless, albeit entirely natural predictions: Franceschino would grow up, we would move, grow old, we would have problems at work, economic problems, our love would fade, our parents would die . . . On thinking all this I made a solemn commitment not to lose heart when the day came, but rather to brandish the memory of that morning as if it were a sword, and to face uncomplaining whatever adversity destiny held in store for me, strong in the knowledge that all the evil in the world could never have taken from me one drop of the happiness I was feeling in that moment. I knew it wouldn't have worked—*Only loving, only knowing / counts, not having loved / not having known*—but at least it served, at the time, to save my happiness from the thought that threatened to sweep it away before its time. Now that time had come, and it had come there of all places—talk about coincidences—right in the point in the world where, seven years before, I had foreseen it.

Fade to:

Metallic sounds. Smell of gasoline. Glass crunching underfoot.

A strange oblique shot of treetops-rooftops-sky, as if a video camera had fallen to the ground without switching itself off. The outlines of things, although askew, were crisp, gleaming, cut out by an extremely pure light. It was a very fine image. But immediately a man's face covered everything: a square face, dark, literally riddled with pimples. He stared at me, opened his lips, revealed his teeth—ugly, small, uneven: it wasn't a smile.

"Can you see me?" he breathed in my face. "Can you hear me? How many are these?"

I presumed he meant the fingers he was waving in front of my eyes. One, two, three . . .

"Four," I replied.

"Good boy. Now don't move . . ."

I was lying on one side, with my head resting on my arm, my body outstretched, abandoned to the heat of the pavement, and I didn't have the slightest intention of moving.

"Can you breathe okay?"

"Yes. I'm all right."

Heads coming and going behind the pimply face. Jeans. And voices, growing and blending into one another and coming nearer and fading away, while everything started getting faster, convulsive.

" . . . *call an ambulance* . . ."

" . . . *move it a bit farther away* . . ."

" . . . *don't touch anything* . . ."

" . . . *it might explode* . . ."

" . . . *don't talk shit* . . ."

"Stand back!" yelled the Pimple King. Then to me once more: "Don't worry. Breathe easy. Don't move."

He was wearing a ridiculous sky-blue jacket. Where the devil was he off to, dressed like that?

"His leg! Don't touch his leg!"

Who had spoken? What leg? I moved both of them, first one then the other, and they seemed all right to me. In fact, they were all right, I couldn't feel the slightest pain.

"Keep still. Don't move . . ."

"I was checking my legs," I said. "There's nothing wrong with them."

"Sure. Don't move now."

" . . . *jeez, every day an accident . . .*"

" . . . *good heavens, the poor thing . . .*"

" . . . *should put in a traffic light, they should . . .*"

" . . . *didn't even brake . . .*"

" . . . *at least if they'd put up a Stop sign . . .*"

" . . . *He's taken a knock on the head!*"

My head? I went to touch my head with one hand but—aaaargh! A stabbing pain lanced through my shoulder, taking my breath away, and sending me slumping back down.

The pain vanished immediately, thank heaven.

"Don't move," repeated the face.

My shoulder, yes. I'd hurt my left shoulder. It was entirely logical, moreover: I had caved in a taxi door. I took a sidelong look at it: no blood, no torn jacket . . .

"*Stop the cars . . .*"

"*Let them pass . . .*"

"*Stay back . . .*"

"*Move forward . . .*"

"*Let's get him out of there . . .*"

"*Don't touch him . . .*"

I stayed down, motionless, because the pain I had just felt was really atrocious, and I didn't fancy feeling it again. I closed my eyes. Once we had done it the other way around: Anna went to get the papers and the hot pizza, and I stayed on the terrace holding Francesco in my arms. We waved to each other. It was really beautiful.

"Hey, can you hear me? Try to stay awake."

I immediately reopened my eyes, The pimples were still here, a few centimeters from my face.

"I'm wide awake," I said.

I managed to touch my face, maneuvering in an unnatural way

the arm that was beneath my head and being very careful not to move the other one. My face seemed all right too. My head didn't hurt, and I still had the helmet on . . .

"Don't move," again.

"Look, I'm all right," I replied. "I must have broken my shoulder. My legs and my head are all right . . ."

He looked at me, puzzled, and didn't say anything. He was doing something with his hands, beyond my field of vision, toward the right, heaven knows what he was doing.

" . . . *didn't even see him* . . ."

" . . . *banged his head* . . ."

". . . *broken his legs* . . ."

"Got that?" I said. "You tell them that. Only my shoulder . . ."

"Yes, but don't you move."

And he stayed there breathing in my face, in his ridiculous sky-blue coat. Who the devil was he? Why was he above me telling me what to do and why the Greek chorus putting a hex on me in the background? I rolled my eyes as much as I could, and my neck a bit too, to see that sky again, those outlines, that light, but his face blocked my view.

"Excuse me, are you a doctor?" I asked.

Nothing, he had vanished. Another man was in his place, now, an older man, with a pale, anxious face, and owl eyes.

"No, I'm the cabbie . . ."

Ah, the *culprit*. He was breathing wheezily, I could see his belly rising and falling a few centimeters from my eyes. He must have been on his knees. He was looking at me with compassion, the poor man. He was upset, and you could see he was ashamed of what he had done. All this mess, he must have been thinking, and it's all my fault. I was struck by an absurd idea: what if it was the taxi that that woman had taken, Cuba 22? What if she were around here somewhere, dazed, and hadn't yet realized that the injured man was me? What if she had found out at that very moment, and in a second or two she would be bent over me, with her scent of the sea, and what if she started weeping and embracing me again, whispering "poor thing" to me as she accompanied me to the hospital?

No, it was impossible. Too much time had gone past. And then again these things don't happen, they don't happen, they don't happen. The cabbie continued to watch over me, with a distraught expression and breathing heavily. He must have been afraid he was in big trouble.

"You know, sometimes . . ." But what did I want to say to him? "You think . . ."

Did I want to console him? I, him?

"Take it easy now, don't you move yourself," him too. "The ambulance is coming now . . ."

" . . . smashed in the window . . ."

". . . he's not moving . . ."

". . . sure he's moving . . ."

" . . . in a bad way . . ."

"Don't listen to them," I whispered. "They're exaggerating. I've only broken my shoulder. If there's blood on my face it's because I cut myself shaving. Is there blood on my face?"

"No."

He must have been a good man, really. He must have been someone's best friend. He must have built himself a house out in the sticks near Nuovo Salario, with a mortgage, which he would pay off by 2010. That's what he must have been thinking of, when he went through the junction: of the future . . .

"Blessed boy," he said, "didn't you see the sign, then?"

"What sign?"

"The one that says to yield," and he pointed to the right.

What what what? Yield sign, what yield sign? I sat up and tried to turn but there was no way, the stab of pain dumped me on the canvas again.

"Stay down . . ."

"What yield sign?"

". . . jeez, every day a car wreck . . ."

". . . you can't see it, can't do sweet fuck all about that . . ."

"... *it's the leaves, y'see?* ..."

"... *how many times have we written to the Town Hall about this business* ..."

What can't you see? What leaves? What business?

I hauled myself up, and to hell with the pain; I did it slowly, gently, even creeping along the tarmac like a snake in order to turn myself around without my shoulder noticing—but it noticed all right—then I hoist myself up on my good elbow and found an acceptable position, a bit languid perhaps, but solid, and above all painless—only a strange form of pins and needles, now, and a wave of heat—which allowed me to keep my gaze parallel to the ground. Finally I could orient it in the direction in which the cabbie had pointed.

"*Don't get up, behave now* ..."

I saw it right away. On the pavement, just before the junction, along the road I had been traveling on, perched on the top of its nice gray iron pole and effectively half hidden by the leaves of a sycamore tree that hung down right in front of it, there was ...

"*Lie down* ..."

... the red and white triangle, shit, the yield sign. I was coming from the right, yet I had to yield to him. It was absurd, I had been passing by there for years and I had never seen it, and then again there wasn't the slightest logical reason, there, to turn the rules on their heads in that way: the two roads are equivalent to each other, and in fact the one I was on is undeniably more ...

"*D'you want a sip of water?*"

An arm, a hand, a glass of water. A new face, fat, ruddy, a great big enormous, monumental face, the face of Falstaff.

"*Drink* ..."

My mouth was dry, in fact, I was thirsty. I stretched out my neck, gingerly, while Falstaff's hand came toward me with the glass.

"*Stop! What are you doing?*" the voice of the Pimple King.

The glass moved away abruptly.

"*Don't give him anything! Don't touch him!*"

The glass had vanished, and Falstaff with it. Before my eyes now only shins, jeans, cell phones attached to belts, sweaty bellies.

"*He was thirsty, he wanted a drink . . .*"

No, vile ball of lard, that is false: I didn't want anything. And I didn't even know I was thirsty, until I saw the water. *Then*, I got thirsty . . .

"*Didn't you see the television, only yesterday?*"

"*What about it?*"

"*They said so on TV: never move an injured person, never give any substances before the ambulance arrives . . .*"

"*A drop of water can't do much harm . . .*"

Sheesh. What a crummy bunch of rescuers. And what a crummy injured person, too. How embarrassing, how immensely embarrassing to be here, in the middle of a junction in this Pompeyan pose, nailed to the pavement by a javelin through the shoulder, after having bumped into a taxi *and it was my fault*. How everything changes, damn it, when you shift from being in the right to being in the wrong. I had felt so good in the part of the victim, I was already savoring the warmth of suffering undeserved, the exculpatory relief that is a mercilessly adverse fate, and the consolatory melody of the tale of the unsullied hero brought low by the world's injustice, misunderstood, betrayed in his sentiments and then seriously wounded in his body, a tale to be told to me once more after many years—a tale I hadn't told myself since the days of my adolescence. But it was my fault, and that made everything different, because if I wasn't the victim then I was only the latest jerk who didn't see the yield sign and crashed into the car that had right of way. How embarrassing, really. I wasn't anything anymore; I was worth no more than those marks left on the cement of garage ramps, where if you are going even a fraction too fast by the bottom of the slope the license plate scrapes along the ground, *dreng*, and gets twisted, and the bored doorkeeper looks up from the sports pages and mutters, "*And the next one, pleeease . . .*"

The siren. The Seventh Cavalry was on its way. By that time I could see better, from an angle that was more normal, if not much else, only very low, as if I were, let's say, a puppy: there was rather a lot of people, and all around the junction a swastika of traffic had already formed; yelling, horns blowing, dashing about, make way, the siren louder and louder; there was Falstaff, there was the Pimple King—a *barber?*—there was the blameless cabbie. A youth, sitting on a scooter, helmet on, was watching the scene; he was sitting a little to one side, detached from all that frenzied activity: he had been passing by, he had stopped, filled his eyes with this chaos, and when he went home he would tell the whole story to his woman: "I saw an accident today . . ." Oh, why couldn't I be him? I could have been him, had I not been on the ground, if I had been a bit younger, if I had not left the scooter with the engine running when I went to get my book back and if I had taken—not a lot, ten seconds let's say—to get her started again, and especially if I still had—ah—a woman to tell things to . . .

Before falling silent the siren emitted a last sound at an unbearable volume, almost a threat— "I'll deafen the lot of you, boys, if you don't behave!" The stretcher on wheels arrived, pushed by a lanky character. *Click-clack,* the stretcher was lowered, brought up alongside me, almost scraping me off the ground, as if I were a bit of flattened chewing gum. As they transferred me onto the stretcher, the javelin impaled in my shoulder moved, sending an angry thrill through my flesh, and the pain took my breath away— lord knows how much more I was going to feel still, as bad as that or even worse, lord knows for how long . . .

Click-clack, the stretcher was raised. Here we go, they were taking me away. The only thing they had done was to take off my helmet: they hadn't strapped me in like Anita's son—there was no reason to do that—they hadn't put a surgical collar on me like they do in American films, and they hadn't even checked to see what was wrong with me, nor had they used the slightest caution; they simply picked me up and took me away, and let this be said to the shame not of the paramedics but of that pimply barber who had not let me drink so much as a glass of water. They rested the stretcher on the lip of the yawning mouth of the ambulance: a few seconds to align it with I don't know what, to slot I don't know what into I don't know what, then they pushed me inside, and the stretcher-bearer's paws vanished, and I slipped almost without resistance into the belly of that fish that had never swallowed me before then, because that was the first time I had been in an ambulance, I am a lucky man . . .

A click, the lanky guy landed beside me, the doors closed, the siren began to wail again—it wasn't so loud, from inside—and we were off, but to what hospital the lord only knows. The tingling in my shoulder became stronger: it was as if after every twinge it had grown entropically without ever diminishing, but if I didn't move there was no pain. Yet there was pain, lots of it, I was literally drowning in a well of pain, and shame, and fear. For there are terrible truths written only on the ceilings of ambulances, and you can see them only if you find yourself lying beneath one, one Tuesday morning, around noon, while they are taking you to the hospital with a broken shoulder and a letter from your wife in your jacket pocket, and outside the sun is shining, and everyone is better off than you are . . .

twenty

I am the man, it was written, who, every day for ten years, crossed a junction near his home and did not see that there was a yield sign. I am the man who, in those ten years, on at least three occasions had seen them pruning the trees whose foliage covers the sign, and who, every time, had reflected at length on how little it takes, after all, to make a familiar panorama seem unfamiliar, and all the while continuing not to see that sign. And I am the father who regularly enters that junction without stopping, together with his son, in the car and sometimes even on the scooter, clutching the boy tightly between his legs after having put on his nonstandard helmet bought in the market at Porta Portese, convinced he could protect him like no one else in the world could possibly do. That man is me. But I am also the son who did not get on with his father, the fault being naturally the father's, and who has never really asked himself who his father really was. I am the husband who strove not to betray his wife, as if that were the only thing that could happen to his marriage, and did not realize that his wife was betraying him. I am the brother who criticized his sister, his sister's political ideas, his sister's friends, his sister's boyfriends, his sister's husband, a brother who was convinced that he was always right, and who now lives a life not that different from his sister's. I am the uncle of three little nephews who are in awe of him. I am the man who always tells the same stories at dinner parties. I am the man who does not improve his house even though he has the money to do so. I am the man who looks for a policeman when he sees a pistol, the man who gives away checks without endorsing them. I am the man who stops smoking and then starts again. I am the chess player who promises marvels and then stops playing because he cannot bear losing. I am the man with the formidable memory who is losing his memory. I am the writer of children's books who steals ideas right and left, and who maintains that he doesn't want to be any more than that, but who lies, because he certainly does . . .

Oh, how much clearer everything is, like this; how much simpler. How satisfying truth is, how bright and ineluctable, when you do not perceive it against your will, in fits and starts, between one attempt to suppress it and the next, and accept it in its entirety. What relief, now, together with the shame; but how different that moment was, how much more gloomy and bleak it was compared to the one I wanted to find myself living again, sooner or later, so that I might take it from there with a new life, a real life: I had thought it would be joyous, full of people and light, like the end of *Eight and a Half*, but . . .

Yes, because I am the man who thought he could learn things from cinema. I have also stated this in public, in a radio interview, not that long ago either: "The cinema has taught me to live," would you believe, or something like that. So, I am the man who in order to be ashamed of having come out with a piece of crap like that has to crash into a taxi, hurt himself, and get carried off on a stretcher.

"How's it going?" said the lanky guy. He was a ghostly silhouette in the half light, looming over me like a vulture.

"Sometimes better than others," I replied, being the man who learns lines from films by heart, and then says them, or resells them in the books he writes, or both, and then one day suddenly forgets them and no longer knows what to write. (This was Paul Newman's line in *The Drowning Pool*: when will I forget that?)

"Does your eye hurt?"

"Which eye?"

He touched my left eye, with a delicacy that, by looking at him, you wouldn't have thought him capable of. (I am the man who judges whether people are capable or not of doing things just by looking at them.)

"This one. The eyeball is bloodshot."

The eyeball is bloodshot . . .

"I don't feel anything," I said.

"A fragment of glass must have gotten in," he said.

Right. Or the famous beam from the Gospels: "*Hypocrite, why beholdest thou the mote that is in thy brother's eye, but considerest not the beam that is in thine own eye?*"

"Try to close the other one."

I obeyed, but I had to help myself with my hand, because otherwise I couldn't manage. I could still see normally, while he was waggling two fingers in front of my face.

"How many are there?"

"Two."

He opened his hand completely, fingers spread out.

"Now?"

"Five."

He closed his fist.

"Now?"

"None."

Come on, keep going, chum: I am the man who always wins at this game, and there are few things in the world as pleasurable as winning without having to struggle . . .

But it was no go, he gave up. He got up again, ran a hand through his hair, looked at the driver, on the other side of the glass partition. The next time I was going to have to remember to make a deliberate mistake, to make the game go on a bit longer.

The siren suddenly fell silent.

"We're here," he said.

The ambulance slowed down, made a right turn, and proceeded slowly for a few seconds, then stopped. The doors were thrown open, and then it was all a series of maneuvers and sounds and horizontal surfaces slipping away above me: the ceiling of the ambulance, the roof of a porch, the ceiling of the emergency room, the filthy ceiling of a corridor. The lanky guy had disappeared, now I was in the hands of a squat, hirsute porter, whose clogs shuffled noisily over the floor. The faces filed past: Africans, old people, cops, until the porter slipped me into an austere room, transferred me onto a cot with no wheels (atrocious pain, during the maneuver), and told me to wait. Through the walls filtered strange sounds, knocking, arguments, even shouting: "Let us get on with our work!" "It's scandalous!" stuff like that, but I couldn't manage to understand what was going on. The porter went off pushing the stretcher with wheels. I was left alone.

I didn't know where I was. I don't know the hospitals, except for the Policlinico Gemelli, where my father died. But this wasn't the Policlinico Gemelli: it was far more run-down, dirty, abandoned. It seemed like a wartime hospital. The shouting from the other side of the wall grew fainter, as if the argument were moving away. I found a position that let me feel less pain, on my good side, with my head leaning against my arm, like the position I had adopted on the pavement a short time before, and I was strangely calm. Whatever the seriousness of my injuries was, I felt that my body had already gotten used to them: it swelled where it had to swell, tingled where it had to tingle, hurt where it had to hurt, without rebelling against this new condition, and the same thing seemed to have happened to my mind as well. Had I had an accident and had I hurt myself? Was my scooter lying crumpled in the middle of a junction in a lake of gasoline? Had they dumped me here, I didn't know where, and forgotten about me right away? Was my father dead? Had my wife betrayed me? I felt all these questions congeal around a single conclusive thought, picked out by a gelid subcortical intelligence with the precision of a record stuck in a groove: there's nothing I can do about it. There's nothing I can do about it, no, there's nothing I can do about it. And that was that.

I don't know how much time I spent like that, immobilized on this dead-end track: in reality it was as if time were not passing, or in any event was not passing *for me*, and this was not making me suffer, and that is all I know. Exclude a man from the flow of time and his troubles will cease.

Finally something happened: suddenly, the whole wall began to slide to one side, as if we were in the theater—and so this is *Endgame*, and I am Hamm, excluded from the flow of time. Silhouetted against the dazzling void that had opened up (surprise: that little room gave directly onto the outside) there appeared an outline I had come to know well by then, but one that still surprised me—as always, for that matter: it surprised me all right, but I was also glad to see it, because it was the silhouette of the person that loved me most in all the world "apart from my closest relatives" . . .

"Ah, here you are," he said.

He closed the sliding wall again, then he came up and looked at me with a worried expression—even though he was smiling, as usual.

"What on earth have you been up to?"

"How . . . ," I stammered, "How did you know that . . ."

"What have you done to yourself?"

"My shoulder. I must have broken it."

He looked at my shoulder, then all of my body, then at my shoulder again, as if making some inscrutable comparison.

"And my eye," I added, "apparently I have a bloodshot eyeball . . ."

He stooped over me, and examined my eye.

"Hmmm. Can you see out of it?"

"Yes, I can."

He took a step back and went back to contemplating me as a whole.

"Your shoulder, you say?"

"Yes. But how did you know . . ."

"Legs and head all right? Did you bang your head?"

"No."

I raised both my legs, to make my point, and I managed to move them, but it wasn't a good idea, because a stabbing pain took me in the shoulder.

"Sure?"

"Yes. I caved in a taxi door with my shoulder. When I fell to the ground I was practically at a standstill, and I had my helmet on. But are you going to tell me how you came to know that I was . . ."

"I'll explain later," he interrupted me. "There's no time now. We have to get out of here, and in a hurry too. Can you walk?"

"I don't know. Why do we have to get out of here?"

"Because they're quarantining the hospital."

"What?"

He smiled, exhaled through his nose, looked down. He had dropped his usual bombshell, but if anything, this time he seemed aware of it.

"Outside there," he explained, "it's swarming with cars full of Carabinieri and armed police from the inland revenue. They are serving the hospital a sequestration order. By order of the Ministry of Health. I wasn't able to get the details, but it's happening *now*. If you stay inside here you're in the shit. How long have you been here?"

"I don't know. Half an hour, an hour."

"Has someone already examined you?"

"No."

"Have they admitted you? Did you give your particulars, stuff like that?"

"No."

He chuckled.

"They just dumped you in here and that's that . . ."

He closed his eyes, shook his head.

"Well, so much the better," he opined. "Come on, let's hightail it out of here."

"Hightail it": there's an expression my father used all the time.

"And where shall we go?"

"We'll see," he replied. "Can you get up?"

"We'll see," I replied.

I began a laborious hoisting maneuver, and he came nearer again, with his big hands ready to grasp me, but I shook my head in sign that I wanted to try to make it on my own. I slowly heaved myself into a sitting position, and the pain in my shoulder came instantly back to life. In addition, my chest hurt, in the vicinity of my heart, and my head was spinning. My feet were dangling in the air—that cot was high—and I gingerly eased myself down until they touched the ground. Bogliasco continued to follow me with his hands ready to intervene, but without touching me, the way you do with children who are learning to walk.

"Can you manage?" he asked.

I gave a trace of a nod, to save my breath, because talking hurt too, even breathing. Very slowly I drew myself up into an erect position, leaning on him with my good arm. I tried to take a step, then another, but it was as if a power press was crushing my injured shoulder, and the pain was overwhelming. I felt my temples pulsing stronger and stronger, and a wave of scalding heat came rushing down from my head, or rushing up, I'm not very sure, while my vision grew cloudy.

"Catch me," I murmured, and, in the very moment in which I let myself go, a force swung me up, as if I were a bag of wood shavings, a pillow, a sheaf of grain; as if I really were the small thing I felt I was. A second later I was a meter above the ground, with my legs dangling, my good arm around his solid neck and my face crushed against his chest.

"Hey, what's all this, fainting?"

Right, good question: Was I going to faint? At that precise moment it was impossible to say. At that precise moment I was simply suspended in a strange, amniotic hiatus, and anything could have happened, I mean really anything, as I savored once more the completely forgotten bliss of being picked up, and what little sentience I still possessed became as one with the rugged and grandiose mass of the angel who was doing so. With my nose crushed into his jacket I collected all the odors with which it was impregnated—an old, proletarian smell, that blend of smoke, sweat, and inert matter you notice on laborers when they take coffee at the bar, with my ear to his chest I gave myself over to the beating of his heart, hypnotic, robust, regular, and deeper down I could again make out the whistle that was grinding away at his lungs, like the sound of a·key scraping along the bodywork of a car; his big warm belly, expanding and contracting with the piston of his breathing, lulled me with its utterly sweet pneumatic oscillation, and sent my cares drifting away . . .

Then it was as if everything were happening again, but in reverse, and for an amazing, extraordinary moment I noticed that my body possessed a marvelous feeling of reversibility—that reversibility that reality strictly refuses to permit, but in my case, then, suspended as I was in midair in those friendly arms, it was as if it had managed to steal over my body on the sly, the pain eased, my temples stopped pulsing, the heat cooled, the fog thinned . . . This moment would also pass, I knew, I understood, and I would faint or I would not, after which time would start to run in the usual direction once more and I would either struggle against it, or resign myself to its monstrous tyranny, or both; but as long as it lasted I could see what would happen if that moment were not to pass at all, if it were to last and last and last, indefinitely, and I continued to enjoy the gift of living in reverse all the things that had brought me to that point, in an electrifying backward flight in which before finally prevailed over after, and effects were mauled by causes: and so I am returning to the floor again, my legs unsteady, and I sit back down on the cot, and I stretch out on it, slowly, so that it will not hurt, and there's the wall reopening and then closing again, and when it closes again the man is no longer there, and I am alone in my timeless bubble again, then on the stretcher watching ceilings flying past, then inside the ambulance recognizing myself for what I am, then lying on the ground in the middle of the junction realizing that it was my fault, then in the tremendous instant of the collision, powerless and bloated with adrenaline, consoled only by the fact that it wasn't my fault, and my shoulder is all right again and my eyeball is no longer bloodshot and I am riding the scooter, hale, healthy, albeit flayed by the pain of betrayal and appalled by the thought of my marriage falling apart, and there's the moment in which that pang stabs me in the guts, oh, the worst of all, reading Anna's letter and embracing that weeping woman, but now that pain is passing, it really is, for a moment it turns into a fleeting suspicion and then it disappears altogether, giving way to the embarrassment of a check to be endorsed, to the pleasure of a therapeutic caress, to surprise at a mother's beauty, and now my distress is a trifling thing, it is merely a question of a slight lateness and scooters that won't start and neighbors lashed to stretchers and insomnia and cigarettes furtively smoked, and the marriage in rack and ruin is only that of a fellow tenant, and I almost feel ashamed at feeling bad about these trifles, everybody is worse off than me, but now the uneasiness is growing again, and I am in my living room, it is evening, and my disquiet is growing in the presence of the stubbornness with which I am told repeatedly that my father was a Russian, he was a spy on a mission and he had always pretended, and it is growing because I believe it, and my memory is protecting me no longer, not enough, but then finally it protects me, and already I believe it less, barely at all, and I am in the restaurant, and I am reciting Pasolini from memory for all my fellow diners, and this story about my father disturbs me, perhaps, irritates me, but I don't believe it at all, and then it doesn't even bother me at all, it arouses my curiosity, it surprises me, at most it amuses me because it is so ridiculous, and then it vanishes away, that's that, it doesn't

exist anymore, it has never existed, there is only a flash of fear
now, and a flight, and another stronger fear, more unexpected,
never felt before, but then that vanishes too and I am standing in
front of an applauding crowd, and I give fifteen million lire to a
woman and then someone gives it to me, and I am on a train, I am
at home, I am embracing Anna, I am at my father's funeral, I am
at his deathbed, and my father dies, goes into a coma, gets worse,
seems to recover, awakes, undergoes an emergency operation, is
rushed to hospital, loses consciousness, my mother telephones me
in tears, my father feels ill, and then he feels well, there he is sound
as a bell, and my mother is laughing, and I am at dinner in their
house, I am in the car, I am seated at my desk and I cannot write, I
am signing a contract for another book, the book sells very well,
the book comes out, there I am delivering it, I have finished it, I am
about to finish it, I am seated at my desk and I am writing it, it
is summer, Anna is at the seaside with Franceschino, we call
each other every day and we love each other, and I am full of ideas
and I begin to write a new book, and we celebrate with sparkling
wine, and the first book is published, and I am dashing it off, and I
get the idea to write it, and then I don't have the idea anymore,
and all I am doing is telling Franceschino the adventures of
Pizzano Pizza, just like that, making them up, to amuse him, seeing that he has begun to want things, to understand, to talk, to
walk, and I am in the street, at that junction, leaning against that
colonnade, and I wave to Anna, who waves back from the terrace,
and I am happy, and away and away and away, faster and faster,
Franceschino is born, I get married, I leave university, I start going
with Anna, I fall in love with Anna, I meet Anna, I stop playing
chess, I argue and argue and argue with my father, and I am
stronger and stronger and lighter and lighter, and I can see farther
and farther, it is marvelous, it is like a painting by Saul Steinberg,
whole epochs dismissed with one word, youth, adolescence,
infancy, away, until, lo, I am free, I am not yet born and so I am
everywhere, in every place and in every time, it is wonderful,
amazing, I am the first man in space, the first computer, the first

nylon fiber, I am consumerism, black and white television, the Cuban Revolution, the Cold War, the Berlin Wall, the Teddy Boys, I am Fred Astaire dancing, Gandhi fasting, Charlie Parker mainlining, Man O'War outstripping them all, I am the Bay of New York as the *Andrea Doria* slides down into the depths, Superga as the plane carrying the great Turin soccer team of the fifties crashes into it, Nuremberg during the trials, the Tyrrhenian Sea before the eruption of Vesuvius—I am the Siberian steppes in '45, and the war has just ended, and it is dawn on an ordinary day, leaden, frozen, and I am spread all over that immensity, in the wind, in the ice, in the bare birches, and now I know whether it is true or not that my father is blowing my father's brains out, in this precise moment, point blank, to take his place as officer, Italian, and father.

twenty-one

Aaaooooooooooowwww . . .

The woman had started howling again. They had brought her in ten minutes before, anaesthetized and intubated, and shortly afterward she had begun to howl in her sleep: plaintive yowling, animal yelping, as if possessed by the devil. And yet no one was concerned about this, neither the nurse who came and went, and who every so often would stop to see how I was doing, nor her colleague, who spent all her time sitting doing nothing behind a little desk in the back of the room.

The Recovery Room, it was called. It was pervaded by a kind of background murmur, when the woman wasn't howling, as of fans whirring around, machines functioning, stuff that is considered to be silent but isn't.

Aaaooooooooooooowwww . . .

"Excuse me," I said to the nurse who was coming and going,

as she was coming. She stopped. I suspected she might be pretty, but I hadn't yet managed to verify this, because she didn't smile.

"Yes?"

She was tall, slim, flat-chested, with a smooth, girlish face, and she never smiled. Not that she was rude, or unpleasant: quite the opposite, she was kind, professional. Only she didn't smile.

"Is it normal for that lady to howl like that?" I asked.

The nurse did not smile.

"Yes, it's normal," she said.

She had light blue eyes, small and foreign. From the accent she seemed Polish, or Slav?

"I mean, does everyone do it? Did I do it too?" I asked.

The nurse took a couple of steps and came up close to me. She wore a sweet expression, but she did not smile.

"No. You were quiet as a mouse."

Then, while she was at it, she noted down a few things on her sheets of paper. She looked at the bottles hanging from the stands next to my bed, checked the taps of the drips, and wrote again. She was left-handed.

"And is it normal to be quiet as a mouse?" I asked.

She didn't smile this time either.

"Yes," she said, "that's normal too."

A howl echoed around the room once more.

The nurse looked at me. She was well aware that a smile would be the right thing, given the situation, and it really seemed as if she was forcing herself to suppress one. She must have had ugly teeth.

"She is sedated," she explained, "she's dreaming."

And off she went.

But I hadn't dreamed, I was sure of that. I had never had a general anesthetic before, and I must say it was fantastic. It's fantastic that the decisive thing happens when you are asleep, but it's very nice afterward too, the slow peaceful return to life that takes place in this room, and it matters little if it is an artificial, chemically induced peace. I had been awake for almost an hour, by then, and I felt fine, no getting away from that. My head was completely clear and I felt no pain, nor discomfort, only a great hunger—but even hunger is strangely beautiful, when experienced here, it feels like the hunger you felt as a child. Earlier, I had asked the nurse how long I was going to have to stay inside this whale's belly, and she said "not long." But I had asked out of curiosity: I wasn't in a hurry to leave.

Aaaaoooooooooowww . . .

The fact is that my head had been clear right from the start, as soon as I opened my eyes, and a really fascinating thing had happened, something that I had been thinking about ever since. I'm not sure if the nurse would define this as normal too, but I had *witnessed*, so to speak, my return to myself: I really felt memory slip over me, in distinct blocks, from the somewhere else in which the anesthetic had parked it. It was very different from waking up normally in the morning, when you open your eyes and, *wham*, what you are plunges back down on you in a split second: it was a far slower and more gradual process, like when you reboot a computer and it starts to load all the things it needs in order to work—programs, information, memory—fishing them out from the hard disk in a certain order. It was equivalent to perceiving your own awareness of yourself not as a whole—a granitic, cumbersome whole—but as a concatenation of many separate awarenesses. It was like watching moving men putting all your things back in their place, that's it, one after another in the house where you have always lived and that you had to leave for a certain time: in the end everything is the way it was before, but the operation that makes this possible requires a certain time, and during that time you notice for the first time the difference there is between the wall and the bookshelf that usually stands against it.

The beginning had been surprising: a feeling of nudity. I simply realized that I was naked under that green smock; and the first fragment of the past that reached me was the memory of having kept my underpants on, under the smock, when I had put it on; and therefore the first inference that I made was: someone had removed them. This was the beginning, even before I recalled my

name or how it was that I had ended up there, even before I saw
the bandaging that immobilized my shoulder and arm or noticed
the dressing that covered my left eye—before everything else; and
for a long unprecedented moment I was only that elementary
form of life: feeling of nudity, memory of underpants left on,
realization of underpants removed.

Immediately after that came my sorrows, in procession: Anna
had betrayed me. My father was dead. I had had an accident. I
was in a bad way. They had operated on me, etcetera. They came,
they went to take their place in the first row, but they did not
bring with them any unhappiness, any pain—and I really think
that this was thanks to the drugs, and to the artificial sleep. There
was not the slightest trace of the anguish of certain desperate
past awakenings, the memory of which arrived immediately afterward—perhaps precisely because I could appreciate the difference: awakening after Juventus had lost the European Cup Final
against Ajax; awakening after Ilaria Ortoni had left me; awakening after the terrible defeat at the hands of Tavella in the Lugano
chess tournament; awakening after the death of my father . . .

Only at that point did the so-called facts arrive, along with the
first images. Anna: her brown face, radiant; the fact that she was
my wife; the certainty that I loved her. Franceschino: the happiness of having a son; his pale, oblong face, which looks like mine.
And my mother: her green eyes ever ready to be moved; her legendary resemblance to Sophia Loren; her frail limbs in my
embrace. And my father: his aloofness, his severity, my incapacity
to get along with him even as an adult; his body in full dress uniform, also aloof, inside the open coffin surrounded by wreaths
of flowers; the amazing news that none of it was true, that he was
a Russian, that he was a communist, that he was a spy on a
mission . . .

Then, gradually, all the rest arrived, still in sequence, until it
made me the conscious and hungry Gianni Orzan that I was then.
This took, I'm not sure, maybe a quarter of an hour, but before I
had finished rebooting my destiny—because that's what was going

on, after all—I had already begun to live it once more, and to think about it, like Pinocchio, who began to run away even before he was finished. And so, more even than the suffering that Anna had caused me with that letter, more than the worry about my condition and my future, what captured me was the real novelty of this awakening, the real change compared to before: *my father was a Russian, a communist, a spy on a mission.* No doubt, no question marks. I continued recovering memories and facts that contradicted that, but this thesis suddenly found itself at the center of my life, impregnable, as if it had always been there. So the question I posed myself was: when did I start believing it? *How* did this happen? And my thoughts returned to just before the white gash of the anesthesia, to those last hours spent together with Gianni Bogliasco and to the violent familiarity that ensued, from when he had gotten me out of the hospital under sequestration to the point when his face had been erased by the door of the operating theater, in this clinic where *he* had brought me, putting me in the hands of doctors *he* knew—and for whom his name was Gianni Costante, by the way, as it was on his credit card. The answer was found there, in those hours.

For the previous evening that man had lifted me up into his arms for the second time in his life, almost thirty years after the first time, in Amsterdam, then too after an accident, and he had deposited me inside his smelly jeep, triple-parked, and then he had transported me to this clinic on the other side of Rome, and on the way he had stopped at the junction where I had had the accident, and he got out, picked up my Vespa lying abandoned on the pavement, and charitably chained it to a lamppost, recovered the keys, the documents, the helmet, even Carver's book from inside the mangled pannier, and he had stayed at my side as the specialists examined me, my shoulder, and then my eye, and then my shoulder again, and he had taken the X-rays in his big paws, examining against the light the fracture of the clavicle, with probable damage to the ligaments, and the cracked ribs, discussed my situation with the doctors, telling me later of the conclusions they had come to, and that is that on the following day, I would undergo surgery on both the shoulder and the eye, a dual operation that was apparently not difficult but delicate all the same, and all at a special discount rate that he had skillfully negotiated so that the costs would have been covered by my insurance even though my insurance company had no arrangement with that clinic. And he did all that without ever asking me anything, always presenting me with a fait accompli, as if he knew how much confusion there was in my mind, and how much need I had of someone to make decisions in my stead. No one before had looked after me in such an intrusive, total fashion; and in fact I remember that, even though the moment was perhaps the blackest one of my entire life, his presence at my side conveyed a sense of security I had never felt before. So, I thought, my life has been put into the hands of a receiver like a company on the verge of bankruptcy: I could abandon myself to the flow of my time run wild, while he would forgive Anna and save my marriage, finish the book and save my bank account, see to the matter of my father's estate and, now, to that of the accident, and, one of these days, he would also find the time to make a flying visit to Austria to see the little boy in a coma, and to embrace his mother on my behalf . . .

That was how I came to believe his story: I believed in him. Night had fallen, the mad round of medical consultations had finished, we were alone in my room, and I believed in him. I was moaning, stunned by the pain and the painkillers, the borders of reality blurred into those of dream, the long hours of that hypnagogic night passed, and I believed in him. He calmed me down, told me ancient jokes, sang the praises of the orthopedic surgeon who was going to operate on me the next day, then he talked about himself, he told me that his official occupation was private investigator even though in reality he did not do that job at all, then he showed me the book he had written on rotisseries and he explained that he had been on his way to give me a copy when he had seen my wrecked scooter lying in the middle of the junction, and the barber had told him I had had an accident and that they had taken me to the hospital, and there he had seen the police affixing the sequestration order, and luckily he had found me right away, luckily I wasn't seriously injured, and luckily they hadn't seen him carrying me away unconscious. Then he would go outside for a smoke, then he would come back and, thinking I was dozing, he sat in silence on the couch rereading his book, on his nose the glasses like my father's, or stood at the window staring at goodness knows what, with his short-sleeved shirt, his heavy breathing, and the whistling in his lungs, but I wasn't sleeping and I was watching him, and at a certain point he noticed this and he asked me if there was anything he could do for me, and his figure wavered in the room, and I said yes, there was something, he could tell me the truth about the DC9 that had crashed over Ustica, seeing that he knew, and about the bomb outrages in piazza Fontana, in piazza della Loggia, and in Bologna railway station, and about the Moro case, and the murder of Pasolini, and he sat down and he told me, it was a French missile, he said, it was the Fascists, it was the secret services, Fioravanti had nothing to do with it but he deserves to be in prison all the same, it was known *perfectly well* that the Red Brigades were holding Moro in via Montalcini, whereas no one ever had any hard information about Pasolini because no one ever gave a damn; and I realized that I too had known the truth, everyone had known it, what mysteries? what invisible Italy? it's like when a magician disappears from inside a box, *there's a trapdoor*, for fuck's sake, it's so simple, even a kid can see that, but naturally the magician says that there is no trapdoor and so everyone sits there wondering how the devil he managed to disappear—*mystery*—and if anyone insists about the business of the trapdoor then he is taken for a shit. Then I dozed off, but the intense pain woke me up again, and he went off to call an orderly, who gave me an injection, and then I felt a bit better, and it was the middle of the night, by that time, and he took off his shoes, sending a fair stink of feet all through the room, and he stretched out on the couch, and fell asleep in a twinkling, a moment before he had been talking about when he had fractured his pelvis ages before and immediately after that he was snoring like a hog, and sleeping a restless sleep, gasping, his bulk barely contained by the couch, and at dawn he awoke, hoisted himself laboriously to his feet in the half light, and did his morning exercises, four—and I mean four—knee-bends on creaking, pathetic, antiquated knees, his arms out-stretched like il Duce; and more and more, in all those moments, I believed in him.

Then, in the morning, shortly before going under the knife, as the anesthesiologist was preparing to drag me off and in my eyes there lingered the image of Bogliasco's big face made ugly by a wretched gray stubble, I remember thinking something I would never have expected to think: if my father were permitted to return to this world, I thought, to tell me what he had never told me in all his life, and if he had had to choose a person in whom to be reincarnated—entirely unlike, logically, the person he had pretended to be, *another* person, a creature so far removed from him that it would show how far removed he had been from himself, at the same time, however, a difficult person, hard to accept, but good and mysterious and strong and romantic and solitary and full of the past the way every father wants to be in the eyes of a son—well, I thought, *he would have chosen Bogliasco.*

After having thought something like that, and after falling asleep right in the middle of it, there is no turning back. And that's how it went.

Aaaoooooooooooowww . . .

The nurse who didn't smile continued to ignore the howling woman, and came to me.

"Everything's normal," I said.

She didn't smile. I wonder if she was the one who had taken off my underpants.

"Well, Mr. Orzan," she said, "let's take you back to your room."

The other nurse arrived too: she was less young, more massive.

She looked like Gabriella Ferri. She attached a clinical record to my bed and set to untangling the tubes of the drip. Poker Face looked at her Swatch and started writing something on a sheet of paper.

Right, *the time* . . .

"What's the time?" I asked.

"Two."

Well, it was getting on, as they say. If instead of operating on me they had put me on a plane, I would have gotten as far as Moscow at least.

"Do you feel any pain?" the rosary had begun anew.

"No," I replied.

"None at all?"

"None."

"Your eye too? Discomfort? Tingling?"

"Nothing."

She transcribed everything onto her sheet of paper.

"Is that normal?" I asked.

This time I had the impression that she was really struggling to restrain herself, but she didn't smile. She kept her eyes fixed on the paper and continued writing.

"That's good," she said, still writing. "That's *very* good . . ."

The sedated woman had begun to moan, in the meantime, and she wasn't howling anymore. Gabriella Ferri took the brake off the casters, and my bed jerked forward. Poker Face gestured at her to wait, and she looked me right in the eye.

"Let's hope not," she said, "but should you feel severe pain later, press this button."

She pointed to a little machine attached to the bed's head-board, then to one of the bottles hanging from the stand.

"The machine will automatically release some morphine," she explained.

"Wow," I said, "Fantastic."

"Naturally," she added, "the machine will stop working after it has released a certain dose. So don't abuse it. Understood?"

"Affirmative."

No hope for it, she resisted and did not smile. The bed began to move. She made as if she were pulling it from the foot, walking backward, but you could see perfectly well that it was the other one who was making all the effort.

"Do you think I might have something to eat?" I asked her, while we slipped past the groaning woman.

"Of course," she replied, still pretending to pull the bed. "Are you very hungry?"

"Extremely."

"That's another good sign," she said, letting go of the bed in order to open the door. The bed slowed down, stopped, and when the door was wide open it moved off again, but she remained standing in the doorway.

"Bon appétit, then," she said as I slid alongside her, and all of a sudden she smiled, and her teeth were perfect, and she even had dimples in her cheeks, and she was even more beautiful than I suspected, she seemed *born* to smile, and so it must have been the management that had asked her not to smile, to avoid creating hassles with the patients, since there must have been some problems, in the past, when she smiled (mute phone calls, embarrassing tips, bunches of flowers), and that was not good for the clinic, not to mention jealous colleagues and the doctors making passes. She fell into line: she was a foreigner, a non-EU immigrant who couldn't afford problems at work, and so she had obeyed, she had buckled down with a will and she had learned to reassure patients without smiling, and now it came to her almost naturally—but someone ought to tell her that if she plays it that way, smiling in the end, treacherously, and if it is the last thing the patient sees her do as he is being wheeled away, and he is already feeling blue on his own account, because his problems are out there and no one can face them on his behalf, then it's all useless, in fact it is worse, because he will turn around, it's a mathematical certainty, or rather he will try to turn around to see her for a second longer, but because he is an invalid he can't manage to do that, and

Gabriella Ferri tells him to be a good boy, and he slumps back down, suddenly agitated and vulnerable as he has always been, and so even the anesthetic, the operation, and that blessed awakening have served no purpose, no, they have not changed his life, if he still hasn't begun to live it again and already he is missing something.

twenty-two

My *mother.*
As I entered the room, my mother got up from the couch. She was pale, grief-stricken, and she didn't even try to hide her concern. She waited until Gabriella Ferri had parked the bed and adjusted the angle of the backrest with the buttons, and then she came up to me, on the side with the good arm.

"Hi, Mom," I said.

Gabriella Ferri went off, with an imperceptible nod of farewell.

"How are you?"

"Well. You?"

She leaned over, kissed me on the face, and I sniffed her perfume. Chanel 19, it's called: I have given it to her many times, for Christmas. She straightened up, caressed my face, and looked at me, a long look full of compassion: at my bandaged chest, at my wrist pierced by the drip, at the bandage over my eye. As a kid I don't know what I would have given to have had an accident and to have been operated on without her knowledge, and then to be looked at like that, the day after, the poor injured son that she had not been able to protect: but nothing ever happened to me. Now that something had happened I was ashamed, that's all, and I felt guilty about not having let her know, the day before, when Bogliasco repeatedly told me to do so, between one decision and the other that he was making for me.

"Really, Mom," I said. "I'm all right."

I drew myself up a little—only a few centimeters in reality— and she caressed me again. Then she took my hand and I smiled again, yielding to her old green eyes, still veiled in mourning, and now also chafed with distress.

Nonetheless I could not sit there and ease her mind as would have been natural, clearing the tangle of problems that was occupying her brain (what happened? what have you done to yourself? why didn't you let me know right away? why didn't you go to Di Stefano? . . .), wallowing in her gaze and her caresses. It would have been natural, it would have even been nice, but there are things beyond the reach of naturalness: now there was an urgent question between us that was entirely new, one that had to be dealt with straight away, before it drifted down to settle in the depths, where the algae of habit would immediately begin to grow upon it, an algae that, in families, conceals everything, smothers everything, compresses everything into that clot of neglected urgent questions known as affection. I had not expected to have to do it there and then, but perhaps it was better that way: I was ready, my head was clear, and if there was a right way to do it I was going to find it. All I had to do was take the initiative and drag her far away from this room, carefully, strenuously, will versus naturalness, toward the fundamental correction we needed to make to our lives.

"How did you find out?" I asked.

"Your friend telephoned me, this morning."

My friend. Great.

"And how did you get here? By train?"

"No. Graziella brought me in the car."

"Graziella? Is Graziella here too?"

"No. She wanted to stay but I sent her back to Sabaudia. She has to breast-feed the baby, otherwise . . ."

"Right. How's her mastitis? Is she better?"

"Yes, it's gone. But if she doesn't breast-feed it could come back."

"And is the little girl well? I bet she's prettier than ever . . ."

"Yes, she's well. She eats and sleeps."

"And the other two little rascals? Are they jealous?"

"No, not for now anyway."

"What are they up to? Do they go to the beach? Swim?"

She looked at me, puzzled: I had never asked so many questions about my sister's family.

"They're going to sailing lessons," she said.

"Already?" I pressed on. "But aren't they still a bit small for that?"

"It would appear not."

"Isn't it dangerous?"

"There are instructors," she replied, more and more puzzled, but not just on my account, now, because it seemed to me that she wasn't too sure about these sailing lessons. (And, by the way, the ingenuousness with which she let herself be drawn into talking about her grandchildren was touching. She hadn't been a widow for so much as a month, her son was in the hospital, and you could see that she would have liked to avoid the subject, but she couldn't: it was impossible for her to resist this immense *respect* for the minor family questions that I was using as a diversion . . .)

"Well, that's true," I said. "And then again it's not as if they are the reckless sort, is it? Like those kids that never see the dangers . . . What was it the little lad said, at the swimming pool, when the instructor asked him why he wouldn't dive in?"

Reluctantly, irresistibly, her face lit up.

"Because if you can't see me I'll drown."

I burst out laughing, a frank, genuine laugh, and, reluctantly, irresistibly, she burst out laughing too. It worked: the vicelike grip of apprehension on her face loosened, her head cleared, she had *seen* I was all right, and whatever it was she had feared until five minutes before, now she was there laughing along with me.

"Get it? *Him,* to the instructor . . ."

"What a character . . ."

"What a complete lack of faith . . ."

It was Bogliasco's strategy, that of the Slavs who always used to beat me: initiative, digression, then two lethal attacks—never one only, *two*—one after the other.

Someone was knocking at the door, however, and that was bad. A nurse I had never seen before peeped in with a trolley: she was anonymous, plain, and so she smiled without scruples.

"Do you want to eat?" she said.

"No, thanks," I replied.

The nurse was dumbfounded but she did not insist, disappeared, and the door closed again. I looked back at my mother, and smiled again.

"I can't eat until this evening," I invented.

In fact it was true, I couldn't. It wasn't time to eat. It was time to do something else.

"And did you meet my friend?" I asked.

"Where?"

And he had been the one to suggest how I should go about this . . .

"Here, when you arrived. Did you see each other?"

"No."

"Do you know who he is?"

"Who?"

"My friend. Didn't you recognize him, by his voice?"

"No. Why, who is he?"

Do that, tell her you've met me.

"He's Gianni Bogliasco, Mom."

Naturally, she will deny knowing me.

"Who?"

But you look her in the eye, while she does so, and with your expert son's eye you'll realize that she is lying.

"Gianni Bogliasco."

Her eyes expressed nothing.

"Gianni Costante."

Nothing.

"Gianni Fusco."

Nothing, there was nothing in her eyes, apart from amazement, which seemed genuine, worthy of someone being questioned by a parliamentary investigative committee. Yet *there was* something, as there had always been, only I couldn't see it, as I have never been able to see it. Bogliasco was wrong: nothing in the world is less expert than a son's eye . . .

"Come on, Mom. The guy who wrote that book."

I pointed to the book, on the bedside table by the telephone. She got to her feet, picked it up, and observed it as if she were looking at a Martian. Of course, as a book it was pretty strange (Gianni Bogliasco, *Under 10*, Edizioni Tam-Tam, with a riceball on the cover) and on a purely theoretical level it could also have been the first time she had seen it, which was why some of her amazement could have been genuine: but I knew she had seen it, and she must have had a copy at home, to be precise in the cupboard in the pantry where she keeps her cookbooks.

"It was he who called you, Mom. Dad's friend. The one of the accident in Amsterdam."

Good girl, Mom. Faced with that look, the parliamentary commission would have given up.

"Gianni," amazed, with book in hand. "What are you talking about?"

But I'm not an undersecretary, Mom, and this is what is called a *forced move*. If you have kept quiet for all these years you're certainly not going to talk now; if you have sworn not to tell me anything, then you will not break your oath; you can do nothing else but make an amazed face. And I had to accept this, because from then on it was going to be like that: I would have to learn to believe it, that's all, exactly as I believed for thirty-seven years in your version of the bourgeois life, without ever dreaming of asking for the proof.

"Sit down, Mom," I said.

But there is a difference, and it is an immense one: now you know that I know. You will continue to do your duty all the way, of course you will, and the first thing you'll do, as soon as you go home, will be to throw away that book on the rotisseries; but at least it will mark the end of the most absurd sacrifice that your destiny had nailed you to, to know that your son was wrestling with mistaken problems and to be unable to tell him. It must have been even tougher for you, you who were never a Russian, a communist, sent off on a mission, you who were only a lower-middle-class girl from the Nomentano, pretty, simple, and with no bees in your bonnet—as a plethora of sisters, cousins, grandchildren, and centenarian aunts who are still alive can document without a shadow of doubt. Yet, in a certain sense, it must have been easier too, since for you it was a matter of loving and nothing else, even though it was loving *twice*: loving the man who pulled the trigger and loving the man who was left lying in the snow; loving the husband you could kiss in front of guests and the one you could kiss only in secret; loving the life you led with him and the one you were never able to lead; loving the daughter who never gave you problems as well as the son who gave you lots of them. That's what you were good at, loving, and it's what you did: you loved, and you went on loving, without troubling to draw distinctions between what was real and what was a sham. For you everything was true, at bottom, because in order to avoid making mistakes, faced with such a complicated life, you loved everything. And if the price was twice as high, never mind: you've paid it by now; and if now the price were to be halved, so much the better: it means that it was worth twice the effort.

If I have to believe in something, Mom, why not in this?

"Come on, sit down here," I told her. "I want to tell you a secret."

My mother sat down beside the bed, and her face was now inhabited by a festive throng: I can't see it, naturally, I can still see nothing but amazement, candor, and then preoccupation anew for her poor son who had gone off his head; yet I could see it. My mind was clear, then, and in there I can see all that I need, with a prodigious clarity. Don't worry, Mom, I know what I'm doing. I won't hurt you. It's just that there have to be two attacks, one alone is not enough . . .

"Do you remember," I said, "when I rented my house, ten years ago? Do you remember that in the living room one of the windows was blocked off by a fake fireplace?

"Yes."

"Do you remember how ugly it was, with the built-in drinks cabinet, the bottle-green majolica tiles, and those electric elements that simulated the red of the fire?"

"Yes, it was really ghastly."

"And I told you that the landlord, after having agreed to demolish it, and to reopen the window that was behind it, changed his mind and said no? He was too fond of it, he said, he had spent all the holidays in front of it since he was a child, and he had made a crèche there every Christmas, and it was there that he found his Christmas stockings, and in short he did not demolish it. It was a piece of his past and he didn't want to throw it away, even if this meant going back on his word. Did I tell you this?"

"No."

"Right. I was ashamed because I hadn't managed to get what I wanted, that's why I didn't tell you. I tried to play the tough guy, but you know me, Mom, I'm no good at wheeling and dealing: I liked the house, I was afraid I would get mad and blow the whole thing, and in the end, in order to get rid of it, I agreed to dismantle that fireplace piece by piece, at my expense, with a *written* promise to restore it to its pristine condition when I eventually left the house. A humiliating business, Mom, because it's obvious that the room is far nicer the way it is, brighter, more spacious, more everything, and not even the landlord himself, if he ever goes back to live there, will want that fireplace underfoot; but he insisted on this matter and I complied. An absurd task, and a costly one, just to avoid throwing away a piece of his fucking past . . ."

"Gianni . . ."

"Sorry. And so we photographed it, measured it, drew it in side and front elevation, and in the end we dismantled it, I and the painter who was there to do the walls, the guy you sent over, who died afterward. What was his name?"

"Who, Frate?"

"Frate, yes. Two days, it took us. And this is where the secret comes in, Mom: because after removing all those tiles one by one, all the facing bricks one by one, with a scalpel, chip, chip, very slowly, as if it were the Domus Aurea, do you know what we found inside? In the air space between the fireplace and the wall . . . do you know what there was?"

Mom looked at me, suspended between apprehension and curiosity: and that expression settled the matter once and for all, because it could just as easily have been the expression of a mother humoring a delirious son as it could have been that of a mother listening to a rational son, a mother who simply wanted to know what was behind the fireplace.

"A turd, there was," I whispered. "I swear, there was a human turd. Mummified, desiccated, and wrapped up in a page of the *Messaggero* dated 1953."

Mom made a grimace of disgust and surprise, but she was also mildly amused.

"This is something I have never even told Anna," I continued, "because I was afraid that . . . I don't know why, but I didn't tell her, I never told anyone. But I can still see that scene, as if it were happening now in this room: the bricklayer, who had just built that fireplace, in 1953, when my landlord was a four-year-old kid who believed that Father Christmas would emerge from that chimney to bring him his presents, *crapped on a piece of newspaper, wrapped it up, climbed up to the top of the steps, tossed the packet into the air space, laid the last few bricks, and calmly went off to pick up his wages.*

The disgust on her face wiped out everything else.

"Do you understand, Mom? My landlord spent the most beautiful moments of his childhood in front of a turd."

And it was my turn to look at her: our eyes still met as before, but now I was the one doing the staring.

"What would you do, in my place, would you tell him? Frate is dead, as is—in all probability—the practical joker who put it there, more than forty years ago. The only one in the whole world who knows, apart from you, is me. Bear in mind that my landlord is a real scrooge, and he has me sign a company boilerplate contract from year to year so that he can throw me out whenever he feels like it, and I can't even use the house as my legal address, you know, and in fact officially I am still living in via Tartaglia. Let's say he throws me out: if you were in my shoes, would you tell him?"

A knock at the door.

"One moment!" I yell immediately, in irrevocable tones. Then I looked back at my mother.

"Would you tell him?"

"Gianni, what's this all about?"

"Nothing, it's a question. Would you tell him yes or no?"

There was something imploring, now, in her eyes. "Stop it, Gianni," they were saying, "I beg you, I beseech you, stop it, don't go about things the way you always do, don't be cruel, Dad is dead, I am not strong like he was, what has been has been, I love you, stop before it's too late." And in my eyes, if I hadn't gotten the wrong expression, there ought to have been written, "Don't worry, Mom. Trust me. Answer the question and I will stop, and what I have said will only be a load of bullshit induced by the anesthesia. There is a woman who howls, over there, and that's apparently normal: all I have done is to rave for five minutes."

"No," she replied.

What a fantastic business, playing the truth game with your

own mother: you tell each other even the things you don't tell each other . . .

"Come in!" I yelled.

The door opened. It was Anna. Of course: my friend must have let her know too.

twenty-three

The flickering of the television screen in the middle of the night in Confalone's house, and the deadly emptiness it spills onto the street through the desolate open window.

Victor Balanda's violent metasolutions, his incorrigible incapacity to conceive of defeat.

Pannella's verses in the Lucio Battisti song: "Oh, how alive we are / How everything happens / For completely different reasons" . . .

Not that it's always a strength, remembering, but even when it isn't it gives the impression that it is, this is the point. Now, for example: as Anna came forward in silence, after having talked in a low voice with Mom in the doorway, and Mom went out, and left us alone, and we found ourselves standing at a deadly crossroads, and our lives would change or not according to how I was going to behave in the next few seconds; my calm was not due to sangfroid, or mere fatalism, but to a throng of fiercely vivid memories, regenerated by that blessed anesthesia, which were mustering around me like volunteers on the day of battle, and they made me feel strong.

That evening of a few years ago, when we went to the cinema to see Snake Eyes *and we didn't like it, and she took issue with the "unrealistic and cruel" scene—that was how she defined it—in which Harvey Keitel flies to New York to see his wife because her father has died, and while he is there with her, in front of the coffin, still open, he tells her he is having an affair. I wonder if she remembers it: now, in this very moment, as she looks at me with eyes full of emotion and not knowing what to say, waiting for me to say something but I smile and keep quiet, I wonder if Anna remembers how much healthy indignation she got out of what was—after all—a simple bit of stage business. And I wonder if she remembers what I said to her, because that scene was practically the only part of the film I had appreciated, and so I defended it: "If a man does something like that," I told her, "it means that he has no choice."*

Yet, despite all the strength that memories can transmit to me—assuming that it is a matter of strength—I felt extremely fragile. Faced with her touching beauty (touching because it was intact, and not so much because she is aging incredibly well, which is true in any case, but intact and forever intact in my mind, where she will never stop being *that fantastic girl with the wind in her hair and her feet sticking outside the window who suddenly kissed me in the parking lot of the Versilia-Ovest highway café with* Satisfaction *by Devo going baby baby baby baby baby baby and my cigarette fell to the floor and singed the carpet*), I felt that I could allow myself only one attempt to save our marriage, one only, and then I would give up, because whichever way it went I was going to need my strength afterward: if the attempt succeeded, I would need it every time I kissed her, caressed her, or made love with her, in order to bear the thought of that same intimacy with her enjoyed and remembered by another; and if it failed, I was going to need it just the same every day in order to stand life without her, without Franceschino, and without being able so much as to conceive of happiness, as she put it in her letter.

Those greetings full of happiness, she on the terrace with Franceschino in her arms, I down there at the colonnade holding a bundle of newspapers.

Then Anna was there, very close indeed. If she had been tormenting herself, over those last few days, if the news of my accident had upset her, if she had driven like a maniac from Viareggio to get here as soon as possible, she showed no signs of it. She was fresh, tanned, her body supple and desirable despite the extremely chaste blue dress, wearing that look of hers, the level-headed and controlled air of the cool provincial rebel who had straightened out at the right time thus managing to transform herself into a woman, from all points of view far more delicate and profound and sensitive and aware and loved and attractive than when she was younger—but evidently not yet entirely level-headed and controlled. She looked at me and I was lost, as usual, in the well of her eyes: I knew that I meant much more to her than my moribund pride was telling me in that moment, but also much less than I had ingenuously believed until the day before. She too was a mysterious creature, unknowable, despite the fifteen years we had spent living together. She had secret desires, passions still burning, weaknesses entirely unknown to me, about which there was no point in doggedly trying to find out more, delving and probing away, all you could do was take her or leave her. Just take her or leave her. And that was already a piece of luck.

The end of her letter: "And whatever happens, know that I love you." The end of the third act of Adelchi: *"Suffer and be great: this is your destiny." The letters she had written to me every day for over a month, many years before, well before we got married, when I wanted to leave her because I was afraid of her, and especially the one in which she said she would have liked to rest her head on the arm of the sofa and have me suck out all her blood. The Emperor of Japan again, and that phrase of his that really does hold for everything: "Let every man do his duty. May life carry on as normal"* . . .

"How about it, Anna," I said. "Let's say that last week I had a really serious accident, and I went into a coma, and I stayed in a coma for a week. The doctors here have treated me wonderfully well, with techniques they don't even use in Austria, and this morning I reawakened. There has been no permanent damage, only a bad knock: in a couple of days' time they'll discharge me, and I can pick up my life from where I left off. A miracle, Anna: let's say that it has been a kind of miracle."

The strange, at that point, the extremely strange understanding there had always been between her and my father . . .

"How about it?" I repeated.

She leaned over me, her fine hair brushing my good eye, her lips kissing my face.

"Yes," she whispered.

There you go. No arguments, no explanations, no pointless waste of energy. There was a problem and we had solved it, and we loved each other and were noble in spirit, and if we fell we would know how to get to our feet again, and if we hurt each other we would know how to forgive, and we would stay together for the rest of our lives without tormenting ourselves over the past, over the whys and the wherefores—in fact, the past would become our strength, a strength that no one could ever overcome. It was a really beautiful thing, wasn't it? I was happy, wasn't I?

The headline of that Algerian newspaper that went around the world, on the day of certain elections stained with the blood of those massacred by the fundamentalists: "If you vote, you die. If you don't vote, you die. So vote, and die."

Anna carried on covering me with kisses, tenderly, delicately. I raised my free hand, held it in midair for a second, unsure about where to put it, in a kind of hesitant benediction of nothingness. Then I flipped it backward, toward the headboard, where they had attached the little machine, and I pressed the morphine button.

epilogue

(a drawing of the grave of Qlxxzw'kvsfqz/Pizzano Pizza)

Well kids, the real story of Pizzano Pizza ends here.

If it strikes you as a bit sad, as an ending, I cannot say you're wrong. If you think I didn't struggle hard enough to make it end differently, I cannot say you're wrong. If you think I could have done something more to discover the whole truth, all the way, or to find proof of the things I have told you about, just so as not to oblige you to believe and no more, I cannot say you're wrong. And I cannot say you're wrong even if you think that I could have carried on lying to you, at least, inventing other stories with happy and satisfying endings the way lots of people do. But what's done is done, and if I have disappointed you I really don't know how to justify myself, because it's not that it happened by chance, I really did it on purpose: I had to decide, and I decided to do it this way.

But I can tell you one last story, before I leave you, and I'm sure that this one will not disappoint you, and maybe it will even make you laugh. It is a very old story, that many have told in many different ways, even though at bottom it has always been the same: but you are young, and very probably you don't know it yet. It is the story of an unhappy man, who had a golden screw in his belly button that he couldn't get rid of. He had been to doctors, mechanics, coachbuilders, surgeons, goldsmiths, ironmongers, and witches, all over the world, in the hope that one of them would manage to remove that screw: nothing doing, no one had ever managed to move it by so much as a millimeter. But the man did not give up, and he continued to travel the world, stubbornly, in search of someone who might remove that golden screw from his belly button. Until, one day, he went to the Emperor of Japan—who, as often happens in that wise country, was a little boy. The man showed him the screw and, by gestures, since he didn't know a word of Japanese, he made him understand his problem. The boy-Emperor looked at the screw, smiled, then slowly turned around and began to rummage through a big ivory chest he kept hidden behind the throne, until he took out a tiny golden screwdriver, so small that it looked like a pin. He showed it to the man and, still smiling, he uttered an incomprehensible phrase in his native tongue, a phrase however that sounded marvelous, like a handful of silver bells falling on a feather cushion. The man, who had understood nothing, nodded, and so the Emperor took from his chest a piece of purple silk and he spread it out on the floor, with great care. Once he had eliminated even the slightest crease, he had the man kneel, before kneeling in his turn and getting to work.

It really didn't seem possible that such a microscopic screwdriver could loosen such a big screw, but the screw began to turn effortlessly, and, as it turned, it began to emerge from the belly button: one turn, two turns, three turns, the screw came out farther and farther, until it was completely out, and, holding *it between his fingers, the boy-Emperor showed it to the man. Then the man looked at his belly in amazement: for the first time he saw it normal, smooth, and without screws like those of everybody else. He was free: his tenacity had been rewarded, the curse that had accompanied him all his life was over. He leaped to his feet, crazy with joy, and his ass fell off.*